Cycle Four:

# The Pursuit

Piercing the Veil
Home Base
Fairy
At Sea

Bill Myers, Jeff Gerke,
Angela Hunt and
Alton Gansky

Published by Amaris Media International.

Copyright © 2017 Bill Myers, Jeff Gerke, Angela Hunt, and Alton Gansky

Cover Design: Angela Hunt

Photo Credit ©photokitas –fotolia.com.

ISBN-13: 978-1543113259
ISBN-10:1543113257

For more information, visit us on the Web:
www.harbingersseries.com

# HARBINGERS

A novella series by

Bill Myers, Frank Peretti, Angela Hunt, and Alton Gansky

In this fast-paced world with all its demands, the four of us wanted to try something new. Instead of the longer novel format, we wanted to write something equally as engaging but that could be read in one or two sittings—on the plane, waiting to pick up the kids from soccer, or as an evening's read.

We also wanted to play. As friends and seasoned novelists, we thought it would be fun to create a game we could participate in together. The rules were simple:

**Rule #1**

Each of us would write as if we were one of the characters in the series:

Bill Myers would write as Brenda, the street-hustling tattoo artist who sees images of the future.

Frank Peretti would write as the professor, the atheist ex-priest ruled by logic.

Jeff Gerke would write as Chad, the young mind reader with good looks and an arrogance to match.

Angela Hunt would write as Andi, the professor's brilliant-but-geeky assistant who sees inexplicable patterns.

Alton Gansky would write as Tank, the naïve, big-hearted jock with a surprising connection to a healing power.

**Rule #2**

Instead of the four of us writing one novella together (we're friends but not crazy), we would write it like a TV series. There would be an overarching story line into which we'd plug our individual novellas, with each story written from our character's point of view.

Bill's first novella, *The Call*, set the stage. It was followed by Frank's, *The Haunted*, Angela's *The Sentinels*, and Alton's *The Girl*. And now we return to Bill for the next cycle with *The Revealing*, as pieces begin tying together and amping up.

There you have it. We hope you'll find these as entertaining in the reading as we did in the writing.

*Bill, Frank, Jeff, Angie, and Al*

# Piercing The Veil

# Bill Myers

# Jeff Gerke, Angela Hunt, and Alton Gansky

I hate Vegas.

Sorry if that messes with your white, middle class dreams for a vacation. Sorrier still if you're some city councilman that wants to sue my butt for talking trash. (Good luck with that—you can have the trailer—my shop, too, the way all this traveling messes with my business).

Anyway, that's why I didn't take Daniel, why I swung over and dropped him off at my mom's in Arizona before driving over here. I don't care how much he begs, Vegas ain't no place for a kid, 'specially one with his unique sensitivities. I know I said that before, 'specially during our little visit to North Carolina. But there's way too much trash goin' on here that folks don't see (or don't want to). Lucky for me, I was one of the smart ones. Got out before too much damage was done. But there's plenty of other sisters, brothers too, who weren't so lucky.

I'd been on the 93 almost three hours now—the afternoon sun hitting my eyes, and the oven-hot wind roaring through the open windows of my beater Toyota. Not to cool things down, but to dry up sweat so I ain't swimming in it.

Last week I got another one of those texts from "Unknown Caller." It was tellin' me to pick up Andi and Tank, aka Cowboy, at the airport, 3:15 today. It's almost 5:00, courtesy of my overheating radiator. But they know I'll be there. We're always there for each other. Like a bad habit.

Still, these little outings, they're taking their toll. You'd think it would be easier without the professor and his attitude. But no. Not by a long shot. Truth is, I miss him almost as much as Andi does. We were entirely different, fought like cats and dogs, but somehow he got me. And I got him. And now . . . I don't know.

I arrived at the airport and pulled into Terminal One. Sure enough, there was Andi in her flaming red hair. She was melting in the heat and having her ears talked off by Cowboy.

I gave a honk and pulled up.

"There she is!" Cowboy grabbed his duffle bag and, despite Andi's protests, her backpack, too. "Boy, it's good to see you," he said as he opened the door and tossed their stuff in the back.

"It sure is," Andi said.

I could tell by the look of relief she wasn't lying. Cowboy's a great guy, all 6' 4", 275 pounds of him. But he likes to talk. 'Specially when it's to someone he's trying to impress. Course she's told him a dozen times she's not interested, but the loveable lug is as persistent as he is loyal.

He opened the front door, motioning for Andi to take the seat. "Whew," he laughed. "It's so hot here I bet hens are laying hard-boiled eggs."

Andi cut me a look of desperation. She's a sweet kid and doesn't know how to be rude. Come to think of it, Cowboy's the same. But that's where the similarities stop.

As Cowboy shut her door and headed for the back, I asked him, "Sure you don't want the front seat?"

"Thanks, but I'm good," he said. Course he wasn't. You could tell by the way he gasped and grunted, trying to pull in his legs.

"Where's Daniel?" Andi asked as she looked for the seat belt.

"Don't bother," I said. "It hasn't worked for years."

"And Daniel?"

"Not this time."

She gave me a look. "Are you seeing something dangerous?"

"No more than usual. But me and Vegas, we got a history he don't need to be exposed to."

After the usual grinding of gears, I found first and we pulled out.

Cowboy leaned forward to join us. "But you are seeing stuff, right?"

I nodded to the sketchpad on the dashboard.

Andi grabbed it and started flipping pages. There was plenty of drawings from our past encounters— that empty chair in the Vatican, Littlefoot from whatever reality she was in, even the sketch of ourselves (which was also tatted on Cowboy's arm). But it wasn't until she came to the picture of the flying dragon that she came to a stop. It was pretty detailed—red and purple with shiny scales, and little arms and hands under its wings.

"This?" she asked.

"For starters."

She flipped through the other sketches I'd been seeing in my head the past week or so . . . like the green recliner with all sorts of electrical junk around it, or the snowflakes, lots and lots of snowflakes, or the creepy, frog-faced gargoyles. Lots of them, too.

"I sure don't like them things," Cowboy said, referring to the gargoyles.

"Why not?" Andi asked.

"I don't want to get weird on you . . ."

"No, go ahead."

"It's just . . . that's how some folks describe demons."

Andi took a breath and closed the pad. "Well, it looks like we might be in for a wild ride this time."

I flipped the dreads out of my face. "So what else is new?"

She nodded and we all got kind of quiet. 'Cause there's one thing you can say about my sketches: They're never wrong.

# Chapter 2

No problem finding our hotel. Besides the name, Preston Towers, there were two twelve-foot high, hitching posts out front. The internet said it was one of the city's finest, right on the Strip. No surprise there. Our employers, they may be all secretive and stuff, never letting us know who they are . . . but they sure know how to treat us.

The car jockeys, faces leathery from the sun, were all over us—opening doors, grabbing luggage, anything for a tip.

"Nah, fellas, we're good," Cowboy said. "We got it." But they were pretty pushy so our good ol' boy let 'em have their way.

Not me. When they asked for the keys I said I'd park it.

"Actually," a tall brother said. "I'm afraid that's not possible."

"Actually, I'll make it possible."

"We're the only ones with access to the garage."

"Then I'll park outside the garage."

"There's nothing close. The nearest—"

"We good?" I called to Cowboy as he finished loading up the cart.

He nodded.

"Ma'am, if you'll just give me the keys."

"I said *I'll* park it."

"The nearest spot is four blocks away and even at that—"

"I can use the exercise."

I wasn't being a jerk. As a single mom with Daniel and all, I got no need to line someone else's pocket. So after some gear grinding, I pulled onto the Strip leaving behind my customary cloud of blue smoke.

I eventually took a left on Stan Mallin Drive. I'd gone a couple more blocks when this kid, I don't know where he came from, is suddenly in front of me. I slammed on my brakes, but my bumper caught him and, 'fore I knew it, he's sailing onto my hood, then rolling off and onto the road.

I leaped out and ran toward him. "You all right? You okay?"

He lay there, not moving. I dropped to my knees, swearing and praying at the same time, when he suddenly jumps up, pushes me out of the way and runs for my car.

"Hey!" I scrambled to my feet. "Hey!" I took off after him. He was already inside, slamming the door, but no way was I going to let him jack my car. Once I got there, I reached through the window and grabbed his shirt. He tried pushing me away, at the same time fighting with the gearshift. But neither of us was goin' anywhere.

I leaned back and punched him in the face. Not hard, but when you aim for the nose it don't take much. He yelped in surprise and I hit him again. This time there was blood. A real gusher. He swore, hands shooting to his face, which gave me plenty of time to grab the door and throw it open.

"What are you doing?" he yelled.

"What am *I* doing?"

"I don't have time for this!"

I tried dragging him out but he wasn't so cooperative, so I began rabbit-punching him. He got the message.

"All right!" he cried, "All right!"

"This is my car!" I threw in some R-rated language. "Mine!"

"I get it, I get it!" He held up hands, protecting his face like a little girl. "You made your point!"

I paused as he climbed out of the car, then hit him one more time just 'cause he pissed me off.

"Alright!"

He was a good-looking kid, early twenties and from what I could tell, pretty ripped. Even with his hands over his face there was no doubt he was a babe magnet. But it wasn't his looks that got me. It was the dragon tattoo on his right arm. Exactly like the one I'd sketched. Down to the little hands under its wings.

"Who are you?" I yelled.

He spotted something behind me. "It doesn't matter."

"What?"

He motioned down the street. "They're the ones to worry about."

I turned and saw two casino thugs in suits racing towards us. "What do they want?"

"Me," he said. "And now you."

They were big guys and no doubt carrying. And by the look on their faces, they weren't from any hospitality center.

"You running from them?" I asked.

He didn't answer. I turned back to look at him. Actually his tattoo. Then I turned to the thugs. They were thirty feet away.

"All right, get in!" I ordered.

He didn't need a second invite. As he ran to the passenger side, I slid behind the wheel. I didn't know who he was or what they wanted, but I did know that tattoo. And, like I said, the boys didn't look like they wanted to chit-chat. I found first, stepped on the gas, and left behind my trademark cloud of choking blue smoke.

# Chapter 3

"Nice friends you got," I said.

He checked his nose for the third or fourth time. "You're not exactly Miss Congeniality."

I motioned to the blood on his hands. "Don't get any of that on my seat."

"I think you broke it."

"Next time try askin' politely. There's napkins in the glove compartment."

He tried opening it. I reached over and slammed it with my fist a couple times before it popped open.

"What they got against you, anyways?" I asked.

He grabbed a couple of the napkins, courtesy of Burger King, and dabbed at the blood. "I come into town every few weeks, do some playing and pick up some cash."

"You that good?"

"I'm better than good, lady."

"You a card counter?"

"Please, even with your limited skills you should know better than that."

I didn't know what he was talking about but I was disliking him already. And since I'd done my community service for the night, I began to pull over.

"What are you doing?"

"Dropping you off."

"Uh, I don't think so. Not me." The kid was as arrogant as he was good looking. "I live over forty miles from here."

"Nice night for a walk," I said.

"But . . . you will take me home."

"In your dreams."

"Actually, it would be in *your* dreams."

I shot him a withering look.

He shrugged. "But don't take it personally. I'm not into older chicks."

I brought the car to a stop, reached past him and opened the door. "Goodnight."

"But . . . you saw the tattoo, right? The dragon? The one you've been drawing for the last two weeks?"

"How did—"

He grinned. "And that image will haunt you, unless you drive me back to my lab."

"Your lab?"

"You didn't see that? You didn't draw it? Man you *are* an amateur." He sighed. "Another reason I'm not interested in joining your team."

"My . . .?"

"Come on, I'm not an idiot, Belinda."

"Belinda?"

"Your name."

"Try Brenda."

"Close enough."

"*Who* are you?"

He gave another sigh. "My name is Chad Thorton. And you and your little band of wannabe warriors have come to recruit me."

"Recruit you?"

"To replace that old fart who disappeared."

He definitely had my attention. "Are you talking about—"

"And I'll tell you just like I told your handlers, I'm not interested in working with rookies." Before I could respond, he explained, "The football jock, the red-headed babe, and your kid—though he's probably got more potential than the rest of you combined—at least that's what you think."

"What do you know what I think?"

"Come on, lady. That's what I do." He tapped his temple. "That's *my* specialty." He glanced out the back window. "Now can we please get going?"

I stared at him.

He turned and grinned.

I swore, found first, and pulled back into traffic.

He settled back into the seat.

I found Chad Thorton to be almost as informative as he was obnoxious. Almost. As his own biggest fan, he spent the entire drive talking about himself . . .

His childhood:

"As far back as I can remember, people, *real important* people have wanted to study and capitalize on my extraordinary abilities."

I cut him another look.

He gave me another shrug. "What can I say, it's a gift. Similar to yours, but obviously far more developed. No offense."

Offense was taken.

After that, he started going on about our organization:

"Oh, yeah, you guys have been trying to recruit me for months. You know, to help you fight the, what do you call it . . . the Gate?"

I gripped the wheel a little tighter.

He saw it and laughed. "Sure, I know about the Gate. Not everything, just what I've read off your handlers. The Gate, they're some uber-secret organization working side by side with extra-dimensionals to take over the world." He chuckled. "And your little group is supposed to help stop them."

I caught my breath, then tried to sound cool and unimpressed. "And that doesn't interest you, stopping them?"

"Nope."

"That's it? *Nope*?"

"That's right."

"And these other people," I said, "what did you call them—our *handlers*?"

"Yeah, the Watchers."

For the second time I caught my breath. Did he actually know their name?

He continued. "Good guys, I suppose. But the odds are definitely not in their favor."

"You called them the Watchers."

He turned to me and cocked his head "Don't tell me you didn't know their name?"

I said nothing.

He broke out laughing. "Priceless, man. You're working for an organization and you don't even know who they are."

"I didn't say that."

"You didn't have to." He flashed me that grin and tapped his temple.

I felt my ears growing hot. I looked back to the road.

He continued. "One thing you can say about them though, they sure got the bucks. And not just for your plane tickets and hotels. These dudes, they got more money than you and I can imagine."

"Why do you say that?"

"How else would you explain San Diego? All those deaths, that building destroyed. And not a word of it in the press? Talk about hush money, or—" he shrugged again— "maybe they got their own mind games."

"You know about San Diego?"

"Only what I've read off the first recruiter. Or the second. I forget."

"You've met them? Personally?"

"The Watchers? Of course. Well, their representatives." He looked back at me. "You haven't?"

Before I could answer he shook his head and chuckled again. "Well I guess that lets you know how important I am, at least compared to you guys."

I glanced at his nose, wondering if it needed more adjusting. Lucky for him, I was able to contain myself. I hoped he appreciated the effort.

# Chapter 4

I'd barely entered the "lab" with the kid before a pretty, twenty-something in wire-rimmed glasses and a white stocking cap ran toward him. "Your nose!"

"It's nothing."

"But . . . it's broken," she said. "How—?"

"It's not broken," he said scornfully. "Don't you think I'd know if it's broken?"

Her eyes shot to me, then back to him. "How did it happen?"

"Long story. Grab us some coffee, will you?"

"But—"

He brushed past her. "Coffee."

She hesitated.

"Now."

"Sure thing." She turned to leave.

"Belinda takes hers black, no cream or sugar." He threw me a look and grinned. "Right?"

I didn't bother to answer.

The building was on Highway 15, north of Vegas, the middle of nowhere. Except for the occasional semi there were no other lights or signs of civilization. It wasn't much to look at, more like a giant shed, one of those old Quonset huts the military used to use.

But inside, things were a little different.

"I've only got a couple minutes to spare," he said, "but I can show you around." Without waiting for an answer, he started the tour.

"The place was used by the Army from the mid-seventies until about 1990. It was called the Dragon Stealth Program." He gestured to a painting over the entrance we'd just walked through. "Look familiar?"

I could only stare. The image was identical to the one I'd been sketching . . . and to the one tatted on his arm.

"The boys and girls at Stanford Research Institute teamed up with Army Intelligence to experiment with remote viewing."

"Remote viewing?"

"You know. Where you send your spirit out of your body to travel and spy on enemy instalations."

I frowned.

"You never heard of it?"

"Yeah, well . . . in a way."

He snickered. "Liar."

Course he was right, but I wasn't going to let him know. Not with his attitude.

"You guys really are amateurs, aren't you?"

I didn't think it possible, but I was liking him

even less. We walked across the worn linoleum floor to a heavy padded door, like they have in recording studios. He pulled it open and we stepped inside. Everything was gray. Gray carpet, gray walls, gray ceiling.

"To cut out mental noise," he said, answering the question I was thinking but hadn't asked.

The room was pretty small with a worn sofa against one wall. The other had a four-foot control panel with TV monitors, speakers, and readouts beneath an observation window.

"This is where Stephie sits to monitor my vitals."

"Stephie?"

He motioned to the other room where the girl had greeted us. "I could have anyone I want, but she's pretty hung up on me so I figured why not give her a thrill."

"Lucky her."

"She keeps track of all the stuff when I bilocate."

"Bi . . . locate?"

"When I leave my body and travel."

I tried not to scoff, but he saw my expression.

"What? You don't think I can do it?"

Actually, with everything I'd seen these past few months I figured just about anything was possible. But no way was he going to know it.

He continued, "Maybe you should ask your professor friend. Oh, wait, he's not around any more, is he? Hmm, I wonder where he's gone?"

I bristled. "What do you know about the professor?"

He just grinned that grin of his.

"You know where he is?"

"I only know he was reading up on Dragon

Stealth before he disappeared."

"How do you know that?"

He gave me another one of those, *are-you-really-that-stupid?* looks which made me want to give him another *let-me-rearrange-your-face* makeovers. I settled for grabbing his arm. "Do you think he was . . . could he have been messing with this kinda stuff?" He looked at my grip and I let go.

Then, with a shrug, he answered. "I don't know what he was doing. When I travel, my spirit leaves my body. As far as I can tell, your pal took the whole package with him."

I stood a moment, trying to drink it in.

"C'mon." He turned and I followed him out of the room.

The girl appeared, all smiles. "Here's your coffee." She held out a tray with a couple mugs on it—along with packets of sugar, a spoon, and that girlie-flavored creamer stuff. I nodded a thanks and took a cup.

Chad didn't bother. He left his on the tray, so she had to hold it while he opened the packets, dumped them into his coffee, and poured in the creamer, talking all the while. "This next room here, it's where all the action takes place. We've been working about nine months now and we're already way past whatever those military goons were doing."

"We sure are," Stephie agreed.

He ignored her.

"What about funding?" I asked. "Where are you getting the money?"

"The casinos." He finished stirring the coffee and finally scooped up his mug. "That's what my little visit tonight was about." He motioned me into the other room.

I gave Stephie another nod of thanks but her eyes were too glued to Chad to notice.

The second room was even smaller than the first. Same gray floor, wall, and ceiling. Two recliners, identical to the ones I'd been sketching, in the middle of the room. They were attached to a bunch of sensors and wires.

Once again the kid grinned. "Look familiar? They're ERV chairs."

"ER—"

"Exended Remote Viewing." He moved between them, patting their backs. "Like I said, this is where it all happens. Where I sit during the sessions."

"When you bilocate," I said.

"Very good."

"Two chairs?"

"They originally had two, but I only need one."

"And you're messin' with all this because—?"

"Obviously, because it's a doorway."

"Into . . ."

"Higher dimensions."

The phrase didn't surprise me. We'd been hearing a lot about them . . . and experiencing them. At least according to Littlefoot. Or was she talking about the Multiverse? I shook my head, musing at how I get the terminology mixed up.

"Me, too," he said. "Multiverse, higher dimensions. It can get confusing." I stiffened. He was doing it again, reading my thoughts. "But it'll all make sense when I finally get everything figured out."

"And you, all by yourself, you're going to do that?"

"Of course. But not if I'm standing around

talking to you. So, if you'll excuse me." He turned back to Stephie. "Time to get the show going."

"On it." She hurried away.

"That's it?" I said as he led me out of the room.

"What's it?"

"I take you all the way out here for a thirty second tour?"

"I said from the start I wasn't interested in being recruited. I've got too much on the ball to be held back by rookies. Steph!"

She poked her head around the corner. "Right here."

"Get Belinda a travel cup for the road."

"Will do." She hurried off again.

He gave me a wink. "Can't give away all our dishware to strangers."

"Listen," I kept my voice steady. "I'm not interested in recruiting you. I'm not even interested in being in the same room with you."

"Which is why you're so angry at me for kicking you out."

"Who says I'm angry?"

The kid smiled.

"I'm not angry."

"You're doing a pretty good immitation of it."

I started to answer, then caught myself.

"Super," he said. "Since you're not angry, it'll make goodbyes a lot easier. Steph—"

"Coming." She reappeared with an empty styrofoam cup.

"Give our guest a hand with that," he said.

"Keep it." I set down the mug, none too gently.

"Suit yourself." He turned and stepped back into the second room. "Let's go, Steph. Don't want to waste the entire night."

I headed for the exit, thinking, *unbelievable.*

"Yeah," he called from the other room. "I get that a lot. Stephie?"

"Coming."

Ninety minutes later Cowboy was glued to the peep-hole in the door of our Preston Towers suite.

"Do you see it?" I asked.

"No ma'am, not yet."

"Good."

"Unless it's out of view," Andi said. She was wrapping a cold towel around my sprained ankle. "The convection of that lens is roughly 190 degrees, leaving 10-20 degrees for an object the size of Brenda's description to hide from view."

"So it could still be out there?" Cowboy asked.

She looked puzzled. "Isn't that what I just said?"

He grinned. "If you say so."

Andi pulled the towel tighter and I tried not to wince. "One thing's for certain," I said, "they know we're here."

"Maybe they followed you from that fella's laboratory, what was his name again?" Cowboy asked.

"Chad." I gritted my teeth against the pain. "Chad Thorton."

Forty minutes earlier, I'd parked the car a few blocks from the hotel and made my way up to the Strip. It was late, but with so many lights you'd swear it was day. Same with the number of people. Youngsters, oldsters, middle-agers. Most had a pretty good buzz going, and 'cept for the belligerent drunk or two, good times were had by all.

Well, almost all.

I didn't see them 'til I entered our hotel and passed through the noisy casino. There were the blurry-eyed smokers playing slots, the studs and students playing tables, and the hostesses delivering drinks. But it was the working girls that tore at me. Youngsters with caked-on makeup trying to look like seasoned vets. Worn-out vets trying to look like youngsters—everyone laughing, joking and flirting . . . and filled with fear, hatred and self-loathing. Memories of another life poured in.

I grabbed a key from the desk and quickly headed for the elevators. I got off on the nineteenth floor. That's when something even more disturbing caught my attention.

A blue metallic orb, about the size of a grapefruit, hovered at the end of the hall. It was exactly like the ones we ran into in Florida and later in LA. We never completely knew what they did, but we did know they belonged to the Gate.

I steeled myself and moved down the hall, pretending not to notice as I headed for the room. I figured it either followed me from Chad Thorton's lab, or someone at the desk had alerted it. Didn't matter. The point was they knew we were here.

I picked up my pace, passed the long line of rooms, including our own, until the stairway at the other end of the hallway came into view. That's when I bolted for the exit. I threw the door open, stepped through, and tried pulling it shut. But no matter how hard I pulled, it took its sweet time closing. I gave up and raced down the stairs as fast as I could. Actually, too fast. When I rounded the landing I rolled my ankle, could actually hear something tear.

I swallowed back the pain and made it to the next floor. I yanked open the door, but knew I couldn't run down the hallway, so I flattened myself against the wall. Just like I figured, the orb shot through the doorway and past me. It flew down the hallway, searching, and I slipped back through the door just before it closed.

I grabbed the railing, pulling myself up one step at a time. I got to the door of our hall, opened it, and limped towards Andi's and my suite. Once I got inside, we called Cowboy. And now here we were, the three of us hiding inside, figuring our next move.

"I say we go into that hallway and face the thing down like we did before," Cowboy said. "Then hightail it out to that fella's place and see what he's up to."

"He's got a point," I said. "We've beat it before."

Andi, who'd had more history with the orbs than us, wasn't so sure. "We were able to do that only with the professor's help," she said.

Of course she was right. At least part right. Which was enough to get me thinking about the old guy again and how much I missed him . . . and wondering if this Chad Thorton had any clues where he might be.

I shook my head at the thought. The last thing I wanted was to go back and put up with his arrogance again. Actually, the second-to-last thing. Facing that orb came in first.

"Mind if I lay hands on it?"

I looked up to see Cowboy staring down at my ankle.

"Knock yourself out," I said. I pulled off the towel. The thing was swollen pretty good. He stooped down and ever so gently wrapped those big paws of his around it. Then he closed his eyes and silently prayed.

Me and Andi watched. More out of respect than any type of faith. Not that we hadn't seen him heal stuff before, but neither of us were as fast at giving God the credit as he was.

After thirty or so seconds, he pulled his hands away. The thing was just as swollen as before.

"Does it feel any better?" he asked.

I tried moving it and winced.

"Sorry," he said.

"Not your fault," I said. "Jesus must got better things to do."

Cowboy nodded, but you could see he wasn't happy about it.

Andi changed subjects. "All right," she said, "this is the pattern I see.

"The orbs are back, which means the Gate is involved and they know we're here."

"Check," Cowboy said.

"This Chad person knows all about the

30

professor?" she asked.

"A little," I said.

"Enough where he may be able to help?"

I gave a reluctant nod.

"And our sponsors, what did he call them?"

"Watchers," I said

Cowboy frowned. "Kind of a weird name."

"Maybe," Andi said. "But look how they've been keeping an eye on everything since we've started."

"Actually before," I said.

"And helpin' us stop stuff," Cowboy admitted.

Andi continued, "So . . . our sponsors, these Watchers, have clearly sent us here and they've clearly been trying to recruit this man."

"So he says," I said.

Andi pushed back. "He knows too much to be making it up."

"Sometimes more than us," Cowboy said.

I hated it, but they were right.

"So . . ."

Cowboy finished her thought. "We gotta go out there and talk to him."

I groaned.

Andi nodded.

And Cowboy? He turned toward the closed door, preparing himself.

# Chapter 6

The good news was there were no floating orbs. Not inside the hotel, not on the Strip. Fact, we got to the car without a single problem with them. But there was another . . .

Since I couldn't drive, Andi had already taken the back seat and Cowboy was helping me into the front. That's when he looked back and asked, "You don't by any chance know them fellas, do you?"

I turned to look and swore. They were the same goons in sunglasses I'd run into before. And they looked just as friendly. "Get in," I ordered. "Hurry."

"Looks like they wanna talk," Cowboy said.

"We gotta go. Now!"

Maybe it was my tone. Maybe it was because they started running toward us. Either way, Cowboy figured it wasn't a bad idea. He crossed to the driver's side and fought to squeeze his giant body behind the wheel. The fact the front seat was broken and wouldn't go back didn't help.

"Hurry!" I yelled. "These guys are serious."

He finally got in, fired up the ignition, and we shot backwards like a rocket.

"You're in reverse!" I shouted.

He ground the gears looking for first. But, like I said, my transmission don't always cooperate. So, still racing backwards and with no other choice, Tank cranked the wheel hard. We missed the car behind us by inches and flew into the street.

Drivers honked, swerved, and cursed. Somehow Cowboy managed to miss them all as the bad guys closed in on us. (Actually we closed in on them). But instead of jumping out of our way, they came straight at us, one from each side.

"Roll up the windows!" Andi yelled.

A nice idea but, again, we're talking my car. The goon on the driver's side got there first. He reached inside and grabbed Cowboy.

"'Scuse me," Cowboy shouted over the roar of the engine, "but yer gonna have to let go."

Before I could point out his good ol' boy manners probably wouldn't help, Goon Two arrived at my side, reached in, and grabbed me.

"Faster!" I shouted to Cowboy.

He punched it. The engine whined and we picked up speed. So did the goons. I don't know if they were running beside us or being dragged. Didn't matter. By the look of things, they weren't letting go.

Cars kept honking and swerving past us. Drivers kept exercising their freedom of speech and hand gestures. And Cowboy kept trying to talk reason to his man. "You're sure makin' it hard to steer this thing," he shouted.

I wasn't so polite. I grabbed the pencil I keep in the cup holder and jabbed it into my guy's face. He yelled and screamed, but still wouldn't let go. So I did it again. Same yelling and screaming, but this time he managed to lose his sunglasses.

That's when I saw he had no eyes. Only empty sockets. Just like those guys in Rome.

"Cowboy!" I shouted.

He glanced over, then yelled, "I thought they looked familiar."

Andi shouted from the back seat. "They're not going to let go! If they're like the others, they'll hang on 'til the end!"

Cowboy nodded, then cranked the wheel hard to the left. We slid our way onto the Strip . . . still going backwards, still drawing irate horns and colorful language.

"Where you going?" I shouted.

"Not sure!" he shouted back. (He was big on honesty).

My guy was still hanging on so I jammed a couple more holes into his face. He yelled and screamed, but still didn't get the message. I glanced over my shoulder and saw we were coming up to our hotel. "Cowboy!"

"Hang on!" he yelled. "I got an idea!"

He swung the car to the right. We bounced up on the curb as pedestrians screamed and jumped out of the way. We headed straight for the front wall, which was mostly glass.

"Cowboy!"

He hit the brakes and we did a perfect 180,

coming to a stop, looking out the windshield at the hotel—complete with bell hops running every direction. But Mr. Toad's wild ride wasn't quite over. Cowboy stomped on the accelerator again.

"Tank!" Andi shouted.

We shot backwards again, this time straight for the street.

"What are you doing?" I yelled.

He motioned to the two giant hitching posts in front of the hotel. The ones spaced as wide apart as my car. Well, almost.

"Just scrapin' off the barnacles!" he shouted. Hang on!"

We flew between the posts and did exactly what he'd hoped . . . removed the unwanted debris, leaving the bad guys in a groaning heap on the sidewalk. In exchange, the sound of scraping metal told me I'd also acquired a racing stripe the length of my car.

"Where'd you learn that?" Andi shouted.

"Barrel racing." He grinned. "I used to do rodeo as a kid."

Chapter 7

"This the place?" Cowboy asked as he crawled out of the car and crossed to my side.

"This is it."

Once he helped me to my feet I got a healthy look at the gouge running from my front fender to my back bumper.

"Sorry about that," he said.

The good news was he'd gotten my car out of reverse. The bad news was it got us to Chad Thorton's.

It's not that I didn't like the kid, it's just—all right. I didn't like him . . . a lot. I didn't like his arrogance. I didn't like how he treated his assistant. And I didn't like him calling us amateurs, particularly after all we'd been through.

"Look," Andi said as she got to the door. "A

note. It's addressed to a Belinda."

"Give that to me." I ripped it down and read:

> *Welcome back. Come in if you must.*
> *But don't disturb. Our work is too*
> *vital.*

"Wow," Cowboy said, reading over my shoulder. "He sounds important."

I crumpled the paper and tossed it to the ground.

Instead of knocking, I pushed at the door. It opened and we stepped inside. Everything was like before, except for the flute and harp music playing in the background. And the two rooms. Both of their doors were shut.

"Where is everybody?" Cowboy whispered.

I limped to the little square window in the door of the observation room. The girl, Stephie, sat at the console in her white stocking cap. I tapped the glass. She looked up, grinned, and motioned for us to come in, but quietly.

We entered, all reverent, like in a funeral home. Once introductions were whispered, she turned back to the console and window looking into the other room. Chad sat in one of the recliners, all sorts of wires and sensors attached to him.

"Is he sleeping?" Cowboy asked.

Stephie shook her head. "Traveling." She glanced up at the digital clock above the window. It read:

02:59:38

"Almost three hours now."

"Traveling?" Andi asked.

"Bilocating." Stephie looked at me, a question on her face like I should have already told them. I shook my head and she continued. "It's a fairly simple technique where you train your phantom body to leave your physical body.

"Lucid dreaming," Andi said.

"In a fashion."

Andi nodded. "There have been multiple studies on the practice. Not always favorable."

Stephie continued, "Unlike lucid dreaming, bilocation occurs when the subject is fully awake." She pressed what must have been an intercom button and spoke, "Coming up to three hours." She looked at the clock, waiting until it clicked over to:

03:00:00

"And mark: Three hours."

"How is that possible?" Andi asked. "While being awake?"

"It takes several months of training—learning to merge the brainwaves of the left and right hemispheres, using various biofeedback techniques to lower breathing and heart rates, dropping brain waves from beta to alpha until they finally reach the target state, which would be theta activity."

I was impressed at how smart and confident she sounded when Chad wasn't around.

"Chad told me it used to be an Army program?" I said.

"That's right. They would find gifted individuals and train them to bilocate—send their phantom bodies into enemy installations and spy on top secret operations."

"When you say phantom bodies, is that like their souls?" Cowboy asked.

Stephie shrugged. "Call it what you like. Either way, the results were quite accurate."

"You said, 'gifted' individuals?'" Andi asked.

"That's right. People like Chad, here. Or," she motioned to me, "Belinda."

"Brenda," I corrected her.

"Really? Because he said it was—"

"Trust me, it's Brenda."

"By *gifted*," Andi said, "what do you mean?"

"People who have a natural psychic ability." She nodded to me. "Like the drawings Chad says you draw. I imagine your psychic rating is quite—"

"She ain't no psychic," Cowboy said.

We turned to him. He was doing his best to be polite, but wasn't quite pulling it off. "Miss Brenda here, her gift is prophetic, like in the Bible. Not psychic. That's occult."

Stephie frowned. "I fail to see the difference."

"Trust me, ma'am, it's a big difference. One is a gift from God, the other, it's a counterfeit used to trick and trap people into—"

"I'm in." Chad's voice came from the console speaker. I looked through the window. His eyes were closed and he seemed totally relaxed, but it was definitely him doing the talking.

Stephie hit the intercom switch. "What do you see?"

"The usual snow. Lots of it."

She scooted to a nearby keyboard and began typing as he continued.

"Same mountains. Everything's the same."

"And the wall?" she asked.

"I'm approaching it now. Seems a lot colder today."

Stephie glanced at another readout. "Your skin temperature is 89.9." She leaned closer to the window. "I see goosebumps on your arms."

"I should have worn a coat."

"Is that possible?" I asked. "Goosebumps?"

She answered while checking other readouts. "There has to be some connection between his phantom and physical body."

"Or?"

"Or he'd be dead."

His voice came back through the speaker. "Still no opening. Still no way to access—wait. What the—"

"Problem?" she asked.

"There's a giant triangle. Can't make out its composition, but it's floating five, six hundred meters above me and to the right. The thing is huge, like an ocean liner and—" He sucked in his breath. "It spotted me. It spotted me and is heading directly for me."

"Chad, get out of there. Now."

"Wait. Something's got hold of me. Nothing physical but . . . like a force field or something."

"Chad?"

No answer.

"Chad, answer me! Chad, I'm ending the session."

"No," he gasped, "too dangerous."

"Dangerous?" I asked.

She answered without looking. "Shock to his limbic system. The transition has to be gentle. And self-initiated. Too abrupt and it could break the connection, his vitals could shut down, go into cardiac arr—"

"It's okay. I'm free." You could hear the strain in his voice, see his chest heaving up and down. "Now if I can just hide behind this outcropping."

Stephie called out another reading. "Heart rate 182. BP is—"

"There. Good. Okay, I'm coming home."

And then silence.

"Chad . . .

More silence.

I looked to Stephie. She waited, nervously watching the clock. Tens seconds. Fifteen. We all figured it was better not to talk.

At twenty seconds, she hit the intercom again. "Chad, can you hear me. Chad, do you—"

He began gasping for breath.

"Chad—"

Suddenly his eyes popped open. He blinked, then lifted his head and looked through the window, grinning.

"You're back!" Stephie cried.

Still breathing hard, he answered, "Of course I'm back." He spotted me and our little group standing beside her. "So the pupil has returned to the teacher, has she? Oh, and look, she's brought her pals."

# Chapter 8

"The Gate?" Andi asked incredulously. "You were at the headquarters of the Gate?"

"Their wall, yeah." Chad didn't bother swallowing his mouthful of eggs. "You want to pass those hash browns here? These little excursions leave me starved."

Cowboy, who'd put away a fair amount of breakfast himself, passed the platter up the table.

It had been a long night. The sun was just peeking over the mountains. Stephie had thrown together a pretty impressive breakfast—unnoticed by Chad, but appreciated by the rest of us. We were eating outside, enjoying the few minutes of cool air before the desert heated up. Well, Cowboy and Chad were eating. Stephie was flitting about the table making sure we were all happy (*we* as in Chad)—while me and Andi nibbled here and there, carefully listening.

The kid continued, doing his best to impress Andi. At twenty-two, he was three or four years her junior. But it didn't stop him from making the moves. Moves she was either too polite to comment on or too naive to notice. Didn't matter. If Boy Wonder was trolling, me and Cowboy would make sure he got both arms broken before reeling her in. "It's their headquarters," he said, "at least here on earth. Or above it."

I frowned.

"From what I've been able to hear, they have plenty more."

We all traded looks, rememberin' Littlefoot's comments during our last outing.

"You've seen 'em?" Cowboy asked.

He shook his head. "Just heard their thoughts."

"And you think they're from another planet," I said.

"Another universe," Andi corrected.

I nodded. "Right, another universe?"

"For starters, yeah. But from what I can tell, there's something more."

"More?" I said.

"We're talking another dimension. Maybe several."

We traded looks some more.

Andi cleared their throat. "You say you've heard their conversations?"

He looked at her and smiled. "Yeah, lots of

times." He gave a little stretch. "Not that I'm one to brag—"

"Since when?" I muttered.

"—but with my gift it's pretty easy to hear what they're thinking. And believe me, sweet cheeks, you folks better worry, because they're thinking a lot."

Andi ignored the flirt and said, "I thought you didn't care what they were thinking, that you weren't interested in stopping them."

"I'm not."

"Then . . ."

"I'm just interested in the money."

"How's that work?" I said.

"Easy. I sell you information. You pass it on to the Watchers. I walk away rich and safe."

"Safe 'cause you're not taking sides," I said.

"Safe's important." He turned to Cowboy. "Which explains that AK-47 you've been wondering about at my front door."

Cowboy's jaw slacked. "How did you know I was thinking . . ." He slowed to a stop as the kid tapped his temple. The big fellow scowled, not liking it one bit.

"And how do we know the information you'll offer is correct?" Andi asked.

"Because I'm never wrong."

"I'll be sure to tell Belinda that," I said.

He smiled. "I'm never wrong about important issues."

"And how do we know we can trust you?" Andi said.

He turned his gaze on her, getting all Barry White. "Because I never lie to people I'm attracted to. Or to those who find me attractive."

I cut in. "And the professor. You've seen him?"

"Maybe."

I scoffed. "How much they supposed to pay for *maybe*?"

Stephie, who was making the rounds with a pitcher of orange juice, came to his defense. "Everything Chad's seen has been carefully recorded. We keep very good logs."

Chad ignored her and leaned across the table to me. "What if I were to show you?"

"Show me what?"

"Like I said, you have a little bit of the gift. Pathetically small, I'll grant you, but you still have it."

"I'm flattered."

"You have enough for me to at least take you for a little spin."

I felt myself stiffen, but managed to look calm. I think.

He turned back to Andi. "And you, there's so much you could learn by watching. By just staying at my side."

"Me?"

"Of course. I can always use another assistant. The more the merrier."

The pitcher slipped from Stephie's hand, crashing to the table. "Gracious me, I'm so sorry." She grabbed a napkin and started mopping up.

I barely noticed. Not because of Chad's flirting or his out-of-control ego. But because of the offer. What if I really could connect with the professor? What if there really was a way to discover the Gate's headquarters?

I turned back to him. "How long would it take?"

"For what?"

He was dangling the bait, but I had to play along. "How long would it take to get me ready for something like that?"

"With me as your teacher? I'd say . . ." He gave us a dramatic pause, then answered: "Now."

I caught my breath.

"If you have the nerve."

I closed my mouth, gave the muscles in my jaw a workout. He was setting the hook all right, there was no doubt about it. And we both knew I had no choice but to swallow it.

"Miss Brenda?"

I looked to Cowboy.

"I don't think that's a very good idea."

"Because?" Chad asked.

"Because it's the occult. You're playing with things you don't understand."

"And you people do?" Chad asked.

"I understand what's forbidden."

"According to?"

"The Bible."

It was the kid's turn to scoff. "Too bad your professor the Bible scholar didn't get that memo."

"You really think she could see the professor?" Andi asked.

"Maybe. Who knows? Like I said to—" he paused, pretending he was trying to remember my name—"Brenda here; the man was definitely researching our stuff." He turned back to me. "I can't promise you the professor, but I can take you to the Gate. At least its perimeter, the one here on Earth."

I felt my ears beginning to burn. Heard the faint pounding of my heart.

"Miss Brenda?" It was Cowboy again. Doing his

best to warn me.

The kid cocked his head sideways, all coy-like. "Well?"

I took the slightest breath to steady myself, then gave the answer. "Of course."

# Chapter 9

"Heartbeat's at forty-eight." Stephie's voice came through the speaker of our room, all soft and gentle. "You can bring it lower than that."

I took a deep breath, trying to relax.

"Don't *try* to relax," Boy Wonder said. He was stretched out in the recliner beside me, talking like he was reading my mind, which he probably was. "Just let it happen."

"Approaching theta," Stephie said. "That's good, very good."

People, they call me a control freak. They're probably right. I been 'round too much to let some stranger call the shots. Even well-meaning, white chicks trying to use their hocus-pocus hypno-voice on me.

"But she's trying to help," the kid answered.

*Will you stop that!* I thought.

"Oops," Stephie said, "you're back up to alpha."

I took another breath. I tried focusing on the soft flute music playing in the background, imagined myself melting into the recliner.

"That's better. Good, good. Keep breathing, nice and slow. In and out. In and out. A little more. Good. And . . . we're there."

For being *there*, I felt exactly the same. Except, well, gradually, I noticed it was like I didn't have any arms and legs. And that I was falling. Falling through darkness. Except it wasn't all dark. There was some sort of tunnel around me. On all sides. And I wasn't falling down, I was floating up.

*Where am I?* I spoke or thought or both.

"Just go with it," Chad said.

I heard wind begin blowing in my ears. Faint at first, but it got pretty loud pretty fast. I actually felt it on my face. That's when the lights or stars or whatever they were started going by. Slow at first, but they picked up speed 'til they were streaking past me, blurring by like one of those Star War movies. And with all that blurring I started seeing faces on the tunnel walls. Actually the walls *were* the faces, some small, some big, most creepy like those gargoyles you see on top of buildings.

Like the ones I'd sketched on my pad.

*Do you see me?* It was Chad's voice again. I couldn't tell if it was inside my head or out.

*I don't—*

*Focus on the center of the tunnel. Away from the faces.*

In my mind, I pretended to squint, looking hard

until . . . there, fifty yards away. Chad was standing waving his arms at me.

*I see you. I see someone.*

*Of course you do.* As usual he was talking down to me like I was a kid. But suddenly things changed. His voice and image rippled like a wave. They did it again, faster. And faster. 'Til everything was a blur, just rippling colors and sound.

*Chad! Chad, You there?*

No answer. Just the flowing colors and sounds. Then the sound of birds. Then voices—a boy and a girl. The colors began taking shape. Patches of blue sky. White, puffy clouds. Tree tops. Then roofs, then porches, front yards. Not ghetto, but lower class. I looked down to see I was standing on an uneven sidewalk, weeds growing between the cracks.

The voices got clearer.

I turned to see the two kids just a few feet away, twelve, maybe thirteen-years-old. A pretty girl in a print blouse and cutoffs. She was doing most of the talking. Arguing, really. And the boy? No doubt. Don't ask me how, but I knew it was a younger version of Chad Thorton, complete with cracking voice.

"Melissa, please. You gotta understand—"

"You ruined my grade! You ruined everything!" The girl pretended to cry, but it was obviously fake. Not that Chad could tell. The boy was a newbie when it came to drama queens.

He tried explaining. "I, I didn't want to do it in the first place. It's cheating and that's wrong, but—"

"You gave me wrong questions for the test and you blame me?"

"No one's blaming—"

"You said you could read Mrs. Snider's mind. You said you could tell me what she'd ask."

"I said I'd try."

"You're such a loser. Everyone says so."

He tried to hide the pain filling his face.

"A freak. That's what they say. Freak!"

"Melis—"

"I should have listened." Before he answered, she repeated: "Freak!" Then turned and ran off.

"Melissa?" You could hear his anguish. And unlike the girl, you could see his tears were real. "Melissa . . ."

I wanted to say something, but doubted he could hear or see me.

His face rippled in another wave. Trees and houses blurred back to colors and light. The ground shook under my feet. Only it wasn't ground. Other faces appeared. All around me. Then seats and walls . . . of a school bus. I was standing inside a moving school bus.

Kids were shouting and laughing. Pushing and shoving to see out the windows on one side. I joined them—surprised, but not scared when I passed through them like they were pockets of air.

I got to the windows. There, at the top of a flagpole, a pair of jockey underwear was flapping in the breeze. But that wasn't what the kids were laughing at. It was the sixteen-year-old who was tied to the bottom of the pole, buck naked, trying to cover his privates. Chad Thorton.

My face grew hot. No one should have to go through that. Particularly a teen. Not even if that teen happened to be wonder boy. I turned and pushed my way through to the front of the bus. I'd barely stepped out before the picture blurred and disappeared. Along with the laughing and jeering. Now there was another voice. Smaller. Helpless.

"Daddy? Daddy, please. I'll be good."

Bits and pieces of a different picture appeared. A closed door. A crack of light under it.

"Daddy . . ."

And the smell. Urine. And worse. Like someone had taken a dump right there in . . . in a closet. I was standing in a closet. Next to me, huddled against a wall, legs pulled in, whimpering, was a little boy, five-years-old—maybe younger. Another version of Chad Thorton.

"Daddy, please, I'll be good, I promise . . ."

Next to the crack under the door was a dog dish, its bowl barely filled with water.

"Daddy . . ."

Suddenly I heard popping. Outside, but close. Fast and rapid. Adrenalin surged through my body. I know gunfire when I hear it. With that realization, came the weight returning to my arms, my legs. Then the pressure of the recliner, the sensors around my chest and arms, the restraints.

"Chad? Brenda?" It was Stephie's voice. "You two need to come back. Guys . . ."

I pried open my eyes. I was back in the room. I turned to see Chad.

More gun fire. Automatic.

I tried speaking. "What's—" My voice was thick and hoarse. I tried again. "What's happening?"

"An attack," Chad said as he began unhooking his monitors. "We're under attack."

It took me a minute to unhook the monitors and get off the restraints. Stephie was still in the observation room, shutting stuff down. Cowboy and Andi were already outside. Not Chad. Boy Wonder had left me behind only to get as far as the front door where he refused to step out.

"What's goin' on?" I shouted as I ran toward him.

"The spheres!" he yelled. "They're back."

I reached the door and looked past him. Not far from my car floated Cowboy. He was fifteen feet above the ground. Around him, forming the corners of a clear box, were not one of the orbs, but eight. Each about ten feet from the other. And, though you could barely see them in the daylight, there were walls stretching between 'em. Six walls, forming a prison with Cowboy inside: a ten-by-ten foot cube he couldn't get out of.

"Cowboy!"

"Shh." Chad took a half step behind the door. "They'll hear you."

I gave him a scowl.

"He'll be okay," he said.

"Okay? They got him locked up in some sort of box."

"He started it."

"What?"

"See those two on the ground?"

I looked back outside and spotted two more orbs. They were in the dirt, ripped apart and smoldering.

"And that?" He motioned to the AK-47 lying on the ground. "Looks like he shot them down."

I swore and started out the door. Chad caught my arm. "You have no idea what they can do."

"Yeah." I shook him off and stepped outside. "I do."

Cowboy saw me and shouted, pounded on the walls, trying to warn me. I couldn't hear him. Didn't matter if I could.

Andi thought the same. She stood out there, not far away, hands on her hips shouting up at them. "Put him down! Put him down this instant!" Granted, it wasn't her best plan, or her brightest. But it was vintage Andi. Don't let her southern politeness fool you. When it came to protecting the rest of our team, she was one mother of a momma bear.

The orbs ignored her. Me, too. They obviously needed more convincing. So I headed for the rifle. I barely got there and scooped it up 'fore they figured what I was up to. Suddenly, the whole cube, Cowboy and all, began spinning . . . and coming straight at me. I didn't even get the gun raised before one of the corner orbs knocked it out of my hand.

The next one knocked me to the ground.

And the next one?

Well there was no next, 'cause suddenly I was inside the cube with Cowboy. The walls still spun, but we hung inside, pretty much stationary. There was so much wind I couldn't hear a thing. But I could see. Andi stood right below us, shouting and carrying on. Until the cube started toward her.

But she still wouldn't back down.

Then, just before we swallowed her up to join the party, my car window blew to pieces. Glass flying everywhere.

Then my side mirror.

Then my left front tire.

I turned and spotted Stephie. She'd raced outside, picked up the gun and was firing away. I appreciated the effort, though she wasn't exactly the best of shots. Still, what she lacked in skill, she made up with enthusiasm. Bullets flew everywhere and in every direction.

Our whirling cube changed direction. Instead of going after Andi, it went after Stephie. But the girl kept firing away, looking like the star in some old Rambo movie. Then, somehow, don't ask me how, she actually got one. The orb exploded into a ball of sparks and fell to the ground.

Without it, one of our walls fizzled and disappeared. And since the cube was still spinning we got thrown out, sailed through the air, and landed a dozen feet away.

And Stephie? She just kept shootin'. Eventually,

she hit another one, that exploded and fell. The cube, which had been wobbling from losing the first orb, went completely out of control. It spun and tumbled every which way until it slammed into the ground, bounced, smashed into my car (leaving a healthy dent at the end of my racing stripe), crashed back to the ground, and then flew apart.

But only for a second. 'Cause the orbs came back together again, forming a tight little circle. They hovered there like they were trying to make up their minds.

Stephie helped them decide by firing a dozen more rounds—mostly into my car. Still, the orbs got the message. They shot straight up into the sky, faster than anything I'd ever seen, 'til they were completely out of sight.

Everything got real quiet. Me and Cowboy, we struggled to our feet, checking for bruises and broken body parts. Andi, too. And Stephie? She looked as surprised at what she'd done as the rest of us. Which explains why she stared at the rifle a moment before throwing it to the ground.

That's when I heard my cell buzzing. I pulled it from my pocket and saw it was a text message from Daniel. It read:

*Are you okay?*

I shook my head, once again amazed at his timing. Even though my fingers were shaking I managed to type back:

*Yes. You?*

I barely finished before his second half came in.

*You have to get out of there.*
*Something bad is coming.*
*Real bad.*

I frowned and was about to answer when I heard Chad's voice.

"We all good?" He stood outside the door, hands in his pockets, looking like nothing ever happened. And it hadn't. At least to him. "Well, will you look at that car."

He strolled up to it . . . shattered window, broken mirror, blown out tire, giant crater, and the steady dribble of water which could only come from my radiator.

"Don't want to be a downer, but it looks like you may be stuck here a while."

Chapter 11

When I was a kid, going twenty-four hours with no sleep wasn't a big deal. But now? Forget it. I barely hit the pillow before I was out. In this case that would be Stephie's pillow.

"You just make yourself comfortable," she'd said. "You've had a long day."

"What about you?"

"I've got some tools in the side shed. Let me see what I can do for that radiator of yours. Looks like it just might be a hose."

I'd like to think she was just bein' helpful, and maybe she was. But I'm guessing some of it had to do with keeping an eye on Chad, not to mention getting

Andi out of there as soon as possible. Not that he'd have a chance with Andi. But to protect her interests, I understand that a girl's gotta do what a girl's gotta do.

Still, whatever she saw in him was beyond me.

Okay, I admit maybe I'd started feeling a little sorry for him, considering what I'd seen in his past—the bullying and all that abuse. And yeah, that probably explains him being such a jerk. But it was going to take more than that to forgive him for being the coward hiding behind the door.

Course he had his excuses which he'd been only too happy to share later, around the table. "It's obvious I'm the one they were after. Considering all I've been accomplishing."

"Don't know about that," I said. "They seemed pretty interested in Cowboy, here."

"Only because he drew their attention with the gun." Leaning past Cowboy, he spoke to Andi. "Would you be a doll and go ask Stephie to get us some more coffee?"

Andi's response—narrowing her gaze and ignoring him—made me proud of her. I got back to the question at hand. The one that had been needling me. "What happened when we were bilocating?"

"You mean the Timefold thing?" he said.

"Is that what you call it?"

"That's what I call it."

"I didn't exactly make it to the Gate's headquarters."

"Yeah, sometimes that happens," he said. "I wondered where you went."

"So it was real?"

"What did you see?"

"Mostly you as a kid. Like when they tied you to the flag pole naked."

"You saw that?"

I nodded. "And when, it must have been your old man, when he locked you in the closet with just a dog's bowl for water and—"

"Right, right," he cut me off. "Time folding."

"So you traveled back in time?" Andi asked.

"In a manner of speaking." He called toward the kitchen door. "Steph? How's that coffee coming?"

"I'll be there in a jiffy," came the voice

He turned back to us. "When we bilocate, we leave behind our three dimensional world and enter a higher dimension."

"The spirit world," Cowboy said.

"If that's what you want to call it, sure. And right next to that dimension is another. Time."

"I thought time was supposed to be the fourth dimension," I said.

He looked at me, musing. "It would be nice if things were that tidy, wouldn't it? Let alone, stable. But as you've experienced, that's not always the case."

"True," Cowboy said. "We've had some pretty crazy adventures."

"Right. Whatever. Stephie!"

So now I'm in Stephie's room, trying to get some sleep. The sleep came, no problem. Not the rest.

Maybe it was Daniel's warning: *Something bad is coming. Real bad.* Or Cowboy's uneasiness about psychics. Or the frog-faced gremlins I'd seen along the edges of the tunnel.

They're what haunted me the most. Seems every time I closed my eyes and drifted off, they were there. On Stephie's walls, her ceiling. Some even on the bed.

For the most part I was able to ignore them. Just tellin' myself they were a dream.

Until a couple of them jumped on my chest.

I actually thought I could feel their weight, like they were makin' it hard to breathe. I tried to shout, but nothing came. I tried to move, but it was like I was paralyzed. When I opened my eyes they were inches from my face, leering down at me. I gasped, tried again to scream.

Nothing came but a croaking cry.

They moved closer to my lips. I clamped my mouth tight, my nostrils flaring, trying to get enough air. I tried screaming again. A pathetic whimper.

"Miss Brenda? Miss Brenda, wake up." I turned and there was Cowboy, kneeling on the floor beside me. "You okay?"

I raised my head and looked. They were gone.

I took a deep breath.

"Are you okay?"

I took another breath and nodded. "Just a bad dream, that's all."

He looked at me skeptically.

"I'm all right. Really."

"Hmm," was all he said. Then, without a word, he turned and, still on the floor, rested his back against the mattress.

"What are you doing?" I said.

"Jus' staying here . . . case you have another one."

# Chapter 12

"Brenda?" Somebody was shaking me . . . again.

I pried open one eye to see Andi staring down at me. "'Sup?" I muttered.

"It's Chad. We've got a problem."

"You think?" I tried turning over, but she stopped me.

"I'm serious."

"What's going on?" Cowboy, who'd fallen asleep on my floor, was doing his own imitation of trying to sound coherent.

"Chad." The fear in Andi's voice told me it was going to be impossible to go back to sleep. "He needs our help."

A minute or two later we were all crowding into the room with the recliners. Stephie was there, doing everything she could to pull Chad out of his trance or whatever he was in. He was all hooked up and strapped into the recliner like before, but this time his body was jerking like he was having some sort of seizure.

"Chad!" She shook him. "Can you hear me?"

An alarm was sounding in the Observation Room.

"What's wrong?" Andi said.

"He's gone."

"He's what?"

"He tried coming back, but something—I don't know. Chad!"

"How often does this happen?" Andi asked.

"Chad!"

"Stephie?" Andi repeated.

"Never."

"You sayin' he *can't* come back or he won't?" I said.

"Chad, can you hear me?"

"Can't or won't?"

"Can't. And the longer he stays—" She couldn't finish and started shaking him again.

"There's got to be somethin' you can do?" Cowboy said.

"Not out here."

"Out here?" Andi asked.

"It has to be from inside. Someone has to join him from the inside—help him out from in there."

"So do it," Cowboy said.

"Not me. It has to be someone with the ability. Someone with experience who can . . ."

She came to a stop and turned to me.

I looked away.

"Someone with the ability?" Andi repeated.

"Yes. Someone who can—"

His body gave a violet jerk. If it wasn't for the restraints he'd have flown out of the chair.

"Chad!" Stephie cried.

His mouth opened like he was trying to scream, but only choking sounds came out.

Andi looked at me. "Brenda?"

I pretended not to hear. I knew exactly what she was thinking and no way was I going back in there, wherever "there" was. Especially for the likes of him.

Another alarm sounded from the Observation Room. Shriller than the other.

"He's going into v-fib!" Stephie yelled. She began ripping off his sensors, fighting with the one wrapped around his chest. "Give me a hand!"

Cowboy obliged, holding down Chad's bucking body, which freed Stephie to struggle with the sensors.

"A crash cart?" Andi shouted. "Do you have a defibrillator?"

Stephie shook her head as she tore open his shirt. "Too expensive. Said we didn't need it."

I stared down at him as he continued to fight and gasp. Then I heard a voice:

*"Daddy . . ."* It didn't come from him, but from the little boy locked in the closet. I looked around. Nobody else heard it. *"Daddy, I'll be good."*

Stephie thumped on his bare chest. Then again. And again.

Nothing. Except . . .

It was no longer his body she pounded. It was the chest of the naked teen, arms stretched out to a flag pole. The boy's cries were drowned out by older kids —laughing, mocking.

"Brenda?"

I blinked, turned to see Andi looking at me.

I shook my head. "No!"

Another alarm began.

"He's flat-lining!" Stephie cried. She shoved the heel of her palm against his chest and began pumping with both hands, giving him CPR.

Only it wasn't him. Or the teenage kid. It was the twelve-year-old version. I still heard the crowd jeering, the little boy crying, but now I saw and heard the twelve-year-old pleading with the girl:

*"Melissa . . ."*

*"You're such a loser. Everyone says so."*

"What are you doing?" I looked up to see Andi shouting to Cowboy.

He glanced up from his cell. "Calling 911."

"They'll never make it!" Stephie cried as she continued to pump. "We're too far!" She threw another look to me.

*"Daddy, please, Daddy, I'll be good.* The laughter was louder. So was the girl, *"Freak. That's what they say. Freak!"*

"Brenda?" Andi asked again.

The images returned, repeated themselves. The naked teen. The twelve-year-old. The kid locked in the closet.

*"Daddy, I'll be good."*

*"Freak!*

The laughter grew to a roar, the voices screaming

over it,

*"Daddy!*
*Freak!*
*I'll be good.*
*Everybody says—*
*Daddy, please—*
*Freak!*
*Daddy I'll be—*
*Freak—*
*Dad—"*

"All right!" I shouted. "All right!"

Cowboy looked up at me.

But Stephie got it. So did Andi.

"Get her into the other chair," Stephie ordered. "Quickly."

Andi said, "Will she be in any danger?"

"Not much. I don't know. Hurry!"

## Chapter 13

The voices still screamed in my head as I flew through the tunnel. Maybe they were in my head, maybe they weren't, who knows? Add to that my snarling, toad-faced friends stuck to the side of the walls, and it was quite a party.

I was coming up to the end of the tunnel and saw what looked like a blizzard—blowing snow, wind growing stronger by the second.

"Looks like a snow storm," I said, or thought, or both.

Stephie answered. "You're approaching the end of the portal. Any sign of Chad?"

"I hear his voices, but don't see anything."

"Follow them. Follow the voices. Chances are they'll lead you to him. But slow down. Start walking."

"I'm flying. How am I supposed to—"

"In your imagination. Think yourself heavy, so heavy you're falling to your feet."

It made no sense. But nothing else did, either, so I gave it a try. I pretended I was big; Jabba-the-Hut big. And it worked. Immediately my feet touched down and I started walking. But I'd only taken a step or two before the whole tunnel disappeared. Now I was surrounded by giant, snow-covered cliffs on every side. And icy wind that cut through my shirt.

"You in the mountains, yet?"

"Yeah, how did you—"

"The Gate's headquarters. This is where we've been going for days. Do you see the wall?"

"Nothing. Just rocks and snow and—wait a minute." Directly in front of me I spotted something flat and coated in snow. It stretched out in every direction as far as I could see.

"What is it? What do you see?"

I reached out and gently touched it. It was freezing. "Some sort of surface," I said. "Flat and smooth."

"The wall. Good. He's got to be around there somewhere."

I pressed harder to get a better feel. That's when my fingers disappeared.

"What the—" I pulled back my hand and my fingers returned.

"What's wrong? What happened?"

I reached out again, hesitated, then pressed the wall again. Same thing. I pushed harder, felt the wind blow against my hand, then my wrist. Just like moving through those kids in the school bus. I pulled my hand out. Checked it. Everything looked good.

"Brenda? What's happening?"

I tried again, this time shoving my whole arm through and pulling it out. Still no problem.

"Brenda?"

I stuck both arms into it. Same thing, which I figured was good enough. I closed my eyes, clenched my jaw and inched forward. The puff of air hit my chest, then my face, and then—

"Bren—"

The snow was gone. The cold too. I was floating again. This time in front of a giant window. One that looked down on, and I know this sounds crazy, but I was looking down on the Earth. It was small, 'bout the size of a soccer ball, with a thin haze around it. And stars. Hundreds, thousands of them. Really breathtaking. And tranquil. Except for the laughter. And the voices:

*I'll be good. Everybody says—Daddy. Melissa, please— Freak! Daddy I'll be— Freak! Dad—*

They were coming from behind me, louder than ever. I turned and caught my breath. There were thousands of floating snowflakes. Beautiful. Each one just a little bigger than a man. Not flat, but round like globes. And they were growing. Large crystals kept forming along their edges making them bigger and bigger. And in each crystal was a scene, like a 3-D movie. Hundreds of them playing at once. More being added by the minute.

"You guys won't believe this," I said.

But there was no answer.

"Hello? Stephie, can you hear me?"

Still nothing. Just the laughter and the voices.

Using my imagination, like I did in the tunnel, I willed myself toward the sound. It worked. I began drifting past one snowflake then another. Just like real snowflakes, each one was different. Each one growing and showing different scenes.

Except, up ahead . . .

One had three children floating around it—actually, on one side of it. Their hands were stretched out and no crystals were growing in that direction. The other sides grew just fine, but the ones closest to the kids' hands had stopped. So, as the snowflake got bigger, it kept getting more and more lopsided. Instead of being beautiful, it was becoming more and more deformed.

The kids must have sensed my presence 'cause all three slowly turned. Goosebumps popped up on my arms. And it had nothing to do with the cold. It was their eyes. They were totally black. Just like the kids we'd seen in Florida.

I gave them a wide birth, and kept following the voices:

*Melissa, please—Freak! Daddy I'll be—*

Finally, I arrived at their source. There was no mistaking it. Somehow, someway this snowflake had to do with Chad Thorton. Not only were the voices the loudest here, but I could actually see a scene of his life playing in the closest crystal. The scene of him hiding behind the door during our fight with the orbs. Beside it was another crystal. This one showing us having breakfast outside with him behind the lab.

"Stephie?" I shouted. "Guys?"

Still no answer.

Carefully, I reached out and touched the outer

crystal. It was frosty and cold, just like the wall. So I pressed harder and my hand passed through, just like with the wall.

Except, I couldn't pull it out. Instead, something powerful grabbed my wrist. It yanked me hard. So hard that before I knew it, I'd fallen inside the giant snowflake.

# Chapter 14

I wasn't lying when I said the snowflakes were 'bout the size of a man. But once I was inside Chad's, I kept falling, going deeper and deeper. And the deeper I went, the more I could see the crystals around me, each one playing a different scene. Things like me driving him to the lab, being chased by the eyeless goons, slamming into him with my car. The deeper I fell, the farther back in his life the scenes went.

Pretty soon I was surrounded by his college years, awkward and nerdy. Even worse were his high school scenes, including the guys stripping him and tying him to the flagpole. Middle school wasn't much better, full of pimples, porn, and, of course, Melissa shutting him down. Finally there were the fights, beatings really, when he was younger. Seemed every wannabe bully practiced on him . . . including his old man.

Then the scenes stopped. As best I could tell I'd reached the center. No more crystals. Just Chad, full grown, on his knees and crying like a baby. Instead of crystals, he was surrounded by shadows. Big ones towering over him. But, as far as I could tell, nothing was making them. They were only shadows, places where the light just sort of vanished.

I called to him. "Chad?"

He looked up, face wet with tears.

"Can you hear me?"

He cocked his head like he heard something. Peered like he was trying to see. But it was obvious he couldn't see through the darkness.

"It's me!" I said.

"Brenda?"

"We gotta get you out of here. Your body, back in the lab, it's—"

"They've caught me. I'm trapped."

"By what? Those things? They're just shadows." I started towards him.

"No! Don't come any closer. It's not safe."

"I didn't come all the way here to be run off by shadows. Now come on, we gotta get you—"

"Go back. Warn the others."

He was starting to piss me off. "They're just shadows. Let's go!" I stepped into the first one. "Let's—" And it hit me. Everything at once. Memories so clear it was like I was there . . .

I'm seven years old, shoplifting Hello Kitty pencils. Other stuff flickers past. Embarrassing stuff.

Shameful. I'm nine years old, giving in to my step-dad, letting him do his thing. Again. And again. Now I'm beating up Jimmy McPherson, torturing the neighbor's cat, breaking school windows. I feel the shadow seeping into me. Icy cold. More stuff. Things I've tried forgetting . . .

Making out with my seventh grade teacher. Doing it with Boyd on the living room floor, Johnson in his Mustang, smoking weed, giving up baby Monique, the meth, breaking into homes. My stomach is turning. I want to puke. I can't catch my breath.

The first abortion. Cussing out Mom. My botched suicide. Her tears sponging up the blood from the bathroom tiles, the second abortion, the DUI's, jail . . .

I begin to sob. Can't help myself. My knees are getting weak. I lower to the ground. No light around me now. Only the shadows. Darkness. And more memories . . .

The dealing. Sex for money. More men than I can count, Caroline's OD, working the Strip. Everything is hopeless. No way out.

When suddenly there is a roar, like a waterfall. The memories shimmer, then break apart. Someone is touching my shoulder. I look up. There's a small patch of light. In it I see the old nun, the one who helped us back in Italy.

"Help . . ." my voice came out as a raspy whisper.

She understood. She took my arm and helped me to my feet. And suddenly . . . the shadows were gone. I could see them, feel them all around me, but they weren't in me, they weren't on me.

"Brenda . . . are you there?"

I turned to Chad. He was just feet away and still

covered in dark. The old lady raised her arm. It wasn't much. A small gesture. But suddenly there was a ripping sound, like a tearing sheet. A thin shaft of light shot through the darkness from above and landed on his head. The shadows pulled back, or maybe the beam got wider, or both. Whatever was happening, he was drenched in light.

"Chad!" This time he saw me. "Let's get out of here!"

He scrambled to his feet and stumbled toward us. The nun turned. More light came down. In front of us. Blinding. And the nun was gone. Vanished. But the light remained, forming a path. I grabbed Chad's hand and we ran as fast as we could.

His scenes began playing in the crystals around us. More than once I had to pull him away—after all they were about him. But we followed the path 'til there were no more, 'til we reached the edge of the snowflake and its frosty wall.

"Now what?" he said.

I had no idea. But since I could see the path kept on going beyond the snowflake, I figured why not. I closed my eyes, walked forward and stepped through the wall. Chad followed.

But instead of being with the other snowflakes or even looking down on Earth, we were outside the Gate's wall, freezing our butts off.

"Miss Brenda?" Cowboy's voice. I could barely hear him through the wind. "Miss Brenda, you there?"

"Yeah," I shouted. "We're here."

"Thank the Lord," he said. "You gotta hurry back. We just lost Chad. Don't need to lose you, too."

"No such luck," I shouted. "He's here with me

now."

"That's not possible."

"Guess you'll have to tell him that." I turned to Chad, but he wasn't moving. His eyes stared lifelessly.

"Hey!" I waved my hand in front of him. Nothing. "Hey!"

"He ain't there, Miss Brenda."

"No." I reached over and shook him. "He's right here." But he didn't move. He didn't breathe. I shook him harder.

"He's gone. Now you gotta get back—"

"No." I grabbed him by the collar. "He's with me."

"Miss Bren—"

Bein' stubborn has its plusses and minuses. I didn't know which this would be. But I did know one thing.

I pulled him forward. "He's with me and we're comin' back!"

# Chapter 15

It wasn't hard willing me and Chad back into the portal. But staying in the center of it was tougher than I thought. Still, we'd come this far, no way was I giving up now. "Keep doing that CPR," I shouted. "Don't let up."

"It's no use." This time it was Andi. "He's gone."

"No! I'm bringing him home!"

Course it might of been easier if the guy wasn't dead weight. It took both hands just to hang on to him, which kept throwing us off balance and causing us to bang along the tunnel's wall like a pinball.

No problem—'cept for those snarling, frog-faced things. Seems every time we slammed into one, we picked it up as a hitchhiker. Creepy? Yeah. But not as creepy as them crawling over us. I tried not to panic, but Stephie and them must of saw it on my sensors.

"You okay?" Cowboy asked.

"Yeah," I said. "It's just these things."

"What things?"

I watched one climbing up Chad's chest toward his face.

"Go on!" I shouted. "Leave him alone!"

"What things?"

"These gremlin things. The ones I sketched, they—" I gasped as it crawled up his neck and onto his face.

"Demons, Miss Brenda? You talkin' 'bout them demons you drew?"

"I don't know what I'm talking about, but—"

I watched as it pried open Chad's lips with its talons then suddenly dissolved. Not dissolved, really. More like turned misty. A mist that shot into his mouth and down his throat.

I might of screamed a little.

"Miss Brenda?"

Another was scampering right behind it. It leaped on his face where it also dissolved and shot down his throat. Then another behind it. Like they were playing follow the leader.

I felt something on my own stomach. I looked down and saw one crawlin' up me, too. "Wake me up," I shouted. "Get me outta here!"

"We can't." Stephie said. You could hear the emotion in her voice. "You've got to do it yourself or it could damage your limbic system."

I watched the first one move up my chest. It was slimy, wart-covered and had a nasty overbite.

"I don't care what it damages. I don't want these

things in me!"

There was no answer.

"Hello? Anybody?"

Cowboy came back on. "Miss Brenda? Will you pray with me?"

"What!?"

"We got the power. We got the authority."

"Cowboy!"

"All we got to do is use it."

The thing had reached the base of my neck. I heard its fangs gnashing and clicking. I clenched my jaw shut. Shouted through gritted teeth: "Anything! Just do it!"

"All right, then," he said. "Demons of hell—"

It crawled up my neck.

"—I command you by the authority of Jesus Christ—"

Now it was on my chin—claws poking and prodding, looking for an opening.

"—leave!" Cowboy shouted. "Go!"

Nothing happened.

"Miss Brenda, you got to agree with me. Brenda?"

I swallowed and gave a hm-mm, which was about all I could come up with. And it was about all I needed. 'Cause when Cowboy shouted, "Go!" again, something happened. Something brushed against my face. Wind, but harder. At the same time I heard a smack and saw the thing flying off, squealing as it fell into the tunnel.

The others that had been following it up my chest froze. But Cowboy wasn't done.

"Do you hear me?" he shouted. "In the name of Jesus Christ, I order you to leave!"

Their heads swiveled, eyes filled with panic.

"All of you! Leave! Now!"

I felt another blast of wind. Heard the things shrieking and screaming as they got swept off, tumbling into the darkness.

But they didn't leave Chad. When I turned to him I saw a line of 'em continuing to run up his chest and leap into his mouth.

"Cowboy," I shouted. "What about Chad? You've got to—"

Stephie interrupted. "You're at level now. Take a breath. Force yourself to wake."

"But—"

"Now! Hurry!"

I did like she said. I took a breath and made my eyes open. The light was bright, but there was Andi and Cowboy staring down at me. It took some doing, but I turned my head toward Chad in the other chair. He was anything but dead. His body twisted and fought against the restraints, his eyes bulging.

"I thought—" my throat was dry as sand. "I thought he was dead."

Cowboy explained as Andi removed the sensors. "We did like you said. We kept up the CPR. But then . . ." He didn't finish.

Stephie stood beside Chad, stroking his head, trying to calm him, but he would have none of it. "We read about this in the Army logs," she said. "We knew it was a risk, but we never—"

"Read about what?" I asked.

"Sometimes the subjects—" she tried to be calm and brave, but that's hard when someone is snapping and snarling at you like a wild animal. "Sometimes they returned with severe mental illness." She looked down at him. "Schizophrenia. Or worse."

"That ain't schizophrenia," Cowboy said. "That's demons."

"Demons?" Andi repeated.

"That's what was attacking Miss Brenda."

They looked to me and I answered. "It was something."

"But she's okay," Stephie said. "How come she's okay and Chad, he's—"

"Cause I took authority," Cowboy said. "Miss Brenda agreed and I used my authority to—"

"Then I'll do it," she said, "with Chad."

"I don't think that's such a—"

She turned to the kid and shouted, "Demons!"

"Miss Stephie, I don't—"

"I command you to leave Chad."

No response. Just more snarling and snapping.

"Like I said—" Cowboy came to a stop as Chad's eyes flew open.

"Chad!" Stephie cried. "You're back." She threw her arms around him.

He opened his mouth, tried to say something.

"What?" she said. She lowered her ear to his lips.

He tried again, a low, raspy whisper.

"Yes!" she said. "Until you're stronger, of course I'll take them. Then we can both find a way to—"

"Miss Steph—!"

But Cowboy was too late. She gave a startled cry. Her head flew back. Her eyes widened and she began choking.

"Stephie?" Andi shouted.

"No," Chad wheezed, trying to talk. "That wasn't me."

"Miss Stephie, are you—"

"A trick." Chad coughed. "They tricked her—"

Stephie cut him off with a scream—more like a howl, deep and from her gut. Then she doubled over, gagging, holding herself up by the medical cart between me and Chad.

"It's them," Cowboy shouted. "They've left him and gone into her."

"Do something!" I yelled. "Cowboy, do—"

"In the name of Jesus." He stepped toward her. "In the name of Jesus Christ, I—"

She came up fast, medical tray in hand. She slammed it hard into his face. Harder than a person her size could swing. Cowboy staggered backward. Andi tried to catch him, but was no match for his weight. They fell to the ground, Cowboy thumping his head on the tile floor. Not bad, but enough to leave him dazed.

"Tank!" Andi shouted to him. "Are you all right?"

Meanwhile Stephie bolted out the door. Out the door and out the building.

"Stop her!" Chad shouted. "Before they—" He broke into a coughing fit. Tried to move, but the sensors and restraints held him down.

I threw my feet over the side of my recliner and rose. Things went white a moment and I had to reach out and steady myself. Andi stayed on the floor helping Cowboy as Chad kept yelling, "Stop her! Somebody!"

I finally got my head clear enough to stumble out of the room. My sprained ankle didn't help. "Stephie!"

Outside, the late afternoon sun blinded me, but I caught movement near the highway and limped after her. "Stephie!"

She heard my voice as she reached the highway

and stopped and turned.

"Come back in," I yelled. "Let Cowboy help. We all can—"

Her voice was deep and guttural. "You have no idea what you're dealing with."

The tone gave me chills and I slowed to a stop.

"You think you can stop us?" she said.

I cleared my throat. "Stop who?"

"Have you not read your own scriptures?" Before I could answer, her face twisted with pain. "Help me." It was Stephie's voice. "Please. Help—" She stooped over, like she was fighting something, then rose with the other voice. "Continue down this path and your fate will be no different than your partner's."

"My part—Are you talking about the professor?"

An approaching eighteen-wheeler hit its horn—the driver obviously not thrilled with someone standing so close to his lane. Stephie turned to it, then back to me. An ugly smile filled her face. More like a leer.

My mind raced, fearing the worse. I started toward her. "No, Stephie. Don't. Whatever you're thinking—"

She turned back to the truck. It was coming fast, horn blasting.

"No!"

She sprinted toward it.

"Steph—"

She darted into its lane. The driver hit the brakes, wheels screeching, smoke rolling off its tires.

If she screamed, I didn't hear. The semi hit her. Dead center. It threw her into the air. She hit the pavement, bouncing like a doll—until the left front tire caught up and rolled over her.

Chad's scream drifted out of the building. "Stephie!" He hadn't seen what happened, but somehow he knew. And even where I stood, you could hear his agony. "Stephie . . ."

# Epilogue

"You sure you ladies are gonna be okay?" Cowboy asked as he tossed Andi's backpack into the rear seat of my car.

"No worries," I said. "Stephie got the hose patched up good enough to get us to town. We'll get it repaired there."

"Or scrap it," Cowboy joked.

"Not this baby." I opened the door and climbed in. "It's a collector's piece. Can't buy nothing like this at a car dealership."

"She's got a point," Andi said, fighting to open the passenger's door. Cowboy joined in and after two or three tugs it cooperated with a sickening groan.

"We'll have them look at that, too," I said.

Andi climbed in, looked back at the lab. "It kills me to know you're going to completely destroy the place."

Chad leaned down to her open window. "Not destroy it. Dismantle it. I'll probably get fifteen, maybe twenty grand for all the stuff."

"But the research, the possibilities. I mean, it brought us to the Gate."

"We don't need the occult to get there," Cowboy said, "not if we're workin' for the good guys."

"You keep using that word, *occult*," I said. "What's the difference between that and what we're doin'?"

"We're using our God-given gifts. The occult is when you try to barge into the supernatural on your own."

Chad agreed. "And with gifts like mine, who needs to barge?"

Andi turned away from him, rolling her eyes. It had been seventy-two hours since we lost Stephie. Chad had been mostly silent and sullen. When we offered to stay and help with the cremation and all, he said it wasn't necessary. But we all noticed he didn't put up much of a fight when we insisted. And later, when we helped pack her stuff to send to her folks, I saw him slip her white stocking cap into his coat pocket. I didn't say nothing. I knew he knew.

But all good things come to an end, and slowly, his pain-in-the-butt ego was resurfacing.

"Sorry we never found your professor friend," he said. I nodded. But he wasn't done. "'Course if I was on my own, it would have been a different matter. But having to hang back and show you the ropes definitely cramped my style."

Andi and I traded looks, wondering what reality the kid was visiting now.

"Yeah," I said. "Sorry for being such a bother."

"It happens," he said. "No worries."

Seriously? He'd not caught my sarcasm?

"What about our bosses," Andi asked him. "The Watchers? Any message you want us to deliver to them?"

"Tell them I may reconsider. If their offer is good enough, I may be willing to talk."

"Offer?" Cowboy said. "As in pay?"

"Naturally. A person would be crazy to do this stuff for free."

We all got silent. Andi might have coughed a little.

He just looked at us. "You're kidding me, right?"

We didn't say a word—which we were finding wasn't so necessary around him.

He shook his head. "Amazing. You guys are amazing"

I fired up the car. "Saving the world?" I called out to him. "That ain't enough for you?"

"Not even close."

I shook my own head and ground the gears 'til I found first.

"Drive safe," Cowboy said. "And give Daniel a howdy for me."

"Will do," I called.

"You boys behave yourselves," Andi said.

"Don't worry about us, sweet cheeks," Chad said. We'll have this place cleared in a week—with plenty of time to take this good ol' boy of yours into town and show him a thing or two."

"I wouldn't be taking any bets on that," I shouted through the window as I pulled up to the highway.

"That's right," Andi called back to them. "He and the good Lord may have a thing or two to show *you*."

"Amen!" I shouted.

We laughed and waved goodbye as we turned onto the highway. It was supposed to be a joke. But when I glanced into the rearview mirror, I saw Cowboy nodding thoughtfully and slapping his big hand on Chad's shoulder.

I had to smile. Chad Thorton had no idea what was in store for him.

Then again, I guess none of us did.

# Home Base

## Jeff Gerke

Angela Hunt, Alton Gansky, and Bill Myers

# SMARTMOUTH AND THE KID

I suppose I should try to rescue her. She *did* save my life, after all. Technically.

Whatever. Okay, fine.

I used the remote control to dim the windows and shut the drapes. Couldn't see much over the Dallas haze today anyway, even from the top floor. But I could still hear the jets taking off, and I probably needed to concentrate. Imminent death to the smartmouth, the kid, and the troll, and all that. And to beautiful Andi.

Yeah, okay. But first things first.

I crossed the living room of my suite—all white fabric and chrome appointments—and went into my white chromy bedroom. I propped the pillows around the headboard and sat up on the bed against them. I shut my eyes and went through the descent protocol.

Right away, I saw the black horizon with a billion options to choose from. It always reminded me of sitting in the middle of a huge black lake and seeing the lights of houses and villages here and there all around me. I thought about the photos of the kid—Daniel or whatever—and saw one of the dots flare at the edge of the blackness. I imagined myself closer to it, and there he was.

Nobody around to say I'd told 'em so, but a pack of black-eyed peas had already surrounded Daniel and were about to strike. In my remote viewing vision, they looked like loose clumps of cloth circling in well water. But I knew they were guided by an intelligent evil in their attack on the kid.

Which meant Brenda, a.k.a., Smartmouth, was probably in danger, too.

Yeah, there she was, flaring nearby in the fog. I might be able to get her attention even now, without training, but Daniel was more open. Plus … imminent death and all.

*Hey, kid,* I thought at him. *It's me, Chad Thorton. You hear me?*

I got a flash of Daniel—skinny geek kid. Pale skin. Typical brainiac. How well I knew what the future held for him. The gestalt I received showed him playing a video game in front of a TV.

*Hi, Chad.*

I had to smile. The kid was good. Quick answer. No apparent strain. Definitely gifted, this one. *You know me?*

An impression of a shrug, plus the TV turning off. *Brenda told me. What's up?*

My vision was clearing and everything looked almost

like reality. I could see their cluttered and tiny home. Every now and then my sight fritzed out and I saw nothing or a glimpse of a memory or interference from some other mind. Even I wasn't perfect. But it worked for the most part.

*You two are kinda in trouble*, I said. *I think the Gate has decided to kill you today. So, you know, you'd best make peace with your creator and stuff like that.*

Daniel didn't seem overly alarmed. I had to give him credit for that. *Why do they want to kill us?*

*Don't take it personal. You and the Merry Men have messed up some of their minor plans here and there, and they're very put out.*

I sensed he was running. Probably to alert Brenda. I felt the black-eyed peas converging. When out of range of my bubble of fuzzy real-ish vision, they looked like those clumps of wet rags. When they passed within the edge of my bubble, they looked like creepy elementary school band nerds. They neared, and I heard a doorbell ring somewhere.

*Don't answer it*, I said.

Another mind butted into the conversation. It was a presence I knew. Belinda, a.k.a., Smartmouth, a.k.a., Brenda. I knew she was brain shouting at me, but without prep and a couch and such, she couldn't do more than make a sound like squealing Styrofoam.

*Ow*, I said. *Kid, tell her to shut up. If she wants to say anything, have her tell you.*

*Okay.* He seemed a little less calm. *Who is at the door? Is it the people who want to kill us?*

*It's your favorite lost children of doom, yes. They'll find a way in soon, but it's best not to just open the door for them.*

A pause, and I sensed the black-eyed peas were almost through the door.

*Brenda wants to know what we're supposed to do.*

I sighed. *You're supposed to not go back to your home states in ones and twos so the Gate can pick you off easily. But I guess your little brain trust couldn't figure that one out. Why don't you tell her to offer to give 'em free tattoos and see if that works?*

A wave of hate enveloped me, and I knew the black-eyed peas had spotted me. I did a little thought shimmy to dodge their gaze. Despite their innocuous appearance as black-eyed children straight out of *The Addams Family*, these creatures were full-on evil. Imagine *The Exorcist* plus a banshee with a migraine.

*Kid, listen to me very carefully. I can't be there to save you, and you don't have your little posse together to pool your meager talents, so you're going to have to work with Brenda and do what I say to get through this.*

I felt the color of Brenda's thought change, which told me the kid had delivered my message. *We're ready,* he said.

*Okay, good. Tell her to concentrate on getting angry at these things. She needs to get ticked off, kid. I'm talking about hellfire kind of anger. Righteous indig-freaking-nation. It's one of the few things that holds them off.*

In the pause, Brenda's color temperature rose, and I could sense the black-eyes get shoved back. Which also had the effect of telling them exactly where she and Daniel were hiding. With the psychic snapshot she sent out, even *I* could see them in the coat closet.

The beasties were inside the house now and coming for them, and even Smartmouth didn't deserve to be torn limb from limb, and especially not by travel sized prep school rejects.

*Kid, listen: You're the key here. I need you to do something you've probably never tried. I need you to create a fire with your mind. Not a real fire—a brain fire. Think of a torch or a—*

JEFF GERKE

In my mind's eye, I saw a flaming sword erupt in the night, like something out of *Legend of Zelda 25*. It was much larger than kid-sized. It was outlandishly huge, like something only animated characters could possibly wield. The flames looked real enough, like those on a very long burning torch, but thankfully they didn't seem to set anything on fire.

I saw Daniel's face illuminated in it. He looked scared but mad. Behind him stood Brenda trying to decide between protecting him and hiding behind him. I couldn't tell if she saw the sword. It didn't matter.

Before I could tell Daniel what to do, he kicked the closet door open and sliced down with the sword.

Five black-eyed school kids scattered back like cats scared by a cucumber. One fell and got up lamely. The sword was metaphysical only, but the metaphor must've held, because it seemed like metaphysical mutants could take damage.

The kid was good.

He strode to the kitchen in the false dark of my remote vision. The black-eyed freaks backed away, hissing like vampires in some stupid SyFy Channel show.

*Behind you, kid!*

He spun around, where two girl creatures had been sneaking up on him. He swung the sword and pulled Brenda behind him, and a blond girl mutant spun away without a metaphysical right hand.

*You need to get the car keys*, I told him. *Get in the car and go to the airport. I will have tickets waiting for you when you get there.*

*Where are we—*

*I'm not going to tell you. Just do it.*

I saw his visage shift color. *In case we're captured and*

95

*tortured?*

*Something like that. Now go.*

I heard the Styrofoam again, and I knew Brenda was brain farting at me.

*What does she want?*

*We can't,* he said. *Her car's in the shop.*

Oh, right. *Figures. Okay, look, just go out front and find someone with a car. Go to the neighbors' or flag somebody down. I'll take care of it.*

Daniel swung the sword all around, keeping the black-eyed peas at bay as if he was a samurai warrior. They made a stand by the front door, but a swing from him and a surprising surge of righteous anger from Brenda, and the thing basically blew open.

Real-world lighting didn't look realistic through when I bilocated, so I couldn't see it, but I suspected Southern California sunlight was flooding the house now. Too bad it didn't make the beasties sparkle and die.

Daniel and Brenda went into the front yard. In the light of the sword, I could see a radius of only about ten feet.

*What do you see, kid? Anyone getting in their car?*

*No, nobody—* Oh, wait. *I see Mr. Hernandez across the street.*

I saw them step off the curb, but then Brenda pulled Daniel back so hard he almost dropped the sword.

*Seriously, woman! What are you doing?*

But into the spot where Daniel had just been rolled the front of a giant brown panel van. A UPS truck. It screeched to a halt and the driver got out, colored afraid and angry, to see if they were all right.

Behind their little drama triangle, the black-eyed peas poured out of the house, and more joined them from the back yard. We didn't have time for Mr. Band-Aid.

*Kid, say this to the driver. Say, 'What would you do if we borrowed your truck?'*

Daniel asked the driver, and I got a mental image from the driver of what he would do. He would run after them and try to stop them. Shoot. I'd been hoping he'd just pull out his cell phone and call the police.

*Okay, he's going to have to come along. Tell him there is a gang of scary arsonists trying to catch you and your...mom, and would he please get you to the police.*

Daniel told him, and he looked at the black-eyed peas. He didn't seem inclined to action, but something changed—probably he saw those all-black eyes—and suddenly he was willing to receive suggestions.

*Get in the van, Daniel. Tell Brenda to get in the passenger side and shut the door. If Mr. Driver gets in and drives, you're golden. If not, Brenda will have to learn how to drive a truck in a hurry.*

I was going to walk them through the whole getaway bit, but other business nagged at me. I sensed that Tank—a.k.a., Cowboy, a.k.a., the troll—was about to have his innards handed to him, and I figured someone would be mad if I didn't at least make a token effort to save his skin too.

In my mind, I disengaged from the fun in SoCal and zoomed back out to the black nether with the encircling horizon of lights I might interact with. Sure enough, Tank had black fog sharks prowling near him too.

In a minute, in a minute. Everybody's so needy! What would they do without me? Seriously.

Even though I wouldn't want Sweet Cheeks mad at me if I didn't at least try to save him, I hated that being in the ether this long and this actively was going to reveal my location to...certain parties.

But what else could I do? I had to help Tank.

I needed to make a stop first. In that hypothetical space "above" the dark plane of my destinations was where the Watchers hung out. "Below" the plane was where the Gate had their icy fortress. Not going there today. This was taxing enough. So I bopped to the center of the black expanse and jetted up, pressing my mind at their ears.

The Watchers preferred talking and letting me pick up on their stuff, like a little psychic dog eating their crumbs. But I knew they also heard my thoughts. Our suite of rooms on the top floor of the DFW Grand Hyatt was proof of that. So I packaged my request into a little thought grenade and lobbed it up where I knew they were. Tickets, clearance at multiple airports, pack up their homes, create cover stories, along with a *Boom, make it happen* chaser. Then I was off to save the troll.

# THE TROLL

Tank was deep in fog.

I'd thought I'd find Tank the Troll Engine physically nearby Brenda and Daniel, since his pad was also in SoCal. But this wasn't L.A. Then I'd thought he was maybe with his uncle in Dicksonville, Oregon, playing junior detective again—assuming they could stitch two police uniform shirts together so it would fit him. But he wasn't there either.

I guess it didn't really matter where he was. What mattered was what floated around him in the pea soup he had gotten himself neck-deep into.

He was alone. Standing in the middle of a highway

ridged with rain forest. Standing beside a yellow road sign that said—what else?—FOG. Sure enough, there was fog here. All around him. Swirling and rising, floating like a ghost, shrouding like the edge of a dream.

And while Tank couldn't see the critters that swam around him, disturbing the mists and slavering for his flesh, I could see them fine. I'd read his memories about the San Diego debacle, of course, so I knew these were the same fog-sharks from before. Or their cousins. These were long snakes that had mouths like twenty fangs of death. Part lamprey eel, part severed tentacle, part chopped cucumber of biting—and all nightmare and murder.

At least with Daniel, I could communicate directly. Even Brenda could probably have heard me, if I'd pushed hard enough. How was I going to reach the captain of the Cro-Magnon wrestling team?

Then it hit me. I didn't know if I could do it, but if I didn't at least try, Sweet Cheeks would be mad at me. And if I *did* pull it off, she'd owe me. If you know what I mean.

I imagined myself heavy and agitated, which helped me climb out of my remote viewing trance. I found myself still sitting in the imperial suite of the Grand Hyatt at the DFW Airport. I was still surrounded by white fabric and silver chrome. I couldn't tell if the sun had moved, with the drapes closed, but I felt a little hungry, so some time must've passed. I was still propped up by plump pillows, so at least I hadn't fallen on my head and drooled on the fancy white carpet.

I scanned the room but didn't see what I wanted, so I went out into the living room-office area. There it was. I grabbed it from the desk and went back to the bed. Propped myself up, started the descent protocol again, and…sent a text.

*Yo, Tank. Chad Thorton here. You're about to die. Get out of the fog.*

I poised my finger over the Send button and jumped back into remote viewing—bilocating—mode. When I'd zoomed back over to Tank and his foggy bottom, I instructed my finger to press the button. Strange how much energy it took to make my body do anything when I was out of it.

Did he even have his phone with him? He was a Christian and therefore probably a Luddite, so it would figure if he'd left his—

I heard a beep that sounded suspiciously like a phone receiving a text.

But of course he didn't check his texts. His aura looked like he was close to wetting the bed, so getting an update about his favorite NFL team or a coupon from Troll-Mart probably wasn't high on his priority list.

Three lampreys coiled together like a Braided Missile of the Apocalypse and started bending in Tank's direction.

*Troll, check your text*, I thought at him.

No response. He spun around, though. Probably the lampreys had showed a hump of their back as they spiraled nearer.

*Cowboy, check your phone. TANK, ya bonehead, I'm trying to save your red neck. Check that doohickey in the pocket of your Wranglers!*

Nothing. But I did see his color change, and I think he was praying.

The death eels were sent tumbling outward as if hit by a sonic detonation.

Yeah, that prayer stuff could be pretty useful

sometimes. About ten times more effective than "righteous anger." He wasn't going to tell that to anyone, though.

*Hey, person who thinks Andi would ever fall for him...get a clue and READ YOUR TEXT.*

No response, and now the creatures were regrouping—angry, this time.

I bundled all my will into a thought and played my last card: *Bjorn Christiansen.*

His color shifted instantly blue, and I knew he'd heard me. He looked around in the fog as it drifted up to the lower branches of the evergreens around him.

I pushed my thought again. *Bjorn, you've got a very important text. Check it right now.*

He reached into his back pocket and pulled out his phone. A few swipes of his sasquatch thumb later, and I could see from his aura that he'd seen my text. The change in his posture suggested that he was trying to communicate with me telepathically, but that wasn't going to work.

I climbed out the bilocation and swiped another message.

**Can c u but not ur thots. Drive out of fog NOW. San Diego monsters.**

His color didn't change much when he read that one, so I thought he'd already figured out his danger. What he'd been doing wading through thick fog—next to a freaking permanent *fog* sign—after what he'd been through, was beyond even my brain's capacity.

Tank dug in his front pocket for his keys but dropped them. He bent down, and that was the opening the nearest death eel had evidently been waiting for. It darted forward, big as a kayak, and slammed Big Bjorn in the back of the neck.

I used my favorite German obscenity.

They went down in a pile of Scandinavian muscle and demon flesh. The troll was strong; I'll give him that. Even with an anaconda-sized monster on him, he fought for all he was worth. He got to his feet, gripping the thing hanging from the back of his neck in some kind of reverse stranglehold. The other eels smelled blood in the water and piled on.

German profanity.

I'd seen Andi's memories of that San Diego massacre, and I knew what generally happened when even one of these things attacked somebody. Generally…just a puff of pink mist and adios muchachos.

One thing was for sure: He wasn't going to be checking his texts anytime soon.

Well, Sweet Cheeks, no one can say I didn't try. Not that I was sad not to have a rival, but nobody deserved to die like—

The eels exploded off Tank like he'd erupted.

It even knocked me back, the wave of spiritual power that blasted off him.

The eel on his neck writhed and shivered like it was trying to get *away* from the guy but was hooked on by its circle of fangs. It stood out from Tank's body like a windsock in a tornado, until bits of it began flaying off. In a flash, it was only a skeleton flapping in the gale, and then even that disintegrated. Last of all, the mouth went to powder and poured away.

Holy bratwurst.

Tank struggled to his feet, blood pouring down the back of his neck onto his shirt. He put his hand back there and brought it forward to look at it. Red goop and lots of it. I was formulating an instruction burst for him, but he was ahead of me. He tore his shirt off and bound it around his neck to stanch the bleeding. I had to say that, even in a remote viewing of his torso, the shirt wasn't the only thing that was ripped.

I needed to be sure Andi didn't get to see him in a swimsuit until she was safely in my pocket.

The death eels were still in the area, swimming upstream against the reverse magnetism Tank was putting out. But unless he passed out from shock or blood loss, it didn't look like they were going to have another shot at him in the near future.

He staggered away from the forested hill he was on, leaving the FOG sign behind and moving toward his vehicle—an old Honda Civic from like 1832. No pickup—really?

The mists of bilocation obscured my vision and I thought I might lose touch with him. That happened sometimes. I heard the sound of a text message received, and I wondered who else might be sending him anything. Then I realized the text was on my end.

I rose from the RV trance and looked at my phone. It was from him.

**Thx man.**

I smiled in spite of myself. He was a dufus, but a plucky one.

Another message from him: **going 2 hsptal – heal didn't work** ☹

**Good call.** I wrote back. **Then take cab to airport. Tix waiting 4 u.** Wait, I had another thought. **wut is nearest airport 2 u?**

**um...** was his first text. Not helpful. Second was better: **Del Norte, I think. crescent city, calif.**

**k, thx**

I put the phone down and went along the RV road again. One more little lamb to save before I could go to the hotel bar and collect a female companion for the evening. I had the very one in mind. There was a bartender named Ashley. Of course there was.

I didn't like the thought niggling my mind. But even if I didn't let myself fully think it, I couldn't escape the image of those creatures flung away from Tank like water off a dog.

That...that was power.

Ah, German profanity.

Never mind that. Now it was time to pay a little disembodied visit to my favorite pair of sweet cheeks.

# A DAMSEL IN DISTRESS

It wasn't hard to locate Andi. I knew she had been planning to visit her grandparents at the beach house, and I'd seen her in transit a few days ago.

I hurried through the descent protocol and zoomed right to her. She was out with that black dog of hers, sitting on chaise lounge on the beach in her blue one-piece suit and with a book in her hands. That red hair rested on creamy white shoulders and contrasted beautifully with the cerulean swimsuit. It was sunny and bright, and beachcombers strolled by in the distance. No attack by evil nasties yet, but I knew from my quick journey here that they were moving in.

Funny how you can get to certain people faster, in remote viewing, when you've checked on them often.

Not that I've checked on her that much. Not saying that. Not saying that I've watched her journaling while sitting up in her bed. Not saying I've watched her fix meals for only herself in her apartment, chopping peppers and cooking stir-fry. Not saying I've learned her rhythms and gauged her aura. Definitely not saying I've been a little slow to pull away when she takes a shower.

Nope. Not saying any of that.

Hey, I'm not a stalker. At least, no one could bring charges.

It's just...she's interesting, that's all. Her mind is...nice. Orderly. Unexpected but always sensible. Even her whimsy is logical and delightful.

Besides, I couldn't be held responsible if, sometimes when I happened to check in on her, she wasn't entirely clothed. The vagaries of bilocating and all.

*Andi,* I thought at her. I hadn't tried this, and I didn't think she was gifted, but it was an experiment to see if intense feelings in the sender amplified the effects of the message. *Andi, can you hear me? It's Chad.*

Her aura permutated a bit and she put her book in her lap. She looked around, shading her eyes, as if thinking she'd heard someone call her name.

Good girl.

Then she made an *I must be hearing things* face and went back to her book.

I was reminded again that by now I had for sure flagged all the bad guys about where I was. *Hey, fellers, wanna come kill me?* Who knew what critters they were sending my way even now? Maybe they'd wait long enough for the whole club to convene at the hotel.

Maybe they wouldn't.

Back to Sweet Cheeks. I was looking at her in a little, full-color holo-sphere in the middle of the black nether of remote viewing. Things were almost photorealistic in that bubble. But outside it, everything was symbolic and vague. Tiny lights and flitting clouds and waves of feeling, all churning together in the darkness.

But this wasn't my first rodeo, and I knew what was what. So when I again saw what appeared to be collections of gray rags billowing in the invisible breeze and roiling toward Andi like a wad of seaweed caught in the surf, I knew what they were.

This was not good. I knew without even checking that Sweet Cheeks wouldn't have her phone. She didn't like trying to use it in bright sunlight, and she wanted to unplug by the beach.

Not saying I'd studied her moods.

So…no texting her like I did Tank. And no direct communication like with Daniel.

Too bad my gifts weren't different. Then maybe I could hijack that dog of hers and start speaking through its mouth. Now that would be cool.

The balls of rag were closer now. In Sweet Cheeks' reality, they were probably already within a quarter mile of her. Maybe on the beach, maybe creeping up from the houses behind her, and maybe flying over the water. Maybe high above her or directly below.

What form would they take to get at her, I wondered. Tank's evil death eels? Black-eyed peas? Men in black with dark sunglasses over eyeless sockets?

I couldn't see much beyond the edge of the bubble. But it wouldn't matter for long. Soon enough, their chosen form would be all too clear.

*Andi, you're in danger*, I thought at her. *Andi, run!*

She put the book down again and cocked her head, but she didn't get up and flee.

I racked my prodigious brain for a solution. If I'd known about this earlier, I could've freaking called her and told her what was going on.

No, better: If they were all together in one place, as a team ought to be, none of this would've happened. They would've been grouped and could pool their pitiful resources. And when that didn't work, I could've saved them. But no, apparently they thought that fifty—or however many it had been—calls from the Watchers didn't suggest a pattern or imply that there might be fifty more. So these geniuses go back to their little sewing clubs and badminton teams or whatever and end up getting pounced on one by one. It was just a wonder it hadn't happened before now. Lucky for them, I was there now.

Except…what about my dear cheeks of sweetness? Was I going to have to watch that beautiful flesh torn apart before my eyes? Was that puzzling, delicious brain going to be seagull dinner surprise? If only I—

Right: the grandparents.

I started climbing out of the RV so I could look up their number, but I heard—felt, really—Andi's dog growl, and I knew it was show time.

The rag balls were near. Seven of them, at least. All I could see was Andi in her chaise lounge. Then a shadow fell over her. It was perfectly round.

Those shiny spheres. I'd seen them in action in Vegas. I remembered how brave Stephie had been to take the gun and shoot at them. And even if that weren't true, I'd seen these things often enough in Andi's dreams to know what they were. Odd how they seemed to pick a different form for each member of the team. Wonder what they'd pick for me.

Andi's dog went into crazed attack mode, barking and snarling and snapping at the spheres—I could see some of the golden orbs in my periphery now—and then cowering away and yipping, as if under some dog-frequency assault.

Sweet Cheeks dropped her book and rolled to her feet, but there must've been other spheres behind her, because she stopped as if blocked.

I didn't like feeling helpless.

*Chad?*

The voice startled me worse than if a golden sphere had been right here in the hotel room with me.

"Who's that?" I asked the air.

*It's Daniel. We're at the airport, but I know Andi's in trouble. I want to help.*

Daniel! "You know what, Junior? You just might be able to help, at that." I let my brain run through the options. "Okay, look, I need to do what I can to protect Andi. You have Brenda use the airplane phone to call Andi's grandparents in Indian Rocks Beach. Tell them to call the police and an ambulance, because I'm afraid Andi's going to need them. Tell them to go out and find Andi on the beach and help her if they can."

*Okay, but…Brenda says this plane doesn't have phones.*

"Of course it doesn't. Okay, have her use her cell phone."

*Um! We're not supposed to—*

"Do it, kid! Screw the FAA. Andi's going to die."

I felt him thinking about it. *Okay.*

Brenda gave her psychic Styrofoam a twist, probably telling me off, but I didn't care, so long as she made the call.

"As for you, Daniel, you can absolutely help me. I've

never tried this, but it might work. I almost got through to Andi a minute ago, alone. But with you and me shouting at her together, I think she might hear us. You up for it?"

Another thoughtful pause. *Well, yeah, but I can't see her. How will I know what to say?*

"I'll tell you, then we'll say it to her together. Got it?"

*Okay.*

I checked in with Andi.

She wasn't dead yet. That was good. But that might change soon. For some reason, she had run toward the water, not away from it. The orbs chased her like giant globular hornets. The dog stayed by her side, leaping at the things and falling hard back to the packed sand.

I caught a glimpse of people watching the spectacle. Not surprisingly, they were dumbfounded. Dumb something else, if you'd asked me.

A couple of slobby surfers ran to Andi's rescue, jabbing their boards at the things like wide poles. One took a wide roundhouse swipe at an orb and slammed it on the side.

It recoiled from the blow and knocked into the sphere next to it, and I had an insane inner vision of pendulum balls merrily smacking into one another. But the two affected balls arrested themselves in the air, made an aggressive move toward the surfers, and then *boom,* the dudes went flying away, feet sailing over their heads.

Gnarly wipeout, dude. Cha.

I couldn't see them, but I sensed that Andi's grandparents were on the case now. I suspected they were on their way over the dunes toward her. Probably both would have heart attacks on the way.

Meanwhile, the spheres were still buzzing Sweet

Cheeks and Wonder-Dog.

Why did the balls of gray rags use the metal orb devices? Part physical conveyance, I knew, but what was scary about shiny cue balls? Still, anyone who knew Andi's dreams like I did would know that it was a good form for them to use against her.

People were fleeing the scene now, and nobody else offered to help. The surfers were limping away with their boards.

An orb dipped too low, and the dog jumped at it, maw open. Not sure what it had in mind, but I couldn't fault its devotion. The sphere sent out a beam of some kind, and I felt the dog's pain across the ether. It fell to the sand in a broken heap, like a deer hit by a truck.

"Abby!" Andi looked at her dog in shock, maybe waiting for it to move. Then she fell to her knees beside it and pulled its head into her lap. I could see her sobbing. The spheres closed in, and things were going to be over very, very quickly.

*Kid,* I thought at Daniel, *I need you to say this with me. Say, 'Andi, you can't stay there. Get up and run.' You ready?*

*I'm ready, Chad.*

*And…now.*

Together, we said, **Andi, you can't stay there. Get up and run.**

She looked up suddenly, and I knew she'd heard us. "Is someone there?"

*Kid,* I said, *say, 'Your grandparents are in danger. They need your help.' And…now.*

**Your grandparents are in danger. They need your help.**

They weren't really in danger, yet, but I figured it would take something like that to get her off her sweet cheeks and into motion.

Andi looked to her left, toward the beach houses. "Sabba? Safta?" Abruptly, she stood, and I figured she'd spotted her grandparents. She ran toward them, and the orbs gave way.

I heard a squeal of Styrofoam, and I knew what that meant.

*Brenda wants to help,* Daniel said.

*No kidding.* I sighed. *Look, I don't have time to… Okay, fine, she can do this: Tap her whenever we're brain-shouting at Andi. Have her join her righteous fury—or her angry eyes or whatever she can bring—to what we're saying. Okay? Tell her, but hurry up.*

After a second, he said they were ready.

Back on the beach, Andi had reached two old people I knew from her memories were her rich grandparents. They looked terrified. Money's nice, but it can't save you from demon balls in the sky, you know what I'm saying?

I figured we had another five minutes before the police got there, unless we got lucky and a car was already in the area. So, now that we had a way to communicate with Sweet Cheeks, what was my plan going to be—hide behind Granny?

As the spheres converged on Andi and her grandparents, I saw in my mind's eye an image of the death eels blasting off Tank back in the rain forest. I didn't like the plan that my usually reliable brain began to tell me about.

*Um, Andi,* I said, knowing she couldn't hear me without my helper, but just trying the idea on for size, *how do you feel about praying?*

I was aware of Daniel in the mindspace around me. *You want me to say that, too?*

*No! Well, I mean…what do you think?*

*I dunno. It works like almost all the time. Against our bad guys, I mean.*

Based on my observations, he was right. But that didn't mean I had to admit it. *I dunno, kid. How about we just have her run into the house until the cops get there?*

I could almost imagine Daniel making a wry face. *You think she's got time?*

Not for a minute. *How about we get her to whip up some of that 'righteous indignation' stuff you guys used?*

*I dunno. Okay.*

I looked in on Andi, and it seemed like she was up to something. She had picked up a hefty driftwood log and was brandishing it like a baseball bat. Moms and Pops backpedaled behind her. Andi seemed to be tracking one certain orb amidst the swarm of balls crossing and floating and throwing their shadows over her. The one she tracked seemed to stay back from her more than the others did.

She'd seen a pattern.

I shook my head. She was a wonder, that one.

Sweet Cheeks hefted the log and stepped backward. Their melee had brought them all the way to the back deck of her grandparents' house. Andi stepped up on it and retreated from the steps. Judging from how her eyes darted to the ground and the orbs, and the calculating look on her face, she was about to do something really brave. Or stupid.

The spheres moved over the deck too, perhaps anticipating that their prey was planning to go inside. One of them darted forward and struck Grams in the shoulder. She went down like a carpet bag, and Gramps bent to catch her.

That's when Andi struck. She sidestepped one orb, leapt forward on the deck, and brought the log crashing right into the face of the sphere she'd been watching.

A knot in the log cracked the golden carapace. A gust of black smoke lit by orange sparks flew out, and the orb lost altitude like a wounded quail. The other orbs hesitated and rose to a stationary orbit ten feet above the deck as if going into some kind of standby mode.

Andi chased the cracked orb off the deck, pounding on it like a woodsman going after a rattlesnake. It dodged and rolled and tried to gain altitude, but a well-placed smack on the top and it fell to the sand lifelessly. She beat it and beat it and beat it some more. I could see she was crying.

*Chad,* Daniel said, shocking me out of my trance, *what's happening? It feels like she's doing better.*

I nodded. *Yeah, she is. We may not have to use the crutch after all. Can't say I'm sorry. She went all Jolly Green Giant on the queen orb, and the rest don't know what to do.*

Andi ascended the steps of the deck like Abraham Lincoln, Vampire Slayer, and checked on Grams. She looked okay.

*Okay, kid,* I thought at him, *say this with me. 'Good job, but they won't be out long. Get everybody inside.' Ready? Go.*

**Good job, but they won't be out long. Get everybody inside.**

Andi dropped the log and opened the door to the house. She pulled Gramps and Grams toward it just as the orbs lowered ominously. One moved to behind the other ones, and if I could see which one was the new queen, Sweet Cheeks sure could.

The two front spheres floated "shoulder to shoulder" and fired a beam that splintered the beach house wall, showering them with kindling.

Andi and her grandparents fell backward into the

house and crab-walked away. A third orb joined the line and I could tell they were about to fire again.

*Andi!*

The leftmost orb shattered and fell.

Black smoke billowed from somewhere, and I registered the blast of a large-barreled weapon. The spheres turned their attention to the newcomer, but two more of them popped like fog balloons. The new queen went down next, its casing caved in.

I saw the four policemen then. Three fired 9mm handguns, but the fourth—a strapping, young, leading man sort of hero—had a pump-action shotgun the likes of which I'd last seen in a zombie apocalypse movie.

The other orbs went into standby mode again, which just made it easier for the Terminator to send them all to the shiny sphere afterlife.

I sighed. With that done, there would be much talkety-talk and the filling out of reports: The detectives-with-notepads sort of scenes you see on every TV police drama. Then the Watchers would send their clean-up crew with their hush money and special "incentives" to make it all go away. The worst of it was that, for the next hour or so at least, my Sweet Cheeks would be all beholden to Police Prince Charming, and I wouldn't even be on her mind.

*Kid, I need you to say one more thing with me.*

*Is Andi okay?*

*She's fine. Better than fine.* I thought again of Ashley the bartender. Did she have a pretty friend? I was going to need a double dose after this.

*What do you want me to say with you?*

*Say, "You did good, Sweet Cheeks. As soon as you can, get to the airport. There will be a ticket." Ready?*

*Uh, I don't want to call her "Sweet Cheeks."*

I smiled in spite of myself. *Okay, we'll call her "Andi." And...whoa, wait.*

As I watched, Andi jumped from the deck and ran for the beach. The police called after her, but I knew where she was going. The dog.

*Hang on a sec,* I thought at Daniel.

She sprinted and I could see the tears flying down her cheeks. Andi shooed away a gaggle of seagulls and crabs and fell beside the black mass on the sand. The tide was coming in, and at that moment the edge of a wave came nearly to where they lay. She was crying from fear and shock and everything else, I knew, but mainly for the loss of her old friend, one who had died trying to protect her.

It was an unselfish love that felt so pure as to be out of my reach. A love only saints and St. Bernards were capable of.

Without permission, a thought of Stephie exploded in my mind. Poor Stephie, my erstwhile assistant in Las Vegas who had helped me master remote viewing. Who had endured my abuse and loved me anyway. Who had taken freaking demons off my soul and onto hers, and had then run into traffic.

I stared at the black landscape of soul travel and felt...

Dead.

I didn't know how many times Daniel had called my name before I finally heard it. *Chad?*

I put away the memories of Stephie. A lot of thoughts I didn't like had come to me today. I put them all away.

*Yeah, kid?*

*Are we going to say that thing to Andi now? I'm afraid I'm going to forget it.*

I felt a smile stretch my cheeks. *Sure. Ready…go.*

**You did good, Andi,** we said together. **As soon as you can, get to the airport. There will be a ticket.**

There's no "camera" in remote viewing. My observing presence is everywhere and nowhere specific at the same time. But when Andi heard our message, I could swear she looked right at me. She raised her head from Abby and gave me a sad smile that I didn't have to be psychic to understand meant *Thank you.*

Chapter 4

# TO THE SWEET SUITE, TOUT SUITE

I greeted them standing up.

Ashley sat in elegant repose on the smart gray couch in the living room portion of my entertaining area, and I stood behind her like a Mexican don with his expensive mistress.

The four of them schlepped in like wet cats pulled from the sewer. The bellhop let them in and stood aside.

Brenda looked more dour than usual. She stepped onto the brown parquet floor, looked over my entertainment area from left to right, and dropped her purse with a fake leather splat.

Tank managed to be taller than I remembered from Vegas, and even hunched from fatigue and the pain from that bandaged wound on the back of his neck, he still looked like he might have to duck through the doorway. His eyes widened at all the white and gray and chrome, and probably at the expanse of windows looking out over the DFW runways. But when the troll's gaze rested on Ashley, I saw that trademark Christian disapproval, and once again, it didn't take superpowers to see what he thought was going on between us.

Sweet Cheeks looked radiant, despite her weariness and the fact that she wore more clothes than I preferred. She'd put that glorious red hair into a quick ponytail—how often I'd seen her do it in just three graceful moves. She wore a brown blouse and khaki capris and brown leather sandals that clapped on the parquet. But her eyes were sad, and something in me lurched.

Daniel was the only one who seemed mostly unchanged. He stepped into the room, spun around to take it all in, then sat next to Ashley on the couch and picked up the TV remote.

"Hi," Ashley said to him.

He gave her a quick smile. "Hi."

I spread my arms magnanimously. "Welcome to Fantasy Island."

They looked at me without comprehension.

"Oh, come on," I said, dropping my arms. "None of you has watched old reruns of that show? Ricardo Montalban? Tattoo? 'Boss! Da plane! Da plane!' Nothing? Seriously? Wow, you guys are missing out."

Brenda trudged over to the white chair beside the couch and flopped into it. "Only thing I'm missing is a bed. You got one in this place, pretty boy, or imma gonna sleep right here?"

The others surged in, as well. Tank took a spot beside Daniel on the couch, all but launching Daniel and Ashley in the air when he sat.

"Please, sit," I said. "We have a moment before dinner."

The troll roused at that. "Dinner?"

"Of course."

Andi rounded the coffee table and came to the matching white chair at the other end of the couch. Before sitting, she met my eyes and gave a fleeting smile. When she sat, she looked forward in the chair and saw something no one else had remarked about. "Ooh, an aquarium!"

Inset in the wall and beside the doorway they'd all entered through was a blue-tinted aquarium the size of a small walk-in bath. Small and medium-sized fish and crabs and other critters circled around in their eternal aquatic boredom. Still, it was nice to look at. And I didn't have to maintain it, so it was a win.

I took a moment to read their thoughts. Mostly they were tired and upset with me for presuming to bring them here—"He ain't the boss of me!" was how Smartmouth was thinking it—and still shaken from their ordeals.

It really wasn't fair, my ability to hear thoughts before, during, and after a discussion with people. Too bad. Fair was for losers.

And with what was going to happen to them tonight, they ought to be extra glad of my gift. I took a sniff of the ether around me and felt sure I knew what had been sent—or drawn—here because of my prolonged time in RV.

I remembered the encounter in Chile all too clearly.

I stifled the ghastly thought and looked down at Ashley. She was gorgeous, dear thing, as all female bartenders should be. Long, dark brown hair now swept across her right shoulder. Beautiful smile and tasty lips. Trim figure, of course, and the palest porcelain skin. She still wore the powder blue button-up shirt and black slacks she'd worn at the bar, and she smelled faintly of wine. But she was an excellent couch decoration and had been—and would continue to be—a delightful companion when other options weren't presenting themselves.

I knelt beside her. "Ash, be a doll and go check on our dinner, won't you, hmm? Our guests are famished."

"Of course," she said. I sensed a bit of upset about being dismissed, but I knew she was into me. She patted my cheek and left the suite.

"Who's that?" Brenda asked. "Your new Stephie? Gotta have one on your arm at all times, playa?"

I ignored her and sat in the spot still warmed by Ashley's pretty backside. "First," I said to all of them, "you're welcome. You know, for saving your lives."

Brenda gave me an *are you serious?* look. "Unbelievable."

I smiled. "Any of the rest of you want to deny it?"

Tank's hand went up to the back of his neck. "So like, how did you know, you know? How'd you know that was going to happen?"

I tapped my temple. "But I didn't have to have the gift to see that one coming. You dolts punch the Gate in the nose and then walk off alone, la-de-da. Might as well wrap yourself in bacon and jump in the lion pen."

"Yeah," Tank said, "but nothing like that's ever happened before, and we've done this a dozen times or more."

"I know you have. And you're just lucky they didn't try it before I was there to save your sorry butts." I turned to Andi. "Except yours isn't sorry, Sweet Cheeks."

She stood and slapped my face.

"Ow!" My cheek stung, but what was worse was that I hadn't seen it coming.

She brought a finger into my face. "That's for being crass."

"That's what I'm talkin' about," Brenda said, giving Andi a high five.

"And there's another one of those for you every time you're crass in the future."

As the sting faded from my face, my admiration rose. Not only could I not figure her out yet, she could surprise me. That was a big deal for mind readers.

"But," Andi said, settling back in her chair, "I do wonder how you knew we were in trouble."

I worked my jaw. "Well, somebody has to look out for your sorry…um, selves. As soon as Moose here got on the plane in Vegas, I came here and started making arrangements. This is your new home now. And I looked in on—"

"Whoa," Daniel said, looking interested for the first time. "We're living *here?* Cool! Can I have a room with an aquarium too?"

Everyone started talking at once. That, plus all their jumbled thoughts, was a lot to sort through. But by now I knew how to endure it. I brought up mental shields, sent my mind to a happy place—which might or might not have included Andi's room—and waited it out.

"No," Brenda finally said. "Nobody's movin' nowhere, no how. Mm-um. I gots bills to pay."

I shook my head. "Not anymore, you don't."

That shut them all up.

"What's that supposed to mean?" Sweet Ch— Um, Andi asked.

"It means," I said, standing and walking behind the couch, my arms sweeping the suite, "that we five, we merry five, are the permanent and sole residents of this entire end of the top floor of the DFW Grand Hyatt. You each have a suite to yourself. Not as nice as this one. This one's mine. But a suite almost as large. Belinda and Daniel—"

"Brenda," Smartmouth corrected.

"—have a two-room executive suite right next door. You, Cowboy-Tank, have a presidential suite, and you, Andi, their finest bridal suite."

They were ridiculously easy to read. And to placate, apparently.

"This," I said, looking around the room where we all were, "will be our headquarters. Except, of course, when I have guests and need my privacy."

Brenda harrumphed. "So, basically, we can't be in here, ever."

I let it go. But she wasn't wrong.

"Wait," Andi said, "let's go back to the part about how this is now our home. That's not going to work for me. I've got to get back to Florida. I've got a—"

"What?" I asked. "You've got a what? An apartment in Cambridge near the university where you worked with the Professor. Except wait, the Professor went body surfing in the nether, didn't he? Which means you're not working with him, which means you don't have a job at the university, which means you don't need to be in Cambridge. Or in Indian Rocks Beach, with your grandparents, as you were about to say next."

Andi opened her mouth and quickly closed it.

I loved being psychic.

"I'm sorry about your Gram-Gram, but she'll be all right. As will Grampa Willy, and their house. They've now been told that those flying orbs were a NASA experiment gone wrong and that you've been offered a prestigious job in a secret facility somewhere and won't be allowed to come back for long stretches at a time." Then something came over me and I felt blue. I didn't like blue. "I am sorry about Abby, though. She was…"

And suddenly I was close to weeping. Me! I shut it down hard.

"As for you," I said to Brenda, "your 'body art' business has, as far as anyone knows, been bought out by a local real estate investor and converted into a Buddhist temple."

"What?"

"No, I don't actually know what they'll put there. I just wanted to see your reaction."

She told me, both verbally and mentally, what she thought of me. Funny girl.

"Oh," I said, "it's also dumb that you're just sort of the kid's guardian. I mean, what does that even mean? So I got that noise all fixed. He's yours now."

"What?" they all said.

"What-what? The adoption. It's finalized. Well, the papers need your final sig. They're over there on the desk." I looked seriously at Daniel. "I know it's a lot of responsibility, Daniel. So are you really sure you want to adopt this girl? She's kind of a wild child."

He giggled and looked at Brenda.

She wanted to object, I knew, but why? Instead, she smiled and called Daniel into a huge hug.

Yeah, that felt pretty good, I guess. And I wasn't

done handing out goodies. Santa had something for one and all.

Besides, you kinda have to keep the person happy who knows your deepest hurts from the past. A happy holder of secrets is a quiet holder of secrets. Or so I hoped.

"How are you doing all this, Chad?" Andi asked.

"Oh, it's not me." I pointed upward. "It's them."

Tank leaned forward. "Angels?"

"No," I said, chuckling. "*Them*. The Watchers. But I guess small minds could think of them as angels. It wouldn't be the first time."

"So, what…" Tank said, and I knew he was smarting from the put-down… "you just send 'em a memo and they say, 'Yes, sir, Chad, sir!' Is that how it goes?"

"Now, now, Cowboy. Maybe he knows a few things we don't." She gave Daniel a squeeze, and I knew she had become a semi-ally, at least for now.

At that moment, there came the sound of a key card in the door to my suite, and the door swung open. Ashley came in and held the door open for a Hispanic waiter pushing a silver cart with silver domes. The dishes clinked and rattled as he drove the wheels over the metal threshold.

I watched this one carefully as they came in. I knew what he was, of course. I'd grappled with them in Chile a few months back. Well, I hadn't been physically there, but it was the same difference. I didn't know yet what this one was planning, and its thoughts were hidden from me. He was too early, but it wasn't as if they were exactly under my control.

We were all in deadly danger.

# A SENSIBLE CHANGE

"Your dinner tonight," Ashley said as the waiter lifted the domes, revealing piles of fancy entrees on oversized dish-bowls, and began arraying the dining table, "is Atlantic halibut, braised artichoke, carrot, fava, and confit tomato, with a lemon and Thai basil sauce." She swept her hand over the table. "Please, come sit."

When the waiter took food, not automatic weapons, from under the domes, I figured we were okay at least for a while longer.

I went to Ashley and gave her a kiss on the lips—an act that surprised but thrilled her, I perceived. But it got no strong reaction from Andi, so it was mostly wasted effort. "Thanks, Ash. This is great. Will I...see you later tonight?"

She tucked her hair behind her ear and smiled without looking at me. "You know where to find me."

"I sure do."

"I'm off at midnight."

"Oh, please," Brenda said, pulling a chair out from the table, "get a room. Wait…I guess you did."

"Good night, all of you," Ashley said. "Enjoy your dinner." She followed the waiter and his trolley out of the room and into the hallway.

The dining table and chairs sat on a square, blue and white throw rug, which looked nice and presumably kept the chair legs from scratching the parquet.

They tore into their food. I cut a piece of halibut and stuck it on my fork.

Tank made a big show of praying first, but then he dug in too. "So, Chad," he said, "save us the trouble. Tell us what you've done. All this." He twirled his fork in the air.

"Well, I could. I could tell you everything, then you'll all tell me why it won't work and how you've got other plans. Then I'll ask Andi to tell us the pattern she's already seen, and then I'll ask Belinda to whip out her sketch book and show us the sketches she's already made of her room here and…a creepy ghast dude I'll explain about later. And finally you'll all agree that I was right." I ate my bite of halibut. "So can we please just skip to that part and enjoy our dinner? There's crème brûlée in the fridge."

They sat there deciding what to say. Then Daniel belched—"Sorry"—and the tension broke.

"You still haven't told us what all you've done," Andi said, sipping sweet tea. "I'd like to hear it."

I took a big breath. "Okay, let's see. First, it's beyond stupid that you guys aren't living together, but I've already covered that. And now you have a headquarters for your Mystery, Inc. clubhouse, and I'm working on a Mystery Machine for us too. What say, Scoob," I said to Tank, "you be the dog and I'll be Shaggy? She's Daphne," I said, looking at Andi, "she's Velma," to Brenda, "and you, kid, can be Fred."

Daniel blinked at me. "I have no idea what you're talking about."

"Never mind. So, now you're all together, as you should've been from the beginning."

Brenda started to speak, but I shushed her.

"Andi," I said, but what I thought was *Sweet Cheeks*, "please tell them the pattern you've seen."

She looked like she'd just been asked to narc on her best friend. She swallowed her tea and set the glass down carefully. "Well, it does seem like the four of us—maybe the five of us now—are being called on again and again. And unless you all haven't been telling me everything, we're not doing other missions on our own or with other groups, right?"

"Right," Tank and Brenda said. How much better they responded to Andi than to me. Would that change over time?

"So if the trend continues," Andi said, "it would mean we will continue to be called upon to come together to meet whatever need arises."

"Until Jesus comes!" the troll said.

"Rrrright," Andi said. "And it does make a certain amount of sense for us to be together so we can respond more quickly, instead of having to first get on planes to reassemble and then fly out again. And," she said with a reluctant look at me, "though I don't relish the thought of living in Texas, I can't argue with the logic of being near a major international airport. Plus,

I've seen today that our being with our loved ones puts them in danger." She sighed as if having to deliver bad news to good people. "Yeah, so, I guess an arrangement like this is actually pretty smart. And…the food's good."

This time it was Tank's turn to belch. "No doubt. But do you think they make cheeseburgers?" He wiped his mouth. "Seriously, though, I basically have no reason to live in California. No reason to live in any specific spot, you know? If I'm not going to be a sheriff's deputy in Dicksonville, and I'm not, I might as well live in Texas, where I grew up, y'all. Plus, Dallas Cowboys Stadium is *right here*." He leaned back and met all their eyes, but his gaze lingered on Sweet Cheeks. "You all are my family now. My team. Of course I want to stick with you. Besides, these digs do beat my roach-trap one bed/one bath, you know?"

"Excellent, Bjorn," I said.

He made a face. "'Tank,' please."

Troll. "Right, 'Tank.'"

"What's mine?" he asked.

"I'm sorry?"

"What's my cover story? Did you tell my uncle and all?"

"Oh, right. Anyone who might be curious has been or will be told that you are doing private bodyguard work for executives and a lucrative firm and won't be reachable for months at a time."

He looked like he'd just won a calf roping contest. "A bodyguard? Woohoo! Look out, ladies, I'm your James Bond security detail for the evening."

Brenda cooed and swiveled her shoulders. "I declare, I feel safer already!"

"Chad," Andi asked me, "what about our apartments and such?"

"It's all taken care of. Your belongings are being shipped here as we speak."

Brenda scratched her head. "Hey, I still owe—"

"All your debts have been paid."

A stunned silence. Even Tank stopped eating.

"You guys are such amateurs," I said. "Do you really think I would forget anything?" I felt Daniel looking at me meaningfully, so I turned an ear to his thoughts.

*What will we do for money?*

"Good question," I replied aloud. "Some of you may be wondering what you'll do for money if you have no job and you disappear from the face of the earth. Not to worry—your Uncle Chadley has taken care of it. For the larger things, like room and board and jetting off to who knows where, that's all being handled by a higher power. No, Tank, not God or angels, but you can think of it that way if it helps."

He didn't like that one either. I was going to have to tone it down around him for a while. "As for spending money, you've each got a monthly allowance of five thousand dollars and no expenses. So...live it up."

I went to the midsize fridge in the little kitchenette beside us and pulled out the tray of crème brûlée.

Brenda looked doubtfully at the fancy little bowl I put before her. "What's the catch?"

"No catch!" I said. "No catch! You're all doing a job here. An important one, even if you're not as skilled as me, at least you've got some ability. I saw that in you this morning. The powers that be seem to think you're useful together, so this, all this, is just you being together. Seriously, what's your problem? Somebody wants to give you tons of money and bring you to live in luxury and do important work, and you're hesitating?

"You know what? Fine. Go on back to your tattoo

parlor, Brenda. Why not? Go back into debt. Then act all surprised when you get called up to another mission and have to hoof it to the airport and come here and get on another plane and fly wherever. Live in squalor, sure. And you haven't signed those papers, so Daniel isn't really yours. I can make that go away in a hurry. That's what you want, I guess."

I was standing, but I didn't remember getting up. "What about the rest of you? Wanna go back to your lonely spots and get picked off one by one? Go right ahead. Anyway, Brutus," I said to Tank, "what in the name of Napoleon's sphincter were you doing all alone out in the middle of a foggy forest? You got a death wish, is that it?"

"No! I didn't think—"

"Of course you didn't. None of you do. If you didn't have me, all of you would be dead right now. So you're welcome. Excuse me for trying to make things smarter, do things better, take care of your needs, and keep you safe. Now go on out and die in the street. Go on, leave."

Nobody moved. Their thoughts were right there for the taking, but I didn't feel like hearing them. So I just stood there staring at the fools and thinking uncontrollably about Stephie and the sound she'd made when those creatures had entered her mouth.

At length, Daniel cracked his dessert with a spoon and had a taste. I could tell he liked it. Tank consumed his in four bites flat. Andi only picked at hers.

Brenda didn't even try it. "Don't take this the wrong way," she said. "I mean, you guys are great. But I like my space. I kinda like seeing you characters once and awhile and then going back to my own place, my own world. You know, ink and needles and home-schooling this kid. But…"

"Me, I'm all for it," Tank said. "Count me in, and grateful. Brenda, you gonna eat that?"

She slid the bowl to him and he attacked it.

"Chad," Andi said, and I melted at the sound, "I have a question."

I sat. "Give it to me, baby."

"How did you arrange all this? I mean, we were all with you in Las Vegas not that long ago. And where did the money come from? I can't imagine how much it had to cost to buy out this suite for just one night, much less have multiple premium suites indefinitely. Plus the way you say our homes have been cleaned out and our debts paid off—thank you for that, by the way—and the cover stories and all. How did you manage it?"

I could look into those green eyes forever. I could've saved her the effort of saying all that, of course, having heard it from her brain already. But why would I miss the chance to have that visage turned upon me for that long and to hear those dulcet tones?

I sighed contentedly. "I only asked for it, Andi. You guys had access to this all along, but I guess none of you thought to ask. Or did you think all the international plane tickets they kept sending you were emptying their piggy bank?" I shook my head disdainfully, but out of respect for Sweet Cheeks managed not to say, *Idiots.*

Brenda stood and walked to the desk. She picked up the pen and looked at the adoption documents. Everyone else watched her, but I didn't need to. I knew what she had decided. In a moment, I heard the pen scribbling on the paper. I figured there would ensue much hugging and blubbering among them, but she surprised me by touching my shoulder.

"Thank you, Chad." Though she blinked under the

effort, Brenda nevertheless held my gaze. "I owe you." She laid two crumpled sheets of notepad paper on the table before me. The one on top showed her bedroom and the view out the window. "I'd like to see this place now, if that would be okay."

"Yeah," I said, my voice raspy despite myself. "Yeah, okay." I stood to lead her to their suite, but then the hugging and blubbering did commence, so I sat back down and looked at the second sheet of paper.

It was a drawing of a female ghost. It looked similar to the one I tangled with in Chile. When showing their true form, ghosts manifested as frighteningly emaciated figures with very long, thin limbs and a penchant for formalwear and gaudy jewelry. They did have facial features, but their faces were obscenely old and wizened, and their eyes were orbs of pure white. To use modern cultural terms, they were the halfway point between Slenderman and Tolkien's barrow wights.

And the hotel was crawling with them.

# WHO YA GONNA CALL?

"Could I have your attention, please?" I said.

Mystery, Inc. had moved back to the couch and were in a completely different mood than what they'd been in when they'd first stepped in. Now they acted like lucky lottery winners just starting to spend their money. They looked at ease in this posh white and chrome suite, and I knew without reading anyone's mind that I had won them over.

Tank shushed them all. "Yeah, Chad, whatcha got, brah?"

"Thanks, Tank," I said, because I needed them to listen. "None of you have brought up the only major concern about us living together and always coming back to one home base."

Brenda harrumphed. "You mean that we'll figure out we don't really like each other? That this is a cage, even if it's coated in gold? That living in a hotel isn't the same as having a home? Am I getting close?"

"Not remotely." I looked at Daniel and raised an eyebrow. I thought *Do you know?* at him, but I knew he couldn't hear me if we weren't bilocating.

But maybe he read my face, because he nodded and pulled away from Brenda's embrace. "It makes us easy to find."

That sent a chill through the room. Only the fish seemed unaffected.

"Are you saying we're in danger here?" Andi was again in the chair where she'd first sat. Funny how people do that.

"We're in danger everywhere we go, Sweet…Andi. I was marked by the Gate years ago, and now even you lot are on their radar. The question isn't whether or not you're in danger, but whether you're in more danger alone or when together."

"Probably more together," Smartmouth said, pulling Daniel back to her. "Now they don't even have to look for us."

I chuckled. "Newsflash, Belinda, but they've never had to look for you. Here, at least, together, we can help each other out." I pulled from my pocket the second sketch Brenda had handed me and smoothed it out on the coffee table in front of the sofa.

They gathered around it. All but Brenda, who looked at me darkly.

"Huh," Tank said. "Looks like a creepy Aunt Skinny."

"What is it?" Brenda asked.

"They're called *ghasts*. Real stinkers, they are."

Daniel sat cross-legged on the parquet. "They're already here, aren't they?"

Everyone spun on him. "Say what?"

"Yup," I said, putting my hands in my pockets. "I've sensed three."

"Where?" Andi said. "Here? In the hotel?"

"Yup. Thanks to how I had to stay bilocated for so long today, it hung a target on my back and drew them here. In fact," I said with a nod to the hallway leading to the front door, "one of them has already been in this room, while you were here."

Now they spun on me. "What? When?"

"It was that bartender girl, wasn't it?" Tank asked. "I knew she was bad news."

"Listen, Moose, just because you don't approve of someone's morals doesn't mean they're minions of the Gate. For your information, no, it wasn't Ashley. It was the waiter."

Andi's mouth dropped open, but it was Brenda who spoke. "You trippin'. He didn't look nothin' like what I drew."

"They don't manifest in that form, Belinda. Not until they're about to strike. They look like normal peeps the rest of the time."

Tank surprised me by shuddering. "Guys, he was right here."

It occurred to me that having these ghasts here might actually help me prove my point to these simpletons. If we could come together, with or without a round of "Kumbaya," and toss out a few minor stink-bugs, my case would be made that much stronger. This could be perfect.

"Right," I said. "Okay, fine. So here's the thing: There are three ghasts here in the hotel. They've been sent by the Gate to kill us. They think we don't know what they are, since you at least haven't encountered them before. Plus I think they're just sort of throwing together a token attack, now that they've seen we're together. But they're dangerous, even alone, and we've got three. And we," I said, holding my arms out like Ricardo Montalban again, "are going to find and defeat them."

Brenda wagged her head. "Do what now?"

I walked to the couch, scooted Tank aside, and sat on the middle cushion. "You guys are such noobs. All this time you've been working together, but it's like you're making things up on the spot every time. It's time you started thinking strategically and tactically about how to use your abilities, lame as they are, and work as a team." I pulled my legs up, yogi-style. "I'm going to sit here and lead, and you Scooby Snacks are going to go find the nasties and send them packing."

Oh, how I did love getting that look of disbelief from them. This was going to be fun.

"Excuse me?" Brenda said, but that's all she had.

"You know," Tank said, "when I was playing football, the team leader led from the field, not the sidelines or the locker room…or the armchair."

"That's because when you were playing football, the quarterback wasn't psychic. So here's how it's going to work. I'm going into remote viewing to locate the ghasts. Then you're—"

"Can you do that from here, Chad?" Andi asked. "Without your couch and…"

She was really kind, wasn't she? "And without Stephie? Yeah, I can. Remember, it was only this morning that I did this with all of you guys. I sat on my bed," I thumbed behind to the left, toward my bedroom door, "and found you out there in those dangerously alone places you all were. Besides, we have our phones."

Tank brought his out of his pocket and grinned at it stupidly. "Oh, right."

What we really ought to have was professional comm units, I realized. So I sent a mental note up to the Watchers for next time and started slowing my breathing while I talked. "You will not break up into pairs, like they do on Scooby Doo. You will all travel together." I thought for a minute. I wanted Andi as far from Cowboy's ripped abs as I could put them. "Moose will go first, as cannon fodder, followed by Daniel, then Belinda and Andi."

"Brenda."

"And it's 'Tank.'"

"Whatever. You will go where I tell you, and when you encounter a ghast, you will each deploy the weapons I saw you use this morning."

They looked at each other.

"What weapons?" Tank asked.

I snickered. "Really? Vunderkind here," I said, looking at Daniel, "wielded a metaphysical sword of fire just a few hours ago. We'll need it again, kid. Swing it at the creatures like you did in the kitchen, okay? Belinda attacks with ink needles and sketchbooks, and occasionally her 'righteous anger' even has a small effect on things. I'll need you to be broadcasting that anger against all things creepy pretty much the whole time you're out," I told her. "It's like your shields."

"What about me?" Tank asked. "What's my secret weapon?"

"You will stand ready to bash in the heads of anything that tries to attack Sweet Cheeks or the kid."

"Hey!" Andi said.

"Yeah," Brenda echoed. "What about me?"

I shrugged but gave her a roguish smile. "Moose," I said to Tank, "you've got some small but fritzy talent to heal. Hopefully you won't need it, because I expect none of you to be hurt and I definitely don't want any civilians hurt. In fact, they can't even know what you're doing. Unlike the Ghostbusters, you have to be discreet when you're clearing a hotel."

I didn't mention that I was holding in reserve a request for him to use whatever power it was he'd exerted that had blasted that pack of death eels off his back. I glanced at the bandage on his neck then looked away.

I looked at Andi, who smiled at me shyly but tried to look defiant. "What about me?"

"You? You're hopeless. I'm not even sure why you're on this team."

She put on mock outrage and slapped my shoulder. "That's not true. I contribute."

"Maybe you can find a pattern in their argyle socks or something. Maybe all ghasts wear stripes with plaids, and you'll see it just in time to save us!"

She folded her arms and turned away.

"No," I said gently, "you're there for intelligence and common sense and a level head. Not to mention the ability to bash things with driftwood. You'll be fine, Sweet...heart."

Tank affected a yawn. "So when are we going to do this? First thing after breakfast?"

"No, Colossus, now."

# SIMPLY GHASTLY

The thing about ghasts was that they were unpredictable. I hadn't known if Jose the Waiter was going to attack us in my suite or what. And since they often acted without forethought, it meant I couldn't read their intentions.

I sat on my couch, cross-legged, with my phone face up on a pillow in my lap. But my spirit was in a foggy sphere just outside the executive boardroom on the first floor of the DFW Grand Hyatt.

My four intrepid adventurers stood huddled at the door, one behind the other in the order I'd outlined, as if about to storm a dragon's den. Daniel had his fiery spirit sword and Brenda was spewing righteous anger.

We even had a tank going first. And Sweet Cheeks was there to beautify and add romantic tension and otherwise round out my little Dungeons & Dragons questing party.

And me…I was dungeon master. What else?

I bent a thought toward the hotel security staff and saw that they were indeed alerted that we were going to be doing some…interesting…things. They were under strict orders not to interfere unless something caught fire or there was blood. Basically, they were crowd control, but I hoped they wouldn't be needed even for that.

"Yes," I said aloud into the phone, "there is one ghast in there. He's posing as hotel staff. Male. A front desk-looking guy with a blue suit and peach tie. But he's not alone, so your first job is to get him away from the others so you can take him down." I moved my view so I was seeing half on their side of the door and half on the other. "Okay, go."

Tank put his hand on the knob lever.

"Hang on," Brenda said.

All our phones were linked in a conference call, and we had cleaned the gift shop out of ear buds, so at least we could communicate without everything being heard by others. It would do until the pro comms arrived.

"What?" I said, trying not to let irritation take me out of my trance.

"How *exactly* is we supposed to 'take him down'? I ain't got no butterfly net, and unless Cowboy's got a nu-cul-ar thingamajig on his back, we got bubkes."

"We went over this, Belinda. You spray your holier-than-thou anger at it, Moose holds it down, Fred Jr. slices and dices it with his sparkle sword, and Andi stands there looking pretty."

"Ugh," Sweet Cheeks said. "How can you be this *annoying?*"

"It's a gift. But you're right, darlin'. Next time, you stay here and sit in my lap, plying me with grapes and margaritas. No sense risking you."

"Ugh!"

I smiled to myself. "Okay, they're done in there. Moose, step back now!"

He pulled his hand back just as the door swung open, and three of the five staffers walked out. The front-ghast-clerk was still inside, along with a petite Asian dustmaid I might just have to pay some attention to in the near future.

"Okay, go now."

Tank opened the door and they went in, crouched and ready to strike.

"Guys," I said, "this isn't a cage fight. Fly casual."

A huge brown wood table dominated the room. It was basically a table-room. Six black, wide executive chairs sat smartly on one side of the table, facing across the shiny surface to six chairs on the other side. Each place setting had a signing pad like a placemat, a short pad of white paper, a pen, and an upside-down water glass.

Both staffers were on the far end of the room next to a widescreen monitor on the wall. They turned to my adventurers.

The ghast-clerk clasped his hands in a fig leaf pose and smiled. "Can I help you folks?" He even had a Texas accent. Nice touch.

"Tell the dustmaid that someone was calling for her," I said.

Brenda said it, and I listened to the maid's thoughts. But of course they were in Mandarin. So I took a chance.

"Tell her her boss wants to see her right away. Make it sound urgent."

Brenda did, and the maid said, "Shyeh-shyeh" and scurried from the boardroom.

I wondered if the ghast could see Daniel's flaming sword or if its vision was limited to the natural. I thought perhaps he would play the desk clerk a little longer, but I was wrong.

With a warping shimmer in the remote viewing plane, the young man vanished and in his place was a skinny old woman ghast with a Roaring Twenties haircut and bangles that slid down a radius and ulna barely covered by skin. I didn't know if they'd be able to see the change or—

Smartmouth swore like a Belinda rat, and I had my answer. It was the one she'd drawn, after all.

"Stay back!" Andi sounded more than a little afraid.

They stayed more or less in their line, all hiding behind their tank. For his part, the troll crouched and held his hands apart like lion claws. He advanced on the ghast as if to grapple with it. I couldn't fault his courage, that was for sure. All he had to do was grab it so Daniel could—

The she-ghast doubled in size and flew at Tank with a flurry of slender limbs, claws, and teeth. All he could do was lean back to keep her head in view, and it was on him, shredding his arms and bloodying his nose and already pawing over him to get at someone else.

Tank's blood sprayed over the table and notepads, and the thing screamed like a goat demon. All four of them fell on their rumps in shock and fear. Daniel's sword went out. "Get away! Get away!" someone shouted.

I didn't know they could get big like that. That hadn't happened in Chile. What exactly were we dealing w—

The ghast sprang over Tank, grabbed Daniel above the right knee, and fled the room, bursting the door to shards and carrying the kid upside-down and flailing.

German profanity.

# PEAR-SHAPED

So much for discretion.

Brenda ran through the conference wing of the Grand Hyatt screaming Daniel's name. Andi came next, shaking and mumbling, "Omigosh, omigosh, omigosh."

Tank thundered after and quickly passed them both. His wounds seemed to have enraged him, and blood flowed over his arms and mouth and chin. He tore across the carpet, leaving about as much damage than the fleeing ghast. Hotel staff shrank against the walls or fell to the floor when the monster and its pursuers passed.

The ghast had to run crouched to keep its head under the ceiling tiles. I'd never seen one grow like that. This could be a problem. Daniel wasn't shrieking or crying, but he wasn't exactly calm and his sword had snuffed out. The creature ran past tasteful abstract paintings on the wall and stylish banded carpet, slavering and screaming like a sheep hit by a truck. My team came close behind.

I roved ahead to keep up, trying to send a powerful-enough suggestion to security to get involved now. I wasn't sure it would work, and I saw Andi stumble, so I had an idea. "Andi, go to security and tell them there's been an incident and that it's ongoing. Tank needs medical help and we need them to keep people away from the conference wing. Can you do that for me?"

"Of course I can," she said into her phone, getting up and running toward the main lobby. "I'm not a child."

"Wait, are you mad?"

"Just help Daniel!"

I zoomed down the hall as the ghast came to the end of the long conference wing lobby and burst through two sets of double doors that led into the hotel's 400-seat presentation hall. Gray chairs sat in neat phalanxes in front of massive blue video screens flanked by blue curtains.

The creature waded into the high-ceilinged room, pushing chairs aside as if walking through water up to its knees. It slowed a bit and transferred Daniel to its other hand.

That was enough for Tank to catch up. He launched himself at the beast's middle, knocking it forward onto gray chairs and spraying his blood on the fabric. The creature lost its grip on Daniel, who hit his head on the back of a chair and lay still.

Great. Without Daniel's metaphysical sword, I didn't know how we were going to destroy the creature.

The ghast twisted its torso and reached those over-long arms at Tank, but he held tight to its middle. It hammered him relentlessly, but he held tight. Daniel moaned and stirred.

Brenda arrived and ran directly for Daniel. The ghast rolled in its struggle with Tank, tossing chairs aside. But Brenda got to Daniel and tried to pick him up. She wasn't big and he wasn't small, and the angle was bad—plus, physical combat nearby—so she settled for grabbing him under his arms and dragging him back toward the busted doors. He lolled his head around.

I felt so helpless. This was pure chaos and I had no clue how to make a difference. I hated that feeling. I had half a mind to cry out to the Almighty, like some oafish peasant.

*I'm okay.* It was a thought from Daniel.

*Seriously? Awesome! Can you get the sword going again?*

In the misty hologram of my RV vision, I saw Daniel's spirit sword flare to life.

The ghast must've seen it too, because it—she?—flailed at Tank to get away. But Cowboy held on, his arms raked by cuts and his face covered in bright blood.

"Daniel, no!" Brenda reached for the kid, but he darted away toward the scrum on the carpet.

The Roaring Twenties slender-hag became frenzied at the approach of the sword. Daniel went into the aisle between the disrupted set of chairs and the pristine phalanx next to them and neared the ghast's head.

*Just hack at anything,* I thought at him. *It should slice through all parts of her. It's like a light saber.*

He raised the sword over his head and lunged

forward. The ghast put up an arm, and he cut it clean off.

The creature shrieked so loud I saw Brenda collapse to the floor with her hands over her ears.

At that moment, on the other side of the huge room, the Hispanic waiter came crashing through the double doors.

With a roar and a ripple of reality, he discarded the illusion of humanity and grew into Slenderman— spindly limbs, an immaculate black tuxedo, and only the barest hint of features on an otherwise blank orb of a face. It was a nightmare creature, and I knew that ghasts in this form had been indirectly responsible for several teenage suicides.

This one seemed more interested in homicide. In its larger size, it consumed the distance to Daniel with astonishing speed.

*Now, kid!* I thought. *Kill that one now!*

It crossed my mind that I shouldn't be asking a little kid to be a monster-slayer, but at the moment, he was what we had.

Daniel drew back his flaming blade and jabbed it forward into the she-ghast's neck. It struggled and moaned, but Daniel kept at it. He hacked and stabbed and thrust. His hits landed true, but the thing was big and strong, and it was taking too long to die. Slenderman was almost on them.

"Stay back, you devil freak!" Brenda stepped into the space between Daniel and the other ghast. She had her right hand forward like a superhero crossing guard, and I could feel her shooting a beam of protective, Mama Bear, stay away from my baby anger at the creature.

It flinched and pulled up short, as if struck by a stun gun.

Brenda advanced on it. "Get back, and go back to whatever hellhole you crawled out of. Leave this hotel and never come near any of us again!"

The thing backpedaled and shuddered, twitching as if being tased. But now and again it snarled and surged forward, only to be halted again, and I didn't know how long her trick would work.

I heard a commotion out of the range of my vision, and it wasn't only the sound of Daniel finally lopping the head off of the Charleston Ghast, either.

"I did it!" he shouted.

That broke Brenda's concentration, and she turned to look.

Whatever had restrained Slenderman snapped, and it rushed at her, its blank features stretched and its hands spread into claws.

"Brenda," I shouted at her, knowing I was too late, "watch o—"

Thunder boomed in the cavernous hall, and the ghast was thrown off its path. Its left arm popped Brenda on the side of the head as it cartwheeled over. She fell and it fell, and a squad of security guards advanced, pistols raised.

A fifth figure—Sweet Cheeks!—ran to Brenda and pulled her aside, while the guards closed on Slenderman. It got to its knees but the thunder clapped again, and it fell back under a barrage of bullets.

There was a break in the tension. Medical personnel came to Tank and Brenda and Andi hugged. I could tell they all thought the danger had passed, but I knew differently. *Daniel,* I thought, *cut that one's head off too, just to be sure.*

*Okay.*

Then even I started to relax. That was when I heard

the sound of commotion again, and I realized it wasn't coming from the bilocating vision. It was much closer. I climbed out of the RV trance and opened my eyes.

The third ghost stood over me. Right there in my suite. It was an oversize version of a teenaged Mowgli, shirtless and horribly thin, with long bedraggled hair over its face and those white, white eyes.

"Uh, guys," I said into the phone still on my lap. "I think I'm going to need some help."

# TOGETHER AT LAST

I flipped over the back of the couch, sending my phone and the pillow flying, and held my hands out toward the ghast.

"Nice jungle boy. Nice Mowgli."

The ghast looked sullen and slightly slouched, as any gangly teen boy should. But with the eyes all white, I couldn't tell if it was looking at me or not. It breathed heavily, as if it had taken the stairs, but it didn't fly into a rage just yet. It merely towered over me, breathing.

I risked a glance down the short passageway to the door. It was closed and not smashed, so I figured "Boy" had been posing as hotel staff and had just let himself in before going native on me.

Could I bolt to the door and run?

I looked back at Mowgli, and he hadn't moved. The constrained violence was disquieting, like the Alpha Male mutant in *I Am Legend*. I took two steps toward the door, and the ghast sprang forward to cut me off. It stood in the passageway and pawed at me listlessly.

I backed away. "Okay, okay. I like it here anyway."

What was the thing doing? Was it depressed that its friends had been decapitated? Was it in need of a battery charge?

Was it waiting?

Outside of my remote viewing trance and without my phone, I had no connection to the others. It was possible the phone was still on, though, wherever it had flown to, so I combined a strong mental warning with a spoken one. "Guys, if you can hear me, watch out. I think this thing is waiting for you to get here."

I backed to the desk and scanned it for something I could use as a weapon. Narrow computer speakers? No. Netbook? No. Not even a letter opener. The dining table had been cleaned, but there were knives in the sink. Better than nothing.

I hadn't more than decided it than the thing leapt at me. It crossed the room in a lunge and reached for my neck. I blocked the sickeningly narrow limbs and tried to run behind the dining table.

It slammed a forearm into my right shoulder and knocked me hard against the window overlooking a ten-story drop to the airport tarmac. The glass held, but the blow had knocked me hard. I stumbled toward the table, but the thing made a wet flaying noise and shoved me in the back.

I fell forward behind the nearest dining chair and

rumpled the throw rug. The creature bent over me like a human praying mantis, batting me with those hideously long arms.

I scooted away and grabbed a chair leg. I tried to use the chair as a weapon, but the ghast knocked it and the whole table away savagely and fluttered its lips at me, gagging me with stink breath.

It slashed my forehead with with a horizontal swipe of its hand, and I felt cuts open from ear to ear. Blood spilled over my eyebrows and into my eyes.

"Help!" I called, feeling wretched and ashamed of my weakness. How had I—*I*—been reduced to this? And since I was that low, I might as well go lower. "Please," I begged, "please. What do you want? I'll do anything." This was how I was going to end, useless and begging.

The ghast grabbed me by the waistband of my pants and dragged me into the open space in front of the desk. I struggled and kicked its torso and rolled against its grip, but all that did was shake sweat from its dangling locks and make it narrow those white eyes.

It sank its claws into my upper arms and lifted me off my feet. I had a mental image of it simply biting my head off and spitting it out to go bouncing on the pretty parquet floor.

As it brought my face up to its mouth level, time seemed to slow. I saw a memory of Stephie receiving the creatures from my soul and thrashing with their evil. I saw her run away toward the highway. I saw what was left of her on the road.

I saw the things Brenda had somehow gotten access to from my past, all the humiliations and rejection. The slit of light under the closet door that was my only illumination for what seemed like my entire childhood.

I couldn't even remember the first time he'd hit me. Probably because it had started so early. But I could remember the time he'd done so when I'd brought him a hand-drawn Father's Day card but had apparently chosen an important moment in the TV show to show it to him.

And suddenly this ghost wasn't a jungle boy anymore. It wasn't even a monster from the Gate anymore. It was William Jackson Thorton. My father, the devourer god.

*Please…help…me.*

The thought shocked me, even in that moment on the doorstep to death. It wasn't a psychic command or even a plea to someone nearby to come to my rescue. It was…

It was a prayer.

The ghost seemed confused. It cocked its head at me and furrowed its brow. Then it seemed to shake it off, and it squeezed its claws into my flesh, ripping the skin and piercing to the bone.

I shouted in pain and surrender to the end.

That was when Mystery, Inc. burst in.

The ghost turned in surprise and tried to drop me, but its claws were stuck in the bloodied muscles of my arms. I came off one of its hands and dangled diagonally from the other, fighting to pull its claws out of me.

A wave of some sort of power washed over me. What I *felt* was Brenda's spiritual anger, but what I *saw* was a tank of a man wrapped in hastily applied bandages and with dried blood on his face running forward like a subway train. He swung a metal table leg at the ghost and connected with the head. I went down with it.

"First the arm!" Sweet Cheeks yelled. "The arm,

Tank."

Tank body-slammed the creature's head on the ground and wrested its free arm behind its back. It shrieked and sputtered, and I was able to use my legs now to pull loose from its other hand. It tore a chunk from my triceps, but I was free.

"Now move!" Andi commanded.

Tank scooted down the creature's body and leaned away from its head. Brenda sidestepped to have a clear view. She reluctantly urged Daniel forward.

Daniel held before him an invisible weapon I knew only too well, though it was strange to not be able to see it.

"In the name of Jesus," Tank said—needlessly, I would've argued, except for my own recent petition of the universe—"be gone!" He nodded to the kid.

Daniel brought the unseen blade down in a mighty chop, and somehow that nevertheless cut into the creature's flesh. Its head came partially off its neck, and Daniel put his foot on its shoulder and chopped again, severing the head entirely.

Just like that, it was over.

The beast's body went utterly still. Cowboy stood and touched his forearms gingerly, and I could see blood seeping through the bandages. His neck wound, too, was bleeding a bit. Daniel opened his hands and I knew he'd extinguished the sword. Brenda brought him into a big hug and pulled him protectively from the thing on the carpet.

Andi knelt in front of me. "You're hurt. Forehead and both arms." She looked me over. "Anywhere else?"

I just stared at them all. I couldn't understand what I was seeing.

The troll crouched beside Andi and snapped his

fingers in front of my face. He kept doing it until I flinched and turned away. He reached his hands to the wounds on my arms.

"You guys came," I said, hating how dazed and stupid I sounded. I blinked blood out of my right eye.

Andi wiped it away with her finger and then with a napkin Daniel brought her. "Of course we came, Chad. We're a team, aren't we?"

Normally I would have had some smart riposte, but my brain felt like Jell-O. "I knew you guys were, you're a team, but…" I shrugged.

Tank put his hand on my forehead. "That means you too, dummy."

I looked at Smartmouth and asked *you too?* with my expression. She rolled her eyes and smiled.

Daniel gave me a fist bump.

I realized that my forehead didn't sting anymore. I brought my hands up and found smooth skin, not the flayed shoe leather I was expecting. My arms stopped hurting too. I looked at Tank. "Did you…?"

"I didn't," he said, then pointed upward. "But someone did."

"Right." I checked my arms and moved them about. "Thank you. All of you. Thanks for coming when I called."

# Epilogue

"What a day!" I said.

The others laughed grimly, like veterans of a military campaign. We lounged in the rooftop saline pool atop the DFW Grand Hyatt, sipping adult beverages—except for Daniel, of course—and watching jets take off into the night sky.

I finished my frozen strawberry margarita and set it on Ashley's tray, which she'd just put in front of me to bring me another of the pink delights.

She swept my hair with her fingers and winked, and I wished she was already off duty. "I'm glad you're going to be with us for a long time."

"Me too, Ash."

Ashley went around to the rest of our group, collecting glasses and handing out fresh ones, then she headed for the elevator. There were a couple of other swimmers here, but she paid them no mind.

Tank sat with his legs in the pool, keeping his arm bandages dry. Apparently, his healing gift didn't work on himself very often. He sat next to Andi, and I cursed the fact that I'd not been able to keep them apart in swimsuits. Still, what was a guy to do? Especially since it had been my idea to have us all live together. It was bound to happen. But curse his sculpted abs!

Brenda hadn't taken her bathrobe off. She sat in a chaise she'd pulled close to where the rest of us sat. Daniel was doing handstands underwater and coming up occasionally for a drink of Sierra Mist.

"I guess that's true?" Brenda said.

I looked at her over my shoulder. "What's true?"

"We're going to be here a long time."

I shrugged. "Unless something better presents itself."

"I don't know," Andi said, swishing her legs in the blue-lit water. "Are you going to be able to live in that suite, after what happened? I don't think I could, no matter how many times they scrub the floor, you know?"

"Yeah," Brenda said, "I keep seeing that thing's neck half chopped through." She shuddered.

I shrugged again. "It's not a problem. And we'll be installing a security system and bringing in specially trained guards ASAP. Anyway, I've seen lots worse than that. You have too, if the stories of your other 'adventures' are even half true. Here, at least we're together, which means safer."

Tank smiled mischievously. "Did you like how we

came into your room that time? Just like you'd said: me first, then Daniel, then Brenda, then Andi. Brenda's angry eyes, my muscles, Andi's brain, and Daniel's Masters of the Universe sword. Hoo-boy, that was good. And it worked just like you'd said, that was the crazy part."

I chuckled with the rest of them. "Yes, sometimes even I have a good idea."

We fell silent. Planes landed and planes took off. Daniel came up for air and went back under. The other swimmers left.

"So this is us," Andi said.

"What do you mean?" I asked.

"Us. This is our team now, us five. And here."

I didn't answer this time. My spidey-sense told me to shut up for once.

Brenda sat forward in her chaise. "It's kinda like we're rich."

They smiled and nodded.

"Livin' like queens and kings," she said. "Havin' people wait on us. Orderin' up room service all *day*, y'all. A girl could get used to it."

"And," Tank said, lifting a finger in the air, "the Cowboys' stadium is right here!"

We laughed.

Daniel surfaced and slurped the entire refilled glass of Sierra Mist, chased by a belch. "Brenda...I mean, 'Mom.'"

"Whoo," Brenda said. "Still gotta get used to that one. What is it, sugah?"

"What if I don't like the tutor they're getting for me? I like learning from you."

"Then I'll teach you. But some things yo mamma don't know how to teach. Aw, you'll be okay, baby."

Andi pulled her legs from the water. "Well, I don't know about the rest of you, but I've had about as much fun as I can stand today." She stood and wrapped herself in a giant white towel. "I'm going to go test out that king-sized mattress in my suite. Good night."

The rest of them departed with her, leaving me to wait another half hour for Ashley to get off work and join me for a swim…et cetera. I'd been moved to the other presidential suite for a day so they could clean my real one. I wondered what they would do with the bodies of the ghasts.

I leaned back in the corner of the pool and nestled my head in the nook. The stars above were dimmed by the airport lights and the glow of the surrounding city, but I could still find the Big Dipper.

*Well, Big Fella, I guess I should say thanks. I didn't know how I was going to get them here, but that sort of got taken care of. And when that thing was about to finish me off…*

*Anyway, yeah. Thanks. And…I guess I'll talk to you later.*

# Fairy

## Angela Hunt

## Alton Gansky, Bill Myers, and Jeff Gerke

"What is this?" I picked up the box Chad had just tossed into my lap.

"The Smartech Simultalk 36G Wireless Communication system," he said, tossing identical boxes to Brenda, Daniel, and Tank. "Now whenever we're out in the field, we won't have to rely on cell phones or extra-sensory perception. We'll rely on this state-of-the art professional communication system."

I opened the box and pulled out a manual and two devices—an earpiece and a mouthpiece.

"I saw Katie Perry wearing something like this the other day," Brenda said, tossing her manual aside. "Looked cool."

I bent the wire attached to the mouth piece—a slender plastic tube—and hooked it over my ear. "Did I do this right?"

Chad nodded. "Looks great—of course, anything would look great on—"

"Got it," I interrupted, cutting him off. "And this little plastic thing goes into my ear?"

"Just like a hearing aid." Chad demonstrated with his earpiece. "See? Practically invisible."

"The mouth piece isn't," Brenda pointed out.

"But that's the beauty of the Smartech Simultalk," Chad said, grinning. "You can slip that little mouthpiece anywhere, as long as it's within thirty-six inches of your face. You could put it in your collar, hide it in the cuff of a sleeve, even slip it in your belt. It's going to pick up any sound in your vicinity."

I glanced at Tank, who hadn't said much. He wore a frown the size of Texas and was still pulling pieces out of his box. "And why do we need this?" he asked.

"Communication, my man," Chad said, flashing that Ultra-bright smile. "An unlimited number of radios can be added to the system in talk or listen-only mode. We can talk simultaneously without wires—and this is a lot less clunky than the old systems where you had to wait for one person to finish before another person could begin."

"Hang on." I pointed to the box. "It says here that we can have one-way or full duplex operation at the touch of a button. What button?"

"Look in the bottom of your box."

I pulled out a couple of pieces of cardboard, then found a black plastic gizmo about the size of a pack of playing cards. The thing featured an antenna and two buttons on top, but not much else.

"I'll teach you noobs how to use it," Chad continued, oozing arrogance with every smile. "In fact, why don't we have a dry run this afternoon? We can walk through the hotel and practice to test the limits of the system. After all, we wouldn't want to head out to some dangerous assignment without knowing what we're doing."

Brenda tipped her head back and laughed, and even Tank joined in.

"What's so funny?" Chad looked from them to me. "Care to let me in on the joke?"

I chuckled. "The thing is, Chad, we've gone out every time without knowing what we're doing, and we've survived."

"Without you," Brenda said, arching a brow.

"Then maybe it's time to try a new approach." He looked around the circle, his eyes serious. "You guys have had some close calls, and most of the time you've been playing defense. Maybe it's time to up the ante. Learn some new plays. Go on the offensive for a change."

"Mixed metaphors aside," I said, resisting the temptation to roll my eyes, "I do think these communication gizmos are a good idea. I hate it when we get separated, and if these can help, great."

"And what's with this *you guys* stuff?" Tank asked, looking at Chad. "For better or worse, you're one of us now. So make that a *we*, all right?"

I looked away, unable to stand the sight of Tank being nice and gentlemanly while most of the time I wanted to slap Chad upside the head. He was smart, he had gifts, but we had to pay for those gifts by tolerating his smarminess, his sexist comments, and his all-round obnoxiousness.

I caught Daniel grinning at Chad as if they shared some kind of private joke. I wasn't sure, but I had a feeling those two were communicating on some level the rest of us couldn't reach. Daniel had never been exceptionally verbal, but he and Chad had become as close as peas in a pod, probably because Chad had been popping into his brain or something to tell him bedtime stories every night . . .

I'd have to speak to Brenda. Chad couldn't possibly be a good influence on an impressionable boy.

"All right—I agree that we need to start playin' offense," Brenda said. "How do we do that?"

She looked at me, I looked at Tank, and Tank looked at Chad—who looked at Daniel. Daniel nodded soberly. "Wait," he said. "Wait for

Watchers."

"There." Chad smiled, looking incredibly pleased with himself. "We wait for the Watchers to give us a clue. And in the meantime, we practice using our comms."

I blew out a breath and caught Brenda's eye. She made a face that seemed to say *Can you believe this?*, but since she had no better ideas, she didn't say anything.

Neither did I.

* * *

"This is Andi." I adjusted my comms mouthpiece, then slipped a straw into the iced tea the waitress had just brought me. "Is anyone listening?"

Chad had promised that the operation of our comm units would be simple. All the remote devices continually monitored whichever unit we designated as the master. To talk, we simply pressed the second button on our transceiver, then waited for someone to respond. Simple, right?

"Andi?" Tank's booming voice filled my ear, causing me to wince. "Are you still in the hotel?"

"I'm in the downstairs restaurant. Where are you?"

He laughed. "I'm at the airport ticket counter. But you sound like you're right around the corner."

I smiled. Considering that the hotel was part of the airport's D terminal, he *was* right around the corner. Sort of.

"That's good. Brenda, Daniel—where are you guys?"

I heard nothing, then Brenda's exasperated sigh filled my ears. "We're at the airport, too—at the ice cream counter in Terminal B. Daniel was hungry."

I smiled. So far, so good. At least we knew the comms worked. "Chad?" I asked. "Where are you?"

No answer.

"Maybe he's out of range," Tank said.

"Or chasing some babe," Brenda suggested.

I groaned. "I hope he catches one," I said. "Someone who'll give him a piece of her—"

"Chad here, at Dallas central. Good to hear all of you."

I exhaled in guilty relief. He was fine. And he hadn't been chasing a babe or one of the ghasts we'd met when we first moved into our suites at the Grand Hyatt. I never wanted to meet another one of those creepy things.

"Were you takin' a nap?" Brenda asked. "You were awfully slow on the uptake."

"Sorry, guys—had to answer the door. We got a special delivery package."

A premonition nipped at the back of my neck. "Who's it from?"

"It's addressed to you, Andi, but the bellman let me sign for it since you didn't answer your door. Should I open it?"

"Wait," I said, signaling the waitress. "I think we should open it together."

"Suit yourself," Chad answered. "I'll be waiting in my love nest."

"Excuse me?"

"My suite. So get yourself up here post haste."

"We're on our way."

# Chapter 2

Twenty minutes later, we had all gathered around the giant television in Chad's suite. I had opened the box and pulled out a letter and a DVD in a plain cardboard sleeve. Chad sat on the floor by the TV, and lifted his hand for the DVD. After slipping it in the slot, he found a seat on the sofa next to Daniel.

We all leaned forward as the black screen filled with two words: THE WATCHERS. Then a voice spoke: "Greetings, team! We hope you are well and rested since your move into the hotel. If you have any problem with the accommodations, or with anything on your journeys, you should memorize our email address:

help@watchers.com. We monitor the site continually, and we'll get help to you as soon as we can."

"A help line." Brenda's mouth curved in a smile. "We coulda used one of those when we first got together. What took 'em so long?"

"Be grateful," I murmured, my eyes intent on the screen. "At least we have a sponsor now."

I couldn't help but wonder why the so-called Watchers were so secretive with us. We were supposed to be on the same team, so why would they be unwilling to show their faces? Would be nice to put a face to the voice, but apparently full disclosure wasn't part of the plan.

"We've hired a plane for you," the resonant baritone continued. "It's a private jet leaving from Hanger 44 tomorrow morning at 10:00 a.m. Be on time, please, and dress in comfortable clothes and shoes. You might have to do a bit of walking. You should also bring your communications system and the video camera."

"What video camera?" Tank asked.

Chad grinned. "No worries—I have it."

Of course he did.

"One more thing," the speaker said. "You'll need your passports. We are sending you to meet Mr. Benedicto Prospero, a television broadcaster and celebrity in his homeland. He speaks English, so you should have no trouble communicating with him. If you speak any Spanish at all, however, it might be useful to brush up on your skills. You might need to interview several people on your journey."

"So where are we goin'?" Brenda growled. "Half the world speaks Español."

"Mr. Prospero is going to show you something unusual," the unnamed speaker continued. "Your mission is to verify the object, determine where it came from, and see if you can establish its purpose. The task may be more difficult than we anticipate, but do your best and send a report when you return. Take photographs, record video, and gather any evidence you can transport home. And if you have any difficulty meeting your contact, you might try asking him about the fairy."

The voice—whoever it was—paused. "Thank you for your willingness to serve in our effort, and Godspeed. Enjoy Mexico City."

We heard a second of silence, a short hiss, and then nothing.

Chad cracked a smile. "Sort of ripping off Mission Impossible, aren't they?"

"Yeah, maybe," I admitted. "But I didn't hear anything about the DVD self-destructing."

"What's this about a fairy?" Brenda asked. "Compared to the monsters we've encountered lately, fairies sound like a nice change."

"Yeah." I parked my chin in my palm and smiled. "When I was a kid, I had a fairy costume. Lots of tulle and sparkles and a magic wand."

"Wings?" Chad asked.

"Oh, for sure. Can't be a fairy without beautiful wings."

"Mexico City." Tank's eyes widened. "Isn't that a humongous place?"

"It is," I said, trying to remember what little I knew about Mexico's capital. I unfolded the letter from the package and skimmed it. "This letter doesn't give us any more information—it has Benedicto Prospero's name and address, and reminds us to send a report when we get back. It also reminds us that we can get help if we send an email."

"I don't get the fairy thing," Tank said. "Sounds crazy."

"Maybe it's some kind of code," Brenda said, shrugging. "A secret password."

"Like Tinkerbell," Daniel suggested.

Brenda groaned. "He's been watching old Disney movies. *Peter Pan* is his latest fave."

"You know, we ought to be able to find out something from that email addy," Chad said, crossing his arms. "Or am I the only one bright enough to be curious about our benefactors?"

"I'm curious," I said, "but not so curious that I want to go snooping in the business of people who are clearly on our side. If they don't want to give us more information, maybe we should respect that."

"It's just a matter of looking up watchers.com and seeing who owns the domain," Chad said. "Nothing wrong with that."

Tank laughed. "I don't know much about computers, but these people are too smart to make it easy."

"Yeah," Brenda agreed. "I'm just grateful they're on our side. If they don't want to provide life histories, I'm good with that."

"And they've given us a way to ask for help." I thumped the folded letter against my palm. "That's amazing."

"Agreed," Brenda said, looking at Daniel. "But is anyone else concerned that they seem pretty sure we're gonna need it?"

\* \* \*

We landed at a private airport outside Mexico City around lunch time—and I was glad the trip didn't take longer.

When Chad met us downstairs, his eyes were watery and his nose red. "I hab a cobe in my nose," he said, wearing a face like a beaten dog's. He shuffled over to me. "Wanna kiss me and make it better?"

I recoiled from the suggestion and backed away from his germs. "Are you really sick? Should you stay home?"

"I'm all right," Chad said, holding a finger under his nose. "I—I—" He sneezed. "Sorry 'bout that. I should be fine in a little while. Just took a heavy duty antihistamine."

"Great," I said, leading the way toward the waiting cab. "We'll be investigating and you'll be asleep."

As I expected, Chad did nod off during the flight. I hoped he'd wake with a clear head and be fully functional, but with Chad, I wasn't sure what "fully functional" was.

He wasn't the only one with physical issues. For the last hour of the flight, Tank's stomach growled so loudly that we could hear it rumbling throughout the cabin. At first, I was embarrassed for the big guy, but when he started talking back to his stomach, it became a running gag. "Who's the big bad on this adventure?" Brenda joked. "A ghast? A flying sphere? No—it's Cowboy's belly!"

I didn't want to laugh, but when Daniel cracked up, I had to chuckle. Poor Tank.

"I had a big breakfast," he said, his face drooping in a woeful expression. "Stack of pancakes, scrambled eggs, six sausage links, grits, orange juice, and biscuits with sausage gravy. I thought that would hold me over 'til lunchtime, but I guess flyin' makes me hungry."

Brenda looked up from her sketchbook and turned to Daniel. "If you plannin' to eat like that when you get bigger, I'm gonna need a second job."

Daniel grinned and looked out the window. While Brenda was distracted, I leaned over the back of my seat to get a peek at what she'd been sketching. The dark figure on her page was vaguely human, with spindly limbs, a knobby skull, jagged teeth, and wings.

I'd seen prettier pictures.

"Had a good look?"

I looked up, my cheeks flushing hot, and met Brenda's gaze. "I was just, um, wondering what we might be heading into. That—" I pointed at her sketchpad—"doesn't look friendly."

"It's probably nothing." She shrugged and flipped the lid of her sketchbook. "I dreamed about it last night, but like I said, Daniel's been into Disney films lately—he's catching up on all the stuff he missed while he was locked up in that psychiatric hospital. I figure that monster is a mix of Maleficent and a dragon, with a little Tinkerbell thrown in for good measure."

"I hope you're right."

We taxied to a private hanger and woke up Chad, then the pilot gave us the all-clear for grabbing our luggage and heading out. We had packed lightly—most of us brought only one small bag or backpack, and we were wearing jeans, short-sleeved shirts, and sneakers. Daniel was wearing a *Walking Dead* tee-shirt, much to Brenda's chagrin.

"I tried to talk him out of buying it," she had told me earlier. "I said nobody wanted to look at zombies and stuff. But then he said the zombies were nuthin' compared to things we'd seen, and he had me there. What could I say?" She shrugged. "Anyway, he knows that stuff is make-believe."

Yet here we were, about to drive into Mexico City to investigate something else that might be make-believe. But considering everything the Watchers had done to prepare us for the trip, something in me doubted that we'd be seeing a fake. Still, we had to keep our eyes, ears, and minds open.

We grabbed our bags and headed into small office, where we had to go show our passports. Getting into Mexico was easy, but we hit a glitch in customs. For some reason, a guy at the customs area opened our bags as we entered the area, then stood behind them with his arms crossed and his face somber.

We waited for Chad, who was moving slower than usual, then motioned for him to join us on a white line painted on the cement floor. The surly customs agent took Chad's bag when he arrived, then opened it and glared at us. "You are bringing forbidden items into Mexico," he snapped, looking as though he wanted to send us straight back home. "You will be arrested and spend the night in jail."

Tank's mouth spread in a good-ol'-boy smile. "Now, hang on a minute, buddy," he began, but the man silenced Tank by moving to the big guy's suitcase. I was afraid he was going to reach in and pull out a bag of crack cocaine or something else he'd planted, but instead he pulled out the box containing Tank's comms gear.

"What is this?" the customs agent snarled.

Tank looked at Chad, and for the first time since I'd met him, Chad appeared at a loss for words. "That is um, a state-of-the-art wireless communications unit," he said. "You know—like a walkie-talkie."

The agent's frown only deepened. "This is forbidden. This violates international order C-475 regarding wireless communications over unsecured frequencies."

"That is perfectly legitimate equipment," Chad argued. "Made by an international company who must certainly sell goods in Mexico."

The man dropped Tank's comms unit on the table, then reached into my bag, Brenda's, Daniel's, and Chad's. In each case, he pulled out the comms unit and dropped it on the table. When we had finished, we were looking at a heap of wires, plastic battery packs, and a couple of instruction manuals. "Confiscated," the man said, his face twisting in an oily smile. He scooped up all the units and left through a swinging door, leaving our bags on the table and us standing behind the white line.

I turned to Chad. "I thought you said those things were good."

"They're the best," he said. "Navy Seals use them."

"Maybe that's the problem," Tank said. "Maybe it's top secret technology, and the Mexicans want to get their hands on it."

"Anyone ever heard of international order C-475?" Brenda asked. "Maybe he made it up. They're going to learn our secrets by studying our gizmos."

"Maybe," Chad said, looking bemused. "Or maybe that guy's a ghost, and this has all been part of a plot to stop us. I could hit him over the head with a chair to see what happens—"

"Why don't you just pop into his brain?" Brenda suggested, her tone sharp. "Save us all a lot of trouble."

Chad blew out a breath. "Reading his thoughts wouldn't help me. I don't speak Spanish. Besides, I think those pills have somehow short-circuited things. My brain feels like it's full of fog."

Brenda burst out laughing and I tried to regain some level of control over the situation.

"Let's not hit anyone or play with their brains." I tapped Chad's arm. "Let's just get our stuff and leave as soon as we can."

A moment later the customs agent returned, empty-handed. He studied our group for a moment, then stepped back and slipped his hands into his pockets. "You are free to go."

We hurried forward to claim our bags and get out of the airport before he changed his mind.

I had hoped our bosses would have a hired car waiting, but apparently the people who thought of everything hadn't thought about having a taxi waiting. Instead we hitched a ride on a couple of airport golf carts, went to the main terminal, and hailed a minivan cab at the curb.

I settled my bag under my feet and tried to relax. At least we had made it to Mexico City.

# Chapter 3

Our cab driver looked at us and frowned. "No speak-e Ingles."

All of the others looked at me. "Okay. Um." I wracked my brain as I fumbled for the letter in my purse. "*Queremos ir aquí.*" Not having the faintest idea if I'd said the right thing, I handed the paper with Benedicto Prospero's address to our cab driver. He squinted at it, and for a moment I was afraid he'd tell us he'd never heard of the place.

"Ah." The man nodded at the paper, then

handed it back to me. "OK. We go."

I leaned back in the seat and looked at Brenda, who sat with Daniel on the bench seat behind me. She shook her head, grinning, and Daniel seemed thrilled by all the hustle and bustle of the airport.

"I don't know about this one," Tank said, turning to look at me from the front passenger seat. "I'm gettin' a bad feelin'."

"You always got a bad feelin'," Brenda said, slipping her arm around Daniel's thin shoulders. "Relax, Cowboy. We're in the land of siestas and margaritas. Of sombreros and—"

"Chupacabras," Tank interrupted. He lowered his voice and turned, cupping his hand to whisper. "Meanin' no disrespect to the country, but haven't you noticed that an awful lot of superstitious stuff comes out of Mexico? I've heard all kinds of things about weepin' paintings and bleedin' statues, and that stuff always seems to come from Mexico or South America. Plus, you've got them Aztecs and their human sacrifices—"

"The Aztecs are long gone, big guy," Brenda said. "And you're probably the last name on any list of possible human sacrifices."

I leaned forward to pat Tank's arm. Brenda and Chad teased him all the time, but I couldn't bring myself to do it. Probably because I knew he had feelings for me (whatever they were, I tried to keep them at bay) and because I knew he was all heart beneath that brawny exterior.

"We're going to be fine," I assured him. "After all, the assignment seems fairly straightforward. After all, no one has tried to kill us yet."

I meant that last bit as a joke, but Tank took it seriously. "I'm not so sure about that." He lifted a bushy brow. "That customs guy looked like he was ready to shoot anyone who spoke out of turn."

"Pfft." Brenda waved the matter away. "That's history. We'll just get some more of those comms thingies and use 'em on our next trip."

As Tank and Chad began to argue about whether people from Mexico were more superstitious than Americans, I looked out the window and watch the country slide by. The international airport was fully as modern as anything in the United States, and the freeway into the capital city was crowded with fast-moving cars. Once we reached the city, we drove along streets filled with skyscrapers that made the trees beneath them look like miniature decorations. "The city is really beautiful," I said to anyone who would listen. "I don't know what I was expecting, but these buildings are architecturally stunning."

The driver must have caught the gist of what I was saying, because he began to point out various buildings. I didn't understand much his description, but as he shifted into the right hand lane, he pointed at one building and said, "*La estación de televisión es dentro de este edificio.*"

"Television station," I repeated. "*Sí. Muchas gracias.*"

"We're here?" Brenda asked.

"I think so."

The driver pulled into an underground parking lot, then turned into an area that would allow him to drop us off and exit without having to park. "*Es un televisión estación?*" I asked.

The driver nodded, so I pulled out my wallet, only to discover that I had completely forgotten about the change in currency. "Um . . ." I showed him three U.S. twenties. "Es okay?"

He grinned. "*Muy okay.*" As everyone else piled out of the minivan, he took the money and gave me a blank receipt and drove off.

Chad, Tank, Brenda, Daniel and I stood in front of the elevator without a clue as to what we should do next. "Well," Chad said, pushing the elevator button, "every building has a lobby, and every lobby should have a receptionist or a list of tenants. Let's find Señor Prospero."

The doors opened and we shuffled inside the elevator car, making room for each other and our luggage.

"Prospero," Chad mused as the doors slid shut. "*Prosperity.* Coincidence, do you think?"

I shrugged. "I've never met the man."

"Well, hold onto your hats," Brenda said as the elevator began to rise. "Because I think we're about to."

* * *

Benedicto Prospero was not listed among the building tenants, but we did spot five television stations: XEW, XHTV, XEQ, XHOF, XAT, and XEIPN. A couple of the stations were owned by Grupo Televisa and TV Azteca, the other by Grupo Prospero.

"There you go," I said, pointing to XAT. "Either our guy owns the station or one of his relatives does."

"Could be coincidence," Chad said.

"The odds are against it." I flashed him a brief smile, then led the way back the elevator. "Going up, anyone?"

We exited on the forty-fourth floor, home to XAT and the offices of Grupo Prospero. With a confidence I didn't exactly feel, I walked through a pair of glass doors and up to an ebony reception desk that stood at the center of a two-story lobby.

"*Hola*," I said, hoping the receptionist spoke English. "*Me amigos y yo de donde los Estados Unidos. Quiero*—we want to see—señor Benedicto Prospero. We believe he'll want to see us."

The pretty receptionist lifted a brow. "Was he expecting you today?"

She understood me! I slumped in relief. "I'm not sure. But it's important that we see him."

She looked at me, an uncertain smile on her face. "I'm sorry, but if you do not have an appointment, I cannot let you see Señor Prospero. He is a very busy man."

"But we've come all the way from Dallas."

"Texas," Tank added. "In the U.S. of A."

The receptionist smiled. "Señor Prospero is in the studio this afternoon and will not be finished recording until late. If you want to come back tomorrow—"

I broke eye contact with her when Brenda elbowed me. Someone was moving on floor above—a middle-aged man in a dress shirt and tie, with paper towels or something tucked over his collar. The guy had apparently just come out of makeup, which meant he was about to go into the studio—

"Señor Prospero? Benedicto Prospero?" I called.

The gentleman did not look happy to be interrupted. "Como?" he said, glancing down at us.

"*Con permiso, señor*—my friends and I would like to talk to you about . . . the fairy." I spoke the last word reluctantly, knowing that I stood in a public place, but we all saw his countenance change at my words. The man who would have brushed us off without hesitation went pale, and the hand he placed on the railing trembled slightly.

"You know . . . about that?"

"Yes. We were sent here to investigate it."

"By whom?"

"Please, señor—may we speak in private?"

He glanced quickly left and right, then pressed

his lips together. After a moment, he seemed to come to a decision. "Conchita, show them the way to the staircase, please. Tell everyone I am not to be interrupted for the next hour."

\* \* \*

We climbed the stairs and met Señor Prospero in a hallway. Keeping his voice low, he led us to a conference room, then indicated that we should drop our luggage against the wall. When we had lightened our load, he crooked a finger and led us into a luxurious office with lots of open space, gorgeous leather guest chairs, and a desk about as wide as a barn door.

I took a moment to introduce everyone. "We work for an organization called the Watchers," I said. "I can't say much about them, but—"

"I know who they are," Señor Prospero said.

While I blinked in amazement, he opened his top desk drawer and pulled out a Bible. Flipping to the center, he ran his finger over the text, then grunted. "*Aqui esta. Para esto ha sido decretado por los observadores—*"

"We don't speak Spanish," Brenda told him.

Prospero nodded. "Ah. Forgive me. 'For this has been decreed by the *watchers*, it is commanded by the holy ones, so that everyone may know that the Most High rules over the kingdoms of the world.' From the book of Daniel, chapter four."

The man looked up as if his explanation should satisfy us, but I could make no sense of it. I looked at Tank, our official Bible gee whiz kid, and he looked as confused as I felt.

"Thank you," I said, ready to move past his explanation. "But we came here to talk about the fairy."

"Yes." He nodded and set his Bible back in the drawer. "I will show you something," he said, stepping over to his desk chair, "and then we will go into the conference room to discuss it. My associate will join us, but no one else. No one else at the station knows about this."

My curiosity was more than piqued. I stepped closer as he sat, then swiveled to the beautiful credenza behind his desk. After taking a key from his pocket, he unlocked a deep drawer in the credenza, then lifted out a glass jar containing clear liquid . . . and a creature that looked identical to the sketch Brenda had drawn on the plane.

I saw her eyes widen, then close tightly. No sense in denying it, I wanted to tell her, when the evidence was right before our eyes.

"*Esta aquí.*" Senior Prospero slid it across the desktop. "*El Hada.* The fairy."

The five of us drew closer. As frightening as Brenda's sketch had been, the creature in the jar was far more terrifying in its gruesome details. The skull was small, but still covered by enough skin that we could see pointed ears and soft fur around the folds. The empty eye sockets were large, and the gaping mouth revealed rows of jagged teeth that reminded me of a shark's. The creature had a visible neck, and a chest covered with what appeared to be black, leathery skin. The skin covered the chest area, two arms, and two legs, both of which ended in hands or feet with five jointed digits each. The creature also had two large wings composed of bone (or cartilage?) and covered with skin.

The thing was incredibly human—far more human than animal. And it was large, for a fairy. About the size of one of my old Barbie dolls.

"Yes," Señor Prospero said, observing our reactions. "It does look like something out of a nightmare. But for the wings, it is humanoid. But you must also see this."

He turned the jar, enabling us to see the oddest feature yet—a tail, long and curving, that ended in a sharp point, almost like a claw or tooth.

"Incredible," Chad whispered.

Tank's response followed: "Jesus, help us."

Brenda said nothing, but kept her arm firmly wrapped around Daniel's shoulders and her gaze on that glass jar.

Chad straightened first. "It has to be a fake," he said, swaying slightly on his feet. "It's a clever fake, but a fake nonetheless."

"How can you know that?" Brenda asked.

Chad shook his head. "These things pop up all the time. Last year two guys in England claimed to find a fairy, and it looked pretty fairy-like. But they released the news on April first, and the thing turned out to be a gigantic April Fool's joke. It was some wire structure with leaves wrapped around it."

Señor Prospero said nothing, but picked up the jar and carried it into the conference room, where he set it in the center of the table. Then he went to a phone, murmured something into it, and sat in the chair at the head of the table, motioning that we should be seated as well.

We had no sooner finished settling into our chairs when another man entered. He wore a white lab coat and glasses.

"I would like to introduce," Señor Prospero said, "Dr. Gregory Wu, an expert in molecular science."

"Great," Brenda whispered under her breath. "We got us a mini-United Nations right here."

When Dr. Wu had seated himself, Prospero leaned forward and clasped his hands on the table. "I own this TV station," he said. "My talk show is live every weekday from one until five. We talk about all kinds of things—politics, religion, economics, and the environment. Many people have encouraged me to run for president, but though I am popular, I am no politician. I am an entertainer. But people see me as more."

He shifted his position, bringing his hand to his face in a gesture I recognized as an anxiety indicator. "Two years ago, a farmer and his twelve-year-old son brought me this—thing." He nodded toward the jar. "They said that since I was on TV, I would know what to do with it. They said they had seen similar things flying at night, but they had never seen a dead specimen. They left it with me, and I put it in this jar of formaldehyde."

He cleared his throat, then gestured to Dr. Wu. "I thought it was a hoax, but wanted to be sure, so I hired Dr. Wu to take X-rays. He did, producing two films—a frontal view and one of the creature in profile." He looked at his associate. "Dr. Wu, would you please distribute the films?"

From a folder, Wu produced two things— actual X-ray films and paper copies of those images. He handed the films to Tank, and the copies to Brenda, indicating that we should pass both around.

For a long while no one said anything. The images were alarming, but the films were obviously genuine. And when viewing the creature straight on, seeing the eye sockets and the mouth open and ringed with teeth—

A ghost spider crawled up my spine as I imagined the fairy alive and moving. What *was* this thing?

"It is one thing," Señor Prospero said, "to cover sticks or wires with leaves and call it a fairy, but what man alive can create a skeleton of bone and cover it with flesh?"

"Hang on," Chad said, slurring his words slightly. "How do you know that's—that's bone?"

"See the calcification at the joints?" Dr. Wu asked. "That is a result of normal wear of bone against bone. And do you see how the calcification is heaviest on the back where the wings join the body? That is what you would expect of a humanoid with wings—the bone is thicker in that area to support the additional weight. That is to be expected, but few would go through such trouble to create a hoax."

Brenda leaned toward me. "Is Chad *drunk*?"

I shook my head. "I think it's his cold medicine. But he does seem a little doped."

"You will also notice," Dr. Wu went on, pointing at a copy of the X-ray, "that the creature has been injured and that injury has been repaired."

I studied my paper copy of the image. I might not have noticed, but Dr. Wu was right—one of the creature's long legs had been broken and the bone clumsily reset. We could see a white spot over the break, as if someone had applied a patch of some sort.

Who would do such a thing? A doctor fairy?

Chad turned the jar to study the creature within. "We could s-settle this question in no time. Have you taken DNA from this—this thing?"

"We have taken samples," Dr. Wu said, "but so far we have been unable to extract DNA because the formaldehyde has destroyed the material. But we have sent samples to other labs in the hope that they can read the DNA sequence."

"That thing is creepy," Brenda said, pushing away from the table as if being near the fairy made her nervous. "It's nasty lookin'."

"It is a *duch*," Daniel said, his wide eyes intent upon the creature.

Señor Prospero frowned. "And what is a duch?"

"We're not sure," I answered, "because sometimes Daniel speaks in his own language. But we do know it's something bad."

"I must admit that Ms. S-Smartmouth makes a good point," Chad said. "If you were going to create a fake creature, you'd want it to look fierce. Just like this."

Brenda cast Chad a killing look, but I pressed on, not wanting the discussion to dissolve into a drug-induced spat.

"Other real animals look terrifying," I argued. "Crocodiles, moray eels, and sharks. They're not fakes."

"Yet people who create hoaxes," Señor Prospero said, "crave and create publicity, but neither the farmer nor his son has ever gone public with this news. I have never mentioned the fairy on my program, nor have I shown it to anyone but my wife and Dr. Wu. But—" he lifted both brows and smiled—"I have been asking God to send me someone who would know what to do with this thing. And here you are."

In that moment I'm not sure who was more dumbfounded—Señor Prospero or our group. Everyone around the table stopped fidgeting as a hush fell over the room.

"We were sent here," I finally said, my voice trembling, "to see this thing, learn about it, and see if we can figure out why it's here."

"It's c-clearly not natural," Chad said, shaking his head. "And I'm not saying it's a fake—I'm saying it's not a natural part of the animal kingdom. I doubt there's anything like it on the planet."

Señor Prospero answered with a sad smile. "Unfortunately, there is." He gestured to Dr. Wu, who pulled out a small box and set a small box on the conference table. When he lifted the lid, we rose from our seats to peer inside. On a soft bed of cotton, we saw the skeleton of another creature, one eerily similar to the first. The skin had desiccated and fallen away, but the skull, the jagged teeth, and the long, slender limbs remained. Along with the wings and the tail.

"You will notice," Dr. Wu said, using his pen to gently probe the remnants of the wings, "this creature has two sets of wings. It was probably—"

"D-deformed?" Chad guessed.

"A prototype," Wu answered. "A first attempt. You will notice that this one is curled up in a fetal position—as if it curled up to die."

I bit my lip. Scientists did not usually make "as

if" statements, but Wu was right—the creature did look as though it had given up.

"Where did you find the second specimen?" I asked.

"A truck driver brought it in," Señor Prospero said. "He struck it with his truck as he was driving one night. When he stopped to see what he had hit, he found it curled up on the truck's fender."

"So . . . you think someone made this," Chad said.

Señor Prospero nodded. "We believe it is a creation, but not a fake. It is a real creature. A hybrid."

I shivered. We had run into hybrids before— the black-eyed children—and the experience had not been pleasant.

Dr. Wu lifted his hand. "This creature is probably 98.5 percent human. As to the remaining 1.5 percent, we can only guess."

"A chimera." Chad smiled. "A blend of two living creatures."

"Exactly." Wu nodded. "The creature could be a chimera composed of human and alien cells. Or human and animal. We will not know its exact makeup until we have an accurate DNA analysis."

"That reminds me," I said. "I just read a newspaper report about this. Apparently the U.S. National Institute of Health is lifting a ban that prevented scientists from creating human-animal chimeras."

Wu shook his head. "The people who are

behind this creature are years ahead of your NIH."

"Does Mexico have a national research program involving chimeras?" I asked.

Señor Prospero shook his head. "Definitely not."

"So whoever is doing this—"

"Is off-book," Prospero said. "Not a national government."

"I have a question," Tank said, lifting the X-ray of the first creature toward the overhead lights. "This creature's skeleton has white dots all through it. What are those?"

Señor Prospero looked at Dr. Wu, then sighed. "We have our theories, but I hesitate to mention them. We are lacking too many facts to be dogmatic."

I looked at Tank and Brenda. "I guess that's where we come in. Our assignment was to verify the creature, try to determine where it came from, and see if we can figure out why it exists."

Prospero smiled. "Not an easy task."

"No," Tank said, meeting the man's gaze. "But we've faced the impossible and survived, so I think we can handle a fairy."

"Hubris," Senor Prospero said, smiling. "You certainly have it in abundance."

"Yes, he does," Chad said, crossing his arms.

Tank beamed . . . I didn't have the heart to tell him the comment wasn't intended to be a compliment.

# Chapter 4

With our shiny new credit cards from the Watchers, we rented rooms at a hotel not far from the TV station. Then we met in my suite to lay out a few plans.

"We need to hire a car," I said, unfolding a map I'd picked up in a small store. "We shouldn't be driving around Mexico without knowing where we're going."

"Roger that," Brenda said, and when our eyes met I suspected that she, like me, was thinking about recent news reports. It might have been an unfair characterization, but our local news networks had featured too many stories about

American tourists running into drug lords and ending up with their heads in one location and their bodies in another.

I didn't want to take any chances.

Tank handed me the contact information Señor Prospero had given us when we left. The man who'd brought the fairy to the TV station was Hector Rodriguez, and he lived on a farm about an hour from Mexico City. I had imagined meeting him in a little cafe somewhere, but after looking at the map and seeing nothing but forest, I realized we'd have to go to the man's house.

"Señor Rodriguez lives in the middle of nowhere, apparently," I said, picking up my iPad to check out a satellite view of the area. I tapped on the maps icon, typed in the address, and found myself staring at a narrow road that wound through an area of heavy forest. I zoomed out and saw that our contact lived inside a national park: *Parque Nacional El Tepozteco.* I could see no road leading to his house, but it probably lay beneath the canopy of trees.

"All right." I did a quick computation. "Google maps says we can reach the farmer's house in about an hour, depending on traffic. We'll visit him tomorrow, interview him and his son, and see what they can tell us about the fairy. And while we're in the area, we can look around to see if we can spot anything else."

"We should spend the night," Chad said.

Four other heads swiveled toward him. "Are

you still drunk?" Brenda asked.

"I'm fine." Chad leaned forward, elbows on his knees. "Think about it—this thing flies, and so far it has eluded most people, so I think it's safe to say it's nocturnal. It may even have luminescent qualities, like a firefly. So if it comes out at night, we should stay and look for it. Our bosses told us to get video."

I blew out a breath. "We can't assume that Señor Rodriguez will have room for us—or even want us hanging around."

"We don't have to stay at his house. We find out where he discovered the creature, and we camp there."

Brenda stiffened. "Did you say *camp*?"

Chad grinned. "Haven't you ever spent the night out under the stars?"

"Not by choice."

"It's easy. We just need to rent a tent, some sleeping bags, and some canteens. We can all share the tent, and Andi and I will double up with a sleeping bag."

"Whoa," I said, my face flushing hot against the air conditioned air. "This is not the time for joking around—and those kinds of jokes aren't welcome here, not now or ever."

Chad lifted his hands in a posture of surrender. "Cool your jets, sweetie. I was only testing the waters."

"Well, stop it." I bit my lip, frustrated that I couldn't think of witty remarks as quickly as a doped-up Chad. "Or I'll . . . you'll regret it."

Chad grinned. He was probably reading my mind, hearing me regret my inability to think on my feet . . .

"Or," Brenda went on, ignoring Chad, "we could pick up some snacks, bottled water, and have someone make us a gourmet picnic basket. There's no law saying we have to rough it out there."

"You guys discuss it," I told them, standing. "I'll be back in a minute."

I left them in the living room and went to the restroom. After washing my hands, I stared in the mirror for a long moment and tried to imagine what I'd look like after a night out in the Mexican woods. Mexico was in the tropics, which meant lots of humidity. It also meant spiders and snakes grew even bigger down here, and maybe more venomous. Not to mention the mosquitoes. We'd not only need a tent, we'd need mosquito repellent, fly swatters, rain ponchos, a couple of lanterns, something to start a fire, and maybe a portable toilet . . .

I laughed and imagined my hair as a big red dish scrubber. Maybe I should get a hat. I'd never been camping in my life, but I was up for anything, as long as everyone else came along.

I dried my hands on a towel, then glanced in the mirror to make sure my hair hadn't gone completely out of control in the humidity. Then I stopped cold.

The professor was in my mirror. He smiled when our eyes met, and my heart did a strange little flipflop. Was I seeing things? Did I miss him so much that I was imagining him in my mirror?

I closed my eyes and counted—one, two, three. I lifted my eyelids and saw him standing there, arms crossed, that funny little smile below his mustache. He was humoring me.

"Where are you?" I asked.

He tapped his left wrist—shorthand for referring to time--then he pointed—not *at* me, but *beyond* me—and the gesture lifted the hairs on my arms. Could he always see us from where he was? If he was in a parallel universe, did his have gruesome fairies, too? I opened my mouth, about to say something else, but before I could speak he vanished. Gone. Just like that.

I exhaled in sharp disappointment. My former boss and good friend had been *right there* . . . unless my brain had conjured him up. Chad would say that I wanted his advice, so my subconscious had provided him, neat and tidy and pointing at me as if to say *You can do it, Andi.*

Except he hadn't been exactly pointing at me. He'd been pointing beyond me, at something in the bedroom.

I turned. And saw a folder on the bed. A striking silver folder with my name on the cover. A folder I had never seen in my life.

As every nerve in my body screamed *impossible*, I walked over and picked it up. And inside I found a biography of Ambrosi Giacomo, a man I'd never heard of.

Moving slowly on legs that felt like wood, I went back to the living room. "Guys," I said, interrupting their conversations. I held up the silver folder. "Anyone ever seen this before?"

They stared at it.

"Where'd you get that?" Brenda asked. "Party City?"

"Never seen it," Tank said, speaking for everyone. His eyes softened with concern. "You okay? You look a little rattled."

I set the folder on the coffee table, then sank back into my chair. "I went into the bathroom and nothing was on the bed. And as I was washing my hands, I saw the professor in the mirror. He pointed behind me, and just as I was about to say something to him, he disappeared. When I turned around, this was on the bed."

Chad brightened. "Cool."

Brenda looked at him as if he'd sprung a brain leak. "Are you insane? This sort of thing doesn't happen . . . much."

"I've seen the professor in mirrors before," I reminded them. "But afterward I've never found anything . . . tangible."

"It's real," Daniel said, smiling. "It's from him."

"I suppose," Chad said, "if your professor traveled to a different dimension via a fold in the space-time continuum, he might have found a way to transport certain materials. Like a folder."

"Never seen one like that," Brenda said. "What's it made of, plastic?"

I ran my fingertips over the folder. "Not plastic. Not paper. Something else."

Tank slapped his blue-jeaned thighs. "Who cares what it's made of? What's in it?"

I opened the folder again, relieved to discover that the contents hadn't changed or disappeared. "It's a bio of some man I've never heard of—Ambrosi Giacomo. Does that name ring a bell with anyone?"

I looked around the circle—Chad, Tank, Brenda, Daniel—nothing.

But Brenda whipped out her phone. "We don't have to stay ignorant." She typed on the keyboard, then nodded. "There's a Wikipedia entry—not a long one, but enough to prove the man exists. In our world, that is."

"And?" Chad prodded.

"Chillax, man, I'm readin'." She skimmed the material, then looked up. "He's some kind of businessman in Italy. Rich, apparently. And that's all it says."

"A photo?" I asked, wondering if Ambrose Giacomo and Benedicto Prospero could be the same person.

Brenda shook her head. "No picture. Says he was born in 1983. In Italy."

I looked at Tank. "Ambrose Giacomo is not another name for Benedicto Prospero. The Italian guy is too young."

"Does the article mention his companies?" Chad asked. "His line of work?"

"No and no." Brenda dropped her phone back into her purse. "Sorry."

"Maybe it's a false name," Chad said. "Or maybe the Italian dude is the Mexican dude's son."

"Maybe this stuff has nothing to do with the fairy," Brenda said. "If the professor is off in another world, how do we know his world matches up with ours? Maybe he's screwed up. Or maybe the worlds are similar, but Señor Prospero is Ambrose Giacomo in the professor's world—and he's younger."

"Or—" Chad lifted a finger—"Maybe the professor is warning us about something in the future. Maybe this Ambrose Giacomo is a kind of Hitler in the professor's world, so he's warning us. Or maybe he just wants us to keep an eye on the guy."

"Maybe the countries are different," Tank said. "Maybe Italy is Mexico in the professor's world and Mexico is something else. Maybe Ambrose whoever is investigating the fairies in the professor's world—"

"Enough." I dropped my head into my hands. "You're giving me a headache."

We sat for a moment in silence, then Chad stood and stretched. "You gals can stay here and rest up if you want, but the big lug and I should go out and get some camping equipment. Andi, be a sweetheart and reserve our car. Do we want to leave this afternoon or tomorrow?"

I bristled at his be a sweetheart comment, but decided to ignore it . . . because he was still under the influence.

"Tomorrow," I said, looking at Brenda to see if she agreed. "I think we need to do a little more planning."

"And we're chargin' batteries," Brenda added. "We're chargin' our phones, our iPads, the camera, the bug zappers, and anything else you guys buy. I'm not headin' into the woods without a full supply of energized gadgets."

"Good idea," I said. "So you guys go shopping and I'll reserve a car for tomorrow morning."

Ready or not, fairies and goblins, we were on our way.

# Chapter 5

By the time our hired car arrived at the hotel the next morning, we looked like a group of city slickers heading out for an overpriced wilderness adventure. Chad and Tank had gone a little overboard collecting supplies. They not only bought a tent, they also purchased cots, mosquito netting, butterfly nets (the perfect thing for catching fairies, Tank said), a Coleman stove, three Coleman lanterns, rain ponchos, a tarp, a folding table (with seats, Chad pointed out), a portable toilet, a bug zapper, toilet paper, a privacy screen, a six pack of flashlights, five sleeping bags, a cooler, and enough water, soft drinks, and groceries to supply us for a week.

Naturally, half of what they brought wouldn't fit into the rented vehicle.

The driver stood outside the hotel shaking his head. "*Esta materia no cabrá.*"

"We can make it work," Chad said. "It's all a matter of design. If we arrange the items geometrically—"

"Not gonna work," Tank said. "You have to shove the stuff in. If we push it all in the back, it'll fit."

I stood in the driveway and looked at the load, then at the space in the large SUV. Add in five passengers, our luggage and personal belongings—

"It won't work," I said firmly. "So here's what you're going to leave behind. The portable table—"

"But—" Chad protested.

"It's too big, and we can sit in the tent. Leave out the toilet and the privacy screen."

Brenda snorted. "You planning on holding it for twenty-four hours?"

"A tree will work fine, and the toilet paper goes with us. But not the giant pack. Two or three rolls, tops."

Chad grinned. "I love it when she plays wilderness woman."

I ignored him. He seemed sharp again, but his eyes were a bit watery and I'd already heard him sneeze three times.

"We take enough food for two meals—and water for two days," I said. "No more. We don't need the stove. We only need one lantern. If we keep the tent zipped, we won't need mosquito netting. You can bring one butterfly net. Ditch the cots, we can sleep on the ground. If there's room, you can bring the sleeping bags, but make sure they're rolled tightly."

Tank peered at me, his eyes narrow. "Were you a Girl Scout?"

"I'm practical. Anyone can see that you guys bought too much."

Thirty minutes later, we had packed the car and pulled away from the hotel, leaving a neat pile of camping gear beneath a sign that read: ¡Gratis! Si te gusta acampar.

\* \* \*

An hour later, I straightened in the front passenger seat and showed my phone and its map app to the driver. "We're close," I said, trying to remember the Spanish words. "Estamos cerca. Maneja lento."

He gave me an uncertain look, but slowed the car so we could search for signs along the road. We had driven about ten miles into the national park when the app indicated that we had reached our destination. Frantic, I looked out the window and spotted a barely visible dirt road snaking through the trees. "¡Aqui! I mean, Por ahi!"

The driver turned. As the SUV rumbled over

the road, jostling our equipment and rattling our teeth, the driver muttered Spanish expletives under his breath. Finally we pulled up in front of a modest house surrounded by several outbuildings. A skinny dog ran over to the car, barking as if there were no tomorrow, but the animal shied away when I opened my door.

"We don't want to scare this farmer," I said, realizing that the sight of a big, black SUV might alarm anyone. "So let me go speak to him. The rest of you can get out and stretch your legs, but don't snoop. And don't wander off."

"Why don't you let me go talk to him?" Chad said, unbuckling his seat belt. "After all, I can read his mind. I could—"

He sneezed so explosively that Brenda's dreads swayed in the resulting breeze.

"Thought you couldn't read a mind that thought in Spanish," Brenda said.

"Yeah, but I can still sense things. Fear. Deception. Irritation."

"You're staying in the car," I told him, feeling irritated myself. "I speak more Spanish than you do, and I'm a woman. Women are less threatening."

"But—"

"No buts, newbie. I can handle this. And by the way—" I exhaled in resignation. "Take another one of those antihistamines. We'll never see a fairy if you scare them off with all that sneezing."

Chad tossed me a mock salute. "Yes, ma'am."

I blew out a breath. I had felt a certain amount of tension between us over the past few days—almost as if Chad expected to be anointed team leader and thought I was usurping his position. But our team didn't actually *have* a leader, so he shouldn't be getting his nose out of joint if I did my best to keep things organized.

I got out and slowly approached the house. The farm might be considered poor by American standards, but it looked pretty prosperous to me. A large water tank sat on the flat roof, and someone had painted the stucco exterior bright blue with coral accents on the door and windowsills. A chicken coop sat behind the house, and a couple of other buildings stood beyond the henhouse. In the distance, a couple of acres had been planted with something that grew lush and green in the hot sun.

"*¡Hola!*" I called. "*¿Alguien en casa?*"

A moment later a man appeared behind the screen door. He wore dark pants and a sleeveless undershirt, and he regarded me with a wary gaze. Behind him, just over his shoulder, I saw a young teenager, probably thirteen or fourteen.

"Hola!" I smiled and waved in an effort to appear friendly. "*¿Hablan ustedes Inglés?*"

The father looked at me, then gestured to the kid, who stepped out from behind him. "My father doesn't speak English," the boy said, "but I can translate."

211

"Good." I smiled in relief. "My name is Andi, and my friends and I are from the United States. Yesterday we spoke to Señor Prospero from the TV station. He gave us your address."

The boy nodded. "Si."

"We'd like to talk to you about the creature you found. And we'd like to see the place—where you found him, that is."

The boy looked at his father and explained in a flood of Spanish. The older man scratched his chin, then looked at me and responded. I didn't catch a word.

"My father," the kid said, "wants me to tell you I found it lying in a ditch. I was riding my bicycle and stopped—" he looked down—"to make water, and that's when I saw it."

I nodded, slowly understanding. So the kid stopped to obey the call of nature. Happens to everyone.

"Was the creature dead when you found it?"

"Si—yes."

"Had you ever seen anything like that before?"

The boy glanced at his father, who nodded.

"Si. Sometimes at night, we see them flying. Once we saw one come out of a tree."

I blinked. "It was in the tree? Up in the branches?"

The boy shook his head. "It was—*¿como dice que?*—it came out of a hole in the tree."

"Ah." I considered his answer, then asked, "Why did you take the creature to Señor

Prospero?"

The kid looked at his father, repeated the question in Spanish, and listened to his father's reply.

"Papa said Señor Prospero always takes questions from the audience and gets answers. But we have not had an answer yet. Señor Prospero has not even talked about the creature."

"Not yet." I glanced back at the others, who appeared to be waiting patiently. "I'm sorry, I forgot to ask your name."

The boy gave me a shy smile. "Tomas."

"Tomas, could you take us to the place where you found the fairy? We would like to spend the night in that spot so we can help Señor Prospero find some answers."

The boy's eyes widened, then he translated for his father. The elder Rodriguez eyed me for a long moment, then nodded and pointed to a bicycle propped against a tree.

"Papa says I am to lead you there and then come home," Tomas said. "I will be ready in a minute."

"Take your time," I said, grateful that the family wanted to cooperate. "We'll follow you."

The boy disappeared into the house, leaving me with Señor Rodriguez. I smiled, then remembered my manners. "Gracias, señor. Muchas gracias."

He nodded, then went back into the house, leaving me to wait for his son.

\* \* \*

"So Tomas is going to take us to the spot," I told the others, "and we can set up camp there."

"This is a national park," Tank pointed out. "Aren't there rules against camping in a national park?"

"You're confused," Chad said, his voice sharp and cynical. "Everybody camps in the national parks. The rules prohibit littering."

I looked at Brenda, who shrugged. "It's not like we're plannin' to live there," she pointed out. "We'll actually only be there a few hours, and we'll clean up. Nonexistent footprint and all that."

"Right." I sighed. "As long as we don't get arrested."

Being jailed in Mexico wasn't my idea of fun, but we hadn't seen any signs that prohibited camping. In fact, since entering the Parque Nacional El Tepozteco, we hadn't seen any signs or any forest rangers. In any case, the Rodriguez family lived within the park boundaries, so how strict could the rules be?

A few moments later Tomas appeared, wearing a button-up shirt, jeans, and sneakers. He picked up his bike and smiled. "Ready?"

"Lead the way, Tomas." I hopped back in the car along with the others. The driver did a three-point turn and we followed Tomas back to the paved two-lane road.

We drove a couple of miles down the

serpentine highway, then Thomas turned onto another dirt road, this one much less-traveled that the one that led to his house. Our driver complained again, but he kept driving, moving slowly over the ruts and maneuvering around fallen trees and branches. Finally the shrubbery and trees at the side of the road opened up to reveal a ditch running along a barren field. The boy stopped and swung his leg over his bike.

Our driver braked to a halt.

"*Aquí.*" Tomas pointed to the ditch. "The fairy was in the ditch."

We piled out of our vehicle. The ditch was nothing extraordinary—only a foot deep, with weeds growing on the banks and a trickle of muddy brown water at the bottom. The field beyond had probably been planted at some point, but now resembled nothing except dry, brown earth. Trees to the right and left provided a curtain of shade for the rutted road, effectively concealing it from overhead planes or helicopters or Google Earth cameras.

Chad stepped closer. "Has it occurred to you—" he scratched his chin—"that this might be the perfect place to grow wacky tabacky?"

"What?"

"Marijuana." He lowered his voice. "Secluded spot, mostly covered from above, no traffic or prying eyes—"

"We're not the DEA," I told him. "We're here to investigate a scientific anomaly."

"But maybe we should consider an illegal drug operation as a reason for the creature," he said, whispering out of the side of his mouth. "Maybe the family made up the story to scare people away from this part of the forest. Maybe some drug lord paid big bucks for a sophisticated fake fairy, and this is all a cover-up—"

"If they wanted to scare people away, they've done a poor job of it," I reminded him. "Did you check the Internet? I did. There was a plastic Tinkerbell that folks in some small Mexican village are charging people to view, and another fake in an unspecified location. But there's been nothing about *this* story. That's *nada* in Spanish."

Chad grinned. "You are *so* cute when you're ticked off. How do you manage it?"

I curled my hands into fists until the urge to slap him had passed.

Moving toward Tomas, I pulled out my phone and showed him a copy of the creature's X-ray. "Does this look like the creature you gave Señor Prospero?"

The boy's eyes widened. "*Si. Claro.* But . . . it looks different."

"This is an X-ray," I said. "The thick parts look white, and the thinner parts are darker." I pointed to one of the strange white spots on the creature's body. "Do you have any idea what those white spots could be?"

He looked closer, then his eyes widened and his expression twisted. He glanced away, then bit his lip and looked at me, guilt written all over his face.

"Tomas—do you know what those spots are?"

He kept his mouth clamped shut as he looked from left to right.

"Tomas, if you help us, we may be able to find answers. Your father would like an answer, right?"

The boy nodded.

"So if you know anything at all—"

"He shot it." The words tripped off his tongue. "The night before I found it, we were outside and we saw them. They came close to the house, and we saw the face. Mama screamed, so Papa got his *escopeta* and shot it."

A dozen thoughts tumbled through my mind. If Señor Rodriguez shot the creature, it should have been blasted to smithereens. But perhaps that depended on what an *escopeta* was.

"Tomas—*¿que es una escopeta?*"

He squinched up his face, then lifted an imaginary gun—or maybe a crossbow—to his face and shoulder, then pulled the trigger.

So . . . rifle? Bow? I didn't know much about weapons.

I walked over to speak to our driver. "*Escopeta, por favor,*" I asked. "*¿Que is escopeta?*"

He gave me a blank look, then pulled a language dictionary from his pocket. After a moment, he looked up. "Shotgun."

I looked at Tank, who had followed me over.

"Buckshot." His smile broadened into a grin. "And, by golly, if those dots aren't the perfect size for buckshot. The thing must have been too quick to get the full blast, but it still got hit by six or seven pellets."

I heard an almost-audible click as the pieces of the puzzle fell into place.

"This is the spot," I told the driver. "We're going to unload here. If you could pick us up here at this time tomorrow, we'll pay double the charge and give you the extra as a gratuity."

In that moment, the man had no problem understanding my English. He hopped out of the car and opened the back hatch. "Okay," he said, grabbing the closest suitcase. "Okey-dokey."

# Chapter 6

An hour later the five of us sat around a pile of logs that was supposed to be a campfire. I couldn't believe it, but though we had purchased everything we could think of to camp successfully, we hadn't bothered to learn how to light a fire.

"A bunch of stupid city slickers, that's what we are," Brenda said, slapping at a bug buzzing her ankles. "Nobody ever told me I'd need to know how to start a fire."

"I can't believe we didn't bring matches," Chad complained for the fourth time. "I assumed one of you ladies would carry them in your purse."

"Nobody smokes anymore," I said. "Lung cancer isn't glamorous."

Chad looked at Tank. "Didn't you learn how to rub two sticks together back there in Podunkville where you grew up?"

Tank glared back. "I haven't seen you creating any sparks. I've seen you *tryin'* to get somethin' goin', but it ain't gonna happen—"

"Guys!" I shouted, aware that they weren't talking about the fire any more.

Sighing, I crossed my legs and looked toward the western horizon, where the sun was about to disappear behind a wall of trees. "Maybe we don't need a fire. We still have a lantern, right?"

Chad grinned. "Yeah . . . and it has ignomatic autonition." He laughed. "I mean automatic ignition."

"His medicine just kicked in," Brenda said, shaking her head.

He opened a box, pulled out the lantern and struggled to read the instructions in the fading light. Fortunately, the lantern blazed into light just as the sun disappeared and the sky turned from blue to blue-black.

"Ouch!" Brenda slapped at her bare arm, then looked at the tent. "Maybe we should get inside before the kamikaze mosquitos come out. I don't want Daniel gettin' a thousand bites."

"Sounds good to me." I picked up my stuff

and moved inside the tent, where earlier Brenda and Daniel had rolled out five sleeping bags and covered nearly all the floor. The tent had several windows, and the guys had rolled up the canvas coverings so we could keep watch from behind the screens.

"Come on, Daniel," Brenda said, practically lifting him from the spot where he'd been playing his hand-held video game. "You're about to wear out the batteries on that thing."

"Yowie!" Tank slapped at his arm, then Chad hit his neck. "Man! Let's get inside!"

The guys followed us into the tent. As Tank zipped up the entrance and Chad powered on the bug zapper, Brenda and I sat before one of the front windows, watching for anything unusual in the air, the trees, or the weeds.

"These things glow, right?" Tank said.

"I'm not sure," I answered. "Dr. Wu didn't say anything about glowing. Neither did Tomas."

"How are we supposed to see 'em if they don't glow?"

"Look for the light," I told him. "The moon is supposed to be full tonight."

"Romantic," Chad said. "I wuv it."

"Not the time or place for such talk," I said, scowling at Chad. "Besides, you're manning the video camera, right?"

"Yep." He patted the pouch hanging from his belt. "I got it covered."

I felt the air move, then heard Tank hit the

canvas floor next to me. "Thought I'd sit here to guard the door," he said, moving so close that his arm brushed mine. "Wouldn't want a bear or anything to come after our food."

"I don't think a bear is going to crash the place for a box of protein bars," Brenda said, her voice as dry as the aforementioned bars. "And that reminds me—Chad, toss me one of those water bottles, will ya?"

I heard the crinkle of plastic behind me, then silence reigned as we settled into position and waited.

"You know," Chad said after a few minutes, "Tank, maybe I should sit in the doorway. I've got the video camera, after all, and that's the biggest opening. I might need all that space to get the shot."

Tank thrust his arm toward Chad. "Hand it over. I can work the camera."

Chad patted the lump on his belt. "No need, I studied the manual. This is going to require a low light setting, and it takes a bit of expertise to get a useable image."

"So set the settings for me," Tank insisted. "Just hand me the camera."

"Naw—let me sit there to tape."

"The taping isn't as important as protection. What if someone or something comes through? Do you think your hundred and thirty pounds could stop a bear?"

"One hundred seventy," Chad said, a thread of

indignation in his voice. "And I don't think there are any bears in Mexico."

"How do you know there aren't?"

"How do you know there *are*?"

"Good grief." Exasperated beyond belief, I got up and moved to the far side of the tent, where I could sit by Daniel. He was paying more attention to his video game than his surroundings.

Brenda snorted.

Chad sank to the canvas, and he and Tank finally stopped bickering.

Time stretched itself thin as we watched and waited. A steady churring of insects rose from the weeds, rising in unison crescendos and diminuendos as if commanded by some invisible director. A sough of wind rustled the branches of the pines around us, sending pine needles spinning to earth. The full moon rose, silvering the landscape and allowing us to see without being seen. Ideal conditions, really. Almost as if our bosses had arranged this, too.

"Look at that." Tank pointed toward the spot where we had been trying to light a fire. Something fluttered there, and once it struck the earth, we heard a high squeal and the soft flap of wings.

"Owl catching mouse," Chad said. "Not fairy."

Tank nodded. "Right."

"That squeak?" Chad laughed. "Reminds me of . . . when I was a kid and my dad . . . used to look at me."

Brenda turned her head. "Who squeaked, you or him?"

He released a hollow laugh. "You'd have squeaked, too, if you'd had William Jack Thorton as your daddy."

The statement hung in the air, inviting questions.

All right, then. "Was your father stern?" I asked.

Chad exhaled in a rush. "Think of the worst father . . . you've ever seen on TV or in a movie, then multiply by two. That was my dad."

"Oh." I sent a sympathetic smile through the gloom. "I'm really sorry."

"'Sokay," Chad said, locking his hands around his bent knees as he stared out the window. The moonlight painted his face with the colors of iron and steel. "I suppose I wouldn't be the stud I am if I . . . hadn't had a terrible childhood. I learned to draw inside myself . . . whenever things got rough, and that's how I . . . discovered my g-gift. I learned that I could leave and g-go places, you know?"

"I'm still sorry you had to suffer like that," I told him. "No kid should survive childhood by the skin of their teeth. But I'm glad you survived."

I studied Chad, wondering if he wanted to keep talking or let the matter rest. Though I suspected he wouldn't have said any of those things if the medicine hadn't made him dopey and emotional, his chin quivered, so I looked away. I had never met a man—sober or under the influence—who wanted to weep in front of friends, so time to keep quiet for a while.

Zzzzzt! At least the battery-powered bug zapper was working.

Time crawled by. I checked my phone and learned that what felt like a couple of hours was only forty minutes. I sighed, realizing that the best thing about sleep was that it made the nighttime hours pass quickly.

I was beginning to wish I had packed my earphones when I saw movement in the moonlight. I squinted through the screen mesh, then rose to my knees and moved closer. Two figures fluttered around the trunk of a pine tree, around and up, in and out in random movements.

"Psst." I looked across the tent, where Brenda and Tank were heavy-lidded and fighting sleep. "Two figures, by that half-dead pine. Whaddya think?"

Tank rose to his knees and knelt behind the entrance screen as if daring the moonlight dancers to do us harm. Chad nudged Brenda and pointed to the creatures, then he moved closer to the window as well. Daniel put down his video game and stood, pressing his hands to the screen as he watched, mesmerized.

The dancing figures came closer. Composed of light and shadow, they circled a bush, teased a flower bud, and hovered over the logs of our unlit fire. Like hands on a clock they moved together, perfectly synchronized, a dance of practiced partners. Then one of them broke away and fluttered toward our tent.

Silence sifted over us, a silence of suspended breathing. We could see it now—this was no bat, no bird, but a creature with a human-like head, arms, legs, and torso. The fairy hovered about four feet from the door, and even from where I sat I could see details on the body—arms, legs, fingers, toes. The head with its downy pointed ears. The lips, closed now, hiding those jagged teeth. And the wings, fanning so quickly they were barely visible.

The creature tilted its head and regarded us, then flew across the front of the tent, peering in at us even as we stared out at—him? Her? Did female fairies wear little dresses made of flower petals?

"Okay," Tank said, and before I could ask what he had in mind, I heard the metallic slide of the zipper. Tank leapt out, the butterfly net in his hand. He sprang forward, the net dipping and swooping and *missing*. The fairy did not flee, but floated up, out of range. Tank took another swipe, and another, but the fairy taunted him, dancing above his flailing arms.

"Tank, will you *m-move*?"

Chad stood outside, the video camera in his hand, his gaze intent on the small screen resting against his palm. He was trying to focus on the fairy, but the thing was elusive and fast, always remaining out of the frame, out of focus—

A bloodcurdling scream shattered the stillness. I turned, horrified by the sound, and saw Daniel arching his back, his mouth open in a paroxysm of terror, his eyes so wide they seemed about to fall out of his face. Somehow, the second fairy had entered the tent and was riding the collar of Daniel's shirt. Not until I moved behind Daniel could I see that the fairy's tail had embedded itself in his clothing, perhaps even into the boy's flesh, because the kid was screaming as if someone had knifed him—

"Get. Away. From. My. Son!"

Brenda picked up the lantern and swung it at the fairy's head, putting everything she had into the blow. The bottom edge of the lantern caught the fairy's chin, knocking it backward, but it remained attached to Daniel's upper back, the tail firmly embedded in his shirt. Not knowing what else to do, I grabbed the creature around the middle, squeezing as I pulled it away from our boy. Something stabbed at my thumb, and I looked down in time to see the creature's teeth at my skin, gnawing my flesh while I tried to pull it away from Daniel—

Brenda approached again, this time with an iPad in one hand and her flashlight in the other. Holding the iPad as a backboard, she slammed the head of the flashlight into the fairy's skull, smashing it and sending a trail of black ooze over my hand and the tablet's shattered screen.

I looked down at the canvas floor where Daniel lay on his tummy, a dark black stain marbling the back of his shirt.

"Is that—is that from that thing?" Brenda asked, her voice trembling. "Or—"

"Help me move him; I can't see."

Together we pulled/dragged an unconscious Daniel into the moonlight, then we pulled up the back of his shirt. I had yanked the fairy away, but the stinger remained—I could see it shining like a polished claw amid a puddle of blood. I tried grasping it with my fingers, but my fingers were slippery and the stinger too firmly embedded—in what? Daniel's skin? His muscle?

Horror snaked down my backbone as I looked up and saw the same emotion reflected in Tank's and Chad's faces. And Brenda—

"My boy." She knelt beside him, terrified to move him, yet aching to draw him into her arms. "What are we gonna do? Andi, we need help, we gotta help him—"

"We're gonna get help." I reached for my phone and pounded 911. Nothing.

"Quick." I looked at Chad. "What's the emergency number for Mexico?"

He looked like a man who had just been told he was dying. "Why s-should I know *that*?"

"It's 66," Brenda said, wringing her hands. "I looked it up before we left—just in case."

I pressed six-six and waited. Nothing.

I stood and moved around, watching the bars on my phone. "I can't get a signal," I said, my panic increasing. "Tank, Chad—you guys got anything?"

As they pulled out their phones to check, I kept pounding the six and waiting for some response. "I had a signal at the Rodriguez house," I said. "How could there be no signal here? We're not that far away."

"We could be in a valley," Chad said, exasperatingly logical, even now. "Or the signal could be blocked by a mountain."

Leaping up, Brenda was on me before I had time to react. "Andi," she said, her fingers gathering up the fabric at the neckline of my shirt. "My boy needs help. I don't know how you're going to get it, but I know you are. Because you always come through. You see things the rest of us miss, so if you ever saw anything, I need you to see a way to help my boy. Now. Right now."

I stared into the whites of her eyes and felt her breath on my face. "Okay," I whispered, placing my hands over hers. "Go—go sit with Daniel. Watch over him."

She obeyed, and I looked up at Tank, who had been watching the treeline for the fairy that got away. "Your gift," I said simply. "Can you help him?"

Tank tilted his head, but immediately sank into the soft earth where Daniel lay. He closed his eyes for what seemed like moments woven of eternity, then he laid his hands on the boy.

We waited. Brenda kept feeling Daniel's forehead and watching the wound on his back as if she expected the stinger to float out and disappear. But nothing happened.

"He's hotter than ever," she said, her voice breaking as she looked up at Tank. "Please." Tears streamed over her cheeks. "Cowboy, you gotta do something for him."

"I'm goin' to."

He looked at me, and in that instant I knew he meant to run. "Okay," I said. "Take Chad—no, Chad needs to stay with Brenda. You and I are going to run to the Rodriguez place and wake them up. We're going to get an ambulance out here."

"Wait." Chad held up his arm, blocking Tank. "You don't need to run. All I hafta do is—you know, go into a trance. I can find someone around here and tell them to get us an ambulance. I'll send firefighters—"

"Medics," I said, grabbing his shirt. "It's not a fire, it's a medical emergency."

Chad waved my hand away. "I can do it. I've done stuff like this my whole life, so I can handle it. You just hafta let me sit here—"

He pointed to the ground, then stumbled forward and fell. "Ya see? I'll go into a trance and find someone. Just watch. You and Tank—you two don't hafta go anywhere alone. That wouldn't be good, no sir. Just sit here where I can keep an eye on ya, and wait while I save the day."

He closed his eyes then and I shifted my gaze to Tank. "He's lost it."

"Leave him," Tank whispered. "Let him see if he can do something while we run to the farm."

"He can't help us," I answered. "He doesn't speak English; his brain is practically out of order—"

"Don't feel sorry for him, Andi," Tank said, his voice surprisingly firm. "We don't have the time."

He pulled his flashlight from his back pocket and shone the light on the road. "Brenda, be careful," he said. "We know there's still one fairy out there somewhere, but there may be others. Okay?"

Brenda nodded, but she didn't seem to be thinking about the threat to herself or Chad. She was focused on Daniel.

"Okay," Tank said, taking my arm. "Let's go."

I paused only long enough to squeeze Brenda's shoulder. "Your boy is going to be okay."

She answered with a heartrending sob.

# Chapter 7

Tank and I jogged about twenty yards before we stopped. "Ya know," Tank said, "we are wastin' a lot of time running south, then west, and then north. Wouldn't it be faster if we just cut through the woods and ran west?"

"But running through the woods—that could be risky. We can't see much in the dark, there could be water or bogs to slog through, or we might run into wild animals or even cliffs—"

"I'm just trying to be smart, Andi."

"I know." I looked into his eyes, so soft and concerned. "But it's still risky."

"I would never want to leave you," he said.

"But if we split up here, one of us might be able to reach the farm faster . . . and every second might count for my little buddy."

I understood his reasoning. Tank was an athlete, a faster and stronger runner than I was. Even going through the woods, he was likely to reach the Rodriguez house before me, because I was not an athlete. In college, I took bowling and archery for physical education because I wouldn't have to run anywhere.

"You'll be safe on the road," he said. "I doubt you'll see any cars at this hour, but be careful anyway. I'm going to take off through the woods."

"Just—" My words died away. I was about to tell him to be careful, but this wasn't the time to be overly cautious. Daniel's life was hanging in the balance, so this wasn't a time to take care, but to take risks.

Somehow I managed a rueful smile. "Sure wish we had those comm units. I'd feel better hearing your voice in my ear."

"Roger that." He grinned. "Okay—I'll meet you at the farm. See ya soon."

I waited, taking a moment to catch my breath as I watched him disappear into the brush. I stood on the dirt road and listened until I could no longer hear twigs snapping and branches rustling, then I took off toward the highway, walking as fast as I could.

I had gone maybe a quarter of a mile when I

saw something that halted me in my steps. Several of the creatures were fluttering in a group just off the road ahead. Knowing that they were anything but harmless, I moved to the other side of the road and kept moving. But when my shoe kicked a pebble, the creatures scattered into the woods.

Curious, I walked to the spot where they had congregated. I thought the fairies had been flying around a hole in a fallen tree, but no tree lay on the ground at that spot. Instead, behind a bush I saw a tall rock with a vertical cleft in it—I suppose *fissure* would be a better word. I wanted to find a stick and probe the opening to see if the creatures had come from a cave, but I couldn't take the time to explore.

I kept walking. The distance from the highway to the campsite had felt short when we were in the car, but on foot, the distance seemed like miles. I walked until a felt a stitch in my side, then I drew deep breaths and tried jogging. When I was certain I couldn't take another step, I bent over, held my knees, and took deep breaths while thinking about Daniel and Brenda. I had to keep going for them.

Finally, I reached the highway. Pavement! I would have done a little happy dance, but I had to keep going. I swung my arms like a power walker and kept going.

I nearly missed the dirt road that led to the Rodriguez house, but I got my second wind when I turned down their driveway and headed for the house. When I saw the blue house glowing in the moonlight, I looked around for Tank—either I had beaten him, or he had already called an ambulance and was inside the house.

But no lights burned in the house. I pounded on the door, knowing that Tank hadn't yet arrived. He would have been outside waiting for me.

No one answered, so I pounded the door again. When a light bloomed in the window and the door opened a crack, I explained as quickly as I could: "Señor Rodriguez, it's me, Andi, and we have a medical emergency. Can you please call an ambulance? *Medico*? Our little boy is hurt."

The door opened, and in the lamplight I saw Señor Rodriguez in a tee shirt and boxer shorts, his shotgun in his hand. He nodded and opened the door, and in the background I saw his wife on the phone, already calling for help.

I collapsed in a chair and wiped sweat from my dripping forehead. I closed my eyes for a moment to catch my breath, and when I looked up, Tomas sat on the couch in front of me. "Are you okay?" he asked.

I nodded. "But Daniel—the little boy with us—he was stung. He's very sick."

Tomas shook his head and pointed to my hand. I turned and gasped when I saw that my right hand was caked in blood, the side of my thumb raw and ravaged from where the creature had exercised its incisors. "Ouch," I said, feeling suddenly woozy. "I guess I could use a Band-Aid, if you have one."

Tomas said something to his mother, then Señora Rodriguez came toward me, pulling the edges of her housecoat together as she exclaimed over my wound. She made motherly clucking sounds, then left and returned a few moments later with a bowl of water and bandages.

As she murmured soothing words and bandaged my thumb, I smiled, whispered "gracias" and tried to be attentive . . . while my thoughts centered on Daniel and Tank, who was still out in the woods fighting only-God-knew-what.

# Chapter 8

It must have been a slow night in Coajomulco, the town nearest the Rodriguez farm, because they sent two ambulances in response to our call. Señor Rodriguez rode with the first one and went to pick up Daniel, but I urged the second to wait for Tank, who had not yet appeared at the farm. I told Tomas about Tank, and he kept trying to tell the medics that we needed help to find Tank. I wasn't exactly sure what the medics were saying, but the gist seemed to be that they weren't searchers, they were medical personnel. "But if

Tank is in the woods," I reminded Tomas, "he might have been attacked by the same creatures that attacked Daniel."

Tomas tried again to explain that we might need medical assistance, but with no success.

As the second ambulance pulled away, I went outside and sat on a tree stump, surprised to find the sky brightening in the east. Sunrise. Blue skies and the touch of reality. A world where dark fairies did not watch through your windows.

I lifted my gaze to that blue-pink sky and found myself yearning for Tank's God. I knew Him too, of course, as HaShem, but Tank seemed to be on a first-name basis with the Deity, while I had always remained at arms' length.

"Master of the Universe," I began—

A huge bush rustled at my left and I tensed, afraid one of the creatures had come back for a last-minute lashing. But then the branches parted and Tank appeared—muddy, rumbled, bleeding, but most definitely alive.

"Tank!" I leapt up and ran forward, throwing my arms around his thick neck. "Are you okay?"

He grinned—apparently the bloodletting wasn't all that serious. "I had quite an adventure," he said. "I slid down a cliff, tangled with a few vampire bats, and nearly jumped out of my skin when I met a bobcat. But I'm here now. And apparently you were right about taking the road." His mood veered to seriousness. "Is Daniel all right?"

"He's at the hospital and Brenda's with him. Chad's with Señor Rodriguez, and I'm here, obviously, waiting for you."

Bright red rushed up from his collar and flooded his face. "That was nice of ya."

"Well—" I shrugged, not wanting him to read too much into it—"we couldn't go off and leave you out there with the vampire bats."

He slipped his arm around my shoulder as I led him toward the house. Señora Rodriguez saw us coming and started making clucking noises as she retreated to get her first-aid supplies.

"She's a sweetheart," I said. "Let her fix you up, then we'll go to the hospital to see Daniel. Brenda would probably appreciate seeing a few familiar faces about now."

"What's this?" Tank took my hand and caressed my bandaged thumb. "What happened?"

"Nasty little sucker tried to chew his way free when I was pulling him off Daniel," I said, shrugging. "Whoever called those things *fairies* had a twisted sense of humor."

"You should probably get a shot," Tank said, completely serious. "Rabies or tetanus, at least."

I blew out a breath. "I hate to admit it, but you're probably right."

\* \* \*

The nearest hospital, we learned, was about an hour from the Rodriguez's farm, in a town called Morelos. We were halfway there when I remembered that our driver would go to the campsite to pick us up in a few hours, but we would no longer be at that spot. I found his number on my phone and was able to cancel our pickup. We weren't going back to Mexico City until Daniel was fit to travel, no matter how long it took.

We found Brenda and Daniel at a trauma center in the heart of the city. Daniel lay inside a curtained cubicle, awake and in such pain that tears streamed down his cheeks at a near-constant rate. His thin frame writhed on the mattress like a cut snake, and to make matters worse, the doctor insisted on keeping him flat on his stomach so they could have access to the stinger in his back.

An X-ray, Brenda told me, her face the color of ashes, had shown that the stinger had worked its way into Daniel's body, almost into the sheath around his spinal column. "I don't know what that thing is," she told me, steel in her voice, "but Daniel is in so much pain that I'm ready to strangle the next person who mentions fairies with my bare hands."

I slipped my arm around her shoulders and told her she should get some rest. "I can't," she said. "They have Daniel on a morphine drip, and even that isn't easing his pain. And the doctors keep quizzing me—they're driving me crazy."

"Quizzing you?"

"Oh, yeah." She looked at the ceiling and sighed, clearly exasperated. "They asked how a black woman came to have a white son. They asked why Daniel doesn't talk much. They asked what stung him—I told them I didn't know for sure, and I don't. They asked what we were doing out in the woods, and why we were in Mexico in the first place. I tried to give them as little information as possible, but I'd tell them anything if it would help Daniel."

"I know." I patted her shoulder again, then led her back to Daniel's cubicle and sat next to her. A nurse was in the cubicle checking Daniel's blood pressure, but she didn't interrupt us. She only smiled and went about her work.

Still, I lowered my voice when I spoke to Brenda. "I feel bad because we came all this way and went through all this, and for what? We still don't know what that thing is."

"But we know it's real," she said. "And we know it's dangerous."

"I didn't even see the stinger at first. I was so fascinated by the face and the wings."

Brenda grabbed my hands. "Andi, what am I gonna do if he doesn't get better?"

Tears welled in her eyes, and I didn't know what to do. So I hugged her, made a bunch of promises I couldn't keep, and found myself wishing that Tank would come around the corner. Even though he hadn't been able to heal Daniel, he was a calming influence, and we certainly could use one . . .

When Brenda finally pulled away, I noticed that the nurse had gone. While Brenda blew her nose and swiped at her eyes, I stood and moved to Daniel's bedside. His head was turned toward me, and I could see his eyes jumping beneath his paper-thin eyelids. The corner of his mouth twitched occasionally, and a muscle at his jaw kept tightening and relaxing, over and over . . .

"Excuse me." I looked up. The nurse had returned, this time without her clipboard. Instead she held a black book.

"Do you have news from the doctor?" Brenda asked, alarmed.

Tank and Chad chose that moment to join us, slipping into the cubicle behind the nurse. Tank nodded and smiled at her, but Chad narrowed his eyes. "Are you assigned to this case?" he asked, his voice curt. "If you're here to read the last rites or something—"

"Chad," I said gently. "Nurses do not administer the last rights." I looked at her. "Do you have news for us?"

A blush crossed the young woman's face. "*Con permiso*, I do not mean to bother you. But I have been overhearing things, and your words reminded me of this." She lifted the book.

"What's that?" Chad asked, practically snatching the book from the woman's grip. "*La Biblia de Estudio*," he read. "What's that?"

"I think," I said, "you should return the woman's study Bible."

He flushed and returned the book. "Sorry."

The nurse smiled.

"Go on," Tank said. "What did their conversation remind you of?"

I narrowed my gaze, wondering why he would encourage the nurse to take up our time with inane words from a centuries-old book, but Tank would listen to a toddler babble if he thought it would make the kid happy. Resigned, I turned back to Daniel, pressing my hand to his forehead. The boy was burning hot.

"*Este*," the nurse said. I heard the rustle of pages, then she began to read:

> The fifth angel sounded his shofar; and I saw a star that had fallen out of heaven onto the earth, and he was given the key to the shaft leading down to the Abyss. He opened the shaft of the Abyss, and there went up smoke from the shaft like the smoke of a huge furnace; the sun was darkened, and the sky too, by the smoke from the shaft. Then out of the smoke onto the earth came locusts, and they were given power like the power scorpions have on earth. They were instructed not to harm the grass on the earth, any green plant or any tree, but only the people who did not have the seal of God on their foreheads. The locusts were not

allowed to kill them, only to inflict pain on them for five months; and the pain they caused was like the pain of a scorpion sting. In those days people will seek death but will not find it; they will long to die, but death will elude them.

Now these locusts looked like horses outfitted for battle. On their heads were what looked like crowns of gold, and their faces were like human faces. They had hair like women's hair, and their teeth were like those of lions. Their chests were like iron breastplates, and the sound their wings made was like the roar of many horses and chariots rushing into battle. They had tails like those of scorpions, with stings; and in their tails was their power to hurt people for five months. They had as king over them the angel of the Abyss, whose name in Hebrew is *Abaddon* and in our language, *Destroyer*.

We had all been listening politely until we heard the words "tails like those of scorpions, with stings." I turned at that point, and Brenda looked at me, her eyes wide. Tank's mouth had fallen open, and though Chad seemed confused, he also seemed to understand that we had just stumbled over something important.

"Thank you," Tank said, placing one hand on the nurse's shoulder and gently guiding her out of the cubicle. "Thank you so much."

When he returned, he pulled the curtain closed, then crossed his arms and looked at me. "Remember what Dr. Wu said? Prototype."

I frowned. "You mean—"

"We know the Gate is doing genetic experiments, combining human DNA with strange DNA—maybe from aliens, maybe from other animals, who knows? But the two specimens in Prospero's office were different—version A and version B. They are working up to Version C, the one that will have—what did it say?—*chests like iron breastplates*."

"They already have teeth like lions," I pointed out, holding up my injured hand. "And when there are lots of them flying around, they could sound like chariots getting ready for battle."

"So they're not fairies," Chad said. "They're locusts."

"Not designed to mow down crops," Tank added. "But men."

Brenda looked at me. "Did you see more than the two at the camp?"

"Oh, yeah." I drew a deep breath. "While I was walking back to the farm, I saw a swarm of them coming from a spot at the edge of the woods. They took off when they saw me, and when I checked out the place where they were gathered, I saw a boulder with an opening in it."

"Like an abyss?" Tank lifted a brow.

"More like a cave," I said. "But I didn't have a chance to look around."

Tank nodded. "No matter where they come from, they're here. And that passage is from the book of Revelation. It's a record of the vision John saw when the Lord let him witness events of the last days. Apparently—if we're reading this right—the Gate is preparing something John saw more than two thousand years ago."

He leaned on the edge of Daniel's bed as a frown settled between his brows. "I don't get it, though. The plagues of the last days are part of God's judgment on the earth, a punishment for sin. How can those creatures be the result of the Gate's work if they are judgments from God? That'd be like terrorists making a bomb for New York City, but the United States stepping in and using it instead."

"You lost me a long time ago," Brenda said, bringing her hands to the sides of her face. "I don't get it and I never will."

"I get it," I said, the picture coming into focus for the first time. "Don't you see? It's brilliant! It's beautiful."

Tank's frown deepened. "What are you talkin' about?"

"HaShem." I nearly laughed aloud with the joy of discovery. "He is above all, right?"

Tank nodded.

"He is omnipotent—more powerful than any force, right?"

Tank nodded again.

"Then how like him to foil the machinations of evil people to suit his own purposes! You are exactly right, Tank—the Gate and whoever might make bombs and creatures and black-eyed children and flying spheres and malignant bacteria, but HaShem can and will thwart their purposes when He is ready. There's no contradiction. Instead, I see evidence of His power and purpose."

Tank tilted his head as a slow smile spread across his face. "Yeah. Yeah, I think I get it."

"I don't." Chad sat next to Brenda, slouching as he buried his hands in his pockets. "Are you planning to tell our bosses that these creatures are harmless because God wins in the end? Sounds a little pat."

"They're not harmless," I said. "Look at Daniel—he's proof that they're not harmless. As long as the Gate's people are testing prototypes, innocent people stand a good chance of being hurt. Just like the people who run into the black-eyed kids or who are infected by the deadly slime."

"The earth suffers, too," Brenda said, her gaze fastened to Daniel's face. "Remember the bird and fish kills? The dolphins that died from the green slime? The people we're fighting against are

ANGELA HUNT

set on destruction. That's evil, pure and simple. And so is what they did to my boy."

"It is," I told her. "But you've gotta see the big picture, too. People will get hurt in skirmishes, but evil is not going to win the war."

248

# Chapter 9

Two days later, the doctors at the trauma center said they were willing to discharge Daniel. They had extracted the stinger, sent it away to be tested at a lab ("I'd like to see those results," Chad quipped), and given Brenda a prescription for extra-strength pain killers. "But you must wean your son off the pills as soon as you can," the doctor warned. "You do not want to foster a dependency on drugs."

Brenda snorted. "Tell me something I don't know."

Brenda was signing papers and preparing for Daniel's discharge while I tried to keep track of our people, our luggage, and the proof we needed to submit to our bosses. Chad and Tank had called our driver and asked to go back to the campsite—to gather the video camera and anything else that might prove important.

I didn't think they'd find much. Maybe the desiccated body of the fairy that bit me and attacked Daniel, but I didn't think the body would last long in the tropical humidity.

While Brenda settled things with the hospital staff, I went to visit Daniel. The kid had been through so much in his life, it hardly seemed fair that he'd been the one to get stung. That fairy— that *imp*—had completely ignored me and Brenda and gone straight for Daniel. Did it *want* to torture a kid? Did it see Daniel as the most vulnerable, or did it sense that he had the ability to see into the spirit world and recognize them for the *duchs* they were . . .

"Hey, kiddo."

Daniel was sitting on the edge of his bed, dressed in new jeans and a new shirt. He grinned when I popped in, and slid off the mattress. "Can we go home now?"

"You bet. Your mom is signing papers, and Tank and Chad will be with us soon."

I'd just finished speaking when Tank lumbered into the room and dropped a big red sombrero on Daniel's head. "Gotcha souvenir," he said, grinning. "And Chad is waiting outside, ready to take you to your mom. Ready?"

"Ready!" Daniel ran outside to meet Chad. As Tank dropped into a chair, I listened to Daniel's chatter as it faded away.

I turned to Tank, but his sunny disposition had evaporated. He was no longer smiling—unusual for him—and he was massaging the skin at the bridge of his nose as if he had a headache.

"You okay?" I asked.

He nodded, then slowly shook his head from left to right. "Yeah," he finally said, opening his eyes, "and no. Yeah, there's nothing wrong with me. But no, because I'm struggling."

"With what?"

He blew out an explosive breath. "I know it's a universal hang-up. I know lots of people can't believe in God because of it. But I never thought I'd stumble over the same thing."

"Enough already." I tapped his hand. "I can't help if you won't explain yourself."

He hesitated, then placed his hand on top of mine. "Why does God allow good people to suffer?"

"Ohh." I sat next to him. "That question has tripped up all kinds of people. Why should you be immune?"

"Because I'm a believer. A strong believer, or so I thought. I know God's in charge, and I'm usually happy to let him be in charge, you know?"

I nodded. "So?"

"So when I looked at my little buddy in that bed—" His voice broke. "Why couldn't God have let that evil thing sting me?"

"Or Chad?" I suggested.

Tank barked a laugh. "Right. But . . . it didn't hurt us, it hurt Daniel. The weakest of us. The one who has already suffered the most."

"I know," I whispered.

"And then when I tried to heal him—God gave me a gift, you know, so why didn't it work when I tried to heal Daniel? If God could give me the power to bring a *dog* back to life, why couldn't he allow me to stop Daniel's pain?"

I shook my head, caught up in the awful memory of when Abby had been dead on the beach, killed by some horrible alien thing . . . but Tank had brought her back. Or HaShem had.

But I couldn't explain why sometimes Tank's gift failed any more than I could explain why sometimes I saw patterns and connections as clear as air and sometimes I only saw confusion . . . like now.

I sat quietly, respecting his confusion and knowing there were no easy answers. I sure didn't have any. Millions of other people had considered his question and come up empty.

But Tank was stronger than he realized. And wiser.

"I guess—" he lowered his head as if he were peering through a passageway filled with obstacles—"it's all a matter of faith, isn't it? We either trust that God knows what He's doing, or we think we know a better answer. Like letting that thing sting me—that'd be a better situation, wouldn't it? But God is good and He knows best, so He has a reason for my little buddy's pain . . . a reason I just can't see."

"Do you have to see it?"

He lifted a brow. "I'd *like* to see it, because then it would all make sense. But no, I guess I don't."

"Why not?"

"Because . . . God's got it covered, and I'm not God." He smiled, not the happy-go-lucky smile that was part of his nature, but a sadder, wiser version that made my heart ache.

**Chapter 10**

Chad and Tank had picked up the video camera from the campsite, but they had neglected to grab all the really important things. "Like my makeup kit," Brenda said, frowning as she searched her back pack. "How could you forget that?"

So before heading to the airport, we had our driver take us back to the campsite so we could grab anything we couldn't leave behind. I found my iPad beneath a sleeping bag, and Brenda found Daniel's video game by the window. And her makeup bag, of course.

We left the tent, lantern, and all that other stuff behind, though we told the driver he could come get it if he wanted to—if no one else beat him to it.

Once we boarded the private plane waiting to take us back to Dallas, I opened my iPad and took a good look around. I had to make a final report to the Watchers, and wanted it to be as complete as possible. We had returned with answers, video proof, and wisdom about the effects of the fairy-locusts, but we had paid a lot for those gains. Daniel had been traumatized, Brenda had suffered, and Tank's faith had been tested. This had not been an easy gig.

Reclining in one of the seats, Tank looked exhausted—not only from our adventure, but from the spiritual struggle he'd faced. I knew he'd come to terms with what happened to Daniel, but if he were God, he would have come up with an alternate plan.

Chad had actually been useful on this trip. He hadn't been able to help get us an ambulance (when I asked about his attempt to find help via a mind-to-mind connection, he said the only person he was able to contact was an old woman in Cleveland who thought she was talking to an angel). He had provided some interesting ideas, and, thanks to his cold meds, he'd actually dropped his snarky facade for a while. Tank still didn't seem very comfortable with the new guy, but he would adjust. We all would.

Brenda—one look at her face told me that she'd been through the wringer and back on this trip. Not only had the fairy freaked her out, but she'd taken Daniel's pain on herself, and her face reflected that agony. For the first time I could see wrinkles in her skin, deep worry lines in her forehead, and shadows beneath her eyes. She remained quiet on the plane, and that was unusual in itself.

And Daniel—the kid had been a trooper, considering all he'd been through. He was resting now, his head in Brenda's lap, a soft smile on his lips, as if he relished the gentle way her fingernails combed his hair. Poor kid. Considering all the years he spent in that psychiatric hospital, I'd bet he was way behind on his fair share of love taps and hair-ruffling. No wonder he lapped up affection the way a kitten laps up cream.

I plugged in my charger, synced my portable keyboard, and typed up a full report on my iPad. I tried not to leave out any important details, though I couldn't escape a niggling feeling that the Watchers already knew everything. I don't know how they would know, but the feeling persisted, all the same.

I also told our bosses about seeing the professor in the mirror before I found the mysterious folder.

*None of us have ever heard of Ambrosi Giacomo,* I

wrote, *but if the professor wanted me to have that information, it must be important. If it's a piece to our puzzle, we haven't found the place where it fits. But I'm sure we will.*

*In the meantime, we will see what we can dig up on Mr. Giacomo. If you have any information you can share, please do. We need all the help we can get.*

*Thank you for the support on this mission. And if you can send another set of communications units, we'll try not to lose them.*

# Chapter 11

Back at the hotel, we walked through the lobby without speaking and went straight to the elevators. Something in our haggard appearance must have been alarming, because once we got into an empty elevator car, no one wanted to join us.

We rode up to the top floor, then stepped out into the lobby.

"I don't care what happens next," Brenda said, her arm firmly around Daniel's shoulder. "Daniel and I are going to our suite and puttin' out the 'do not disturb' sign. Even if there's a massive earthquake or somethin', don't call us."

"You've earned a rest," I told her. "Both of you."

Both Tank and Chad walked me to my door— an exercise in overkill, if ever there was one.

"Thanks, guy," I said, pressing my key to the card reader. "Get some rest, okay? And Chad—" he hesitated— "better find some cold medicine without side effects."

He laughed. "Will do."

They waited for me to open my door, then nodded at me, glared at each other, and went their separate ways.

Blowing out a breath, I stepped into the stillness of my room, dropped my bag in the entrance, and paused before the wall mirror in the hallway. I saw myself reflected there, along with the silk flowers on the foyer table and the wall behind me. Nothing else—no professor, no fairy, no creatures from the black lagoon.

For the moment, at least.

# AUTHOR'S NOTE

¡Hola! Angie here, with two bits of information for you.

First, Al G. is fond of saying that if you have a 100,000 word manuscript and it is 99.9 percent perfect, you're still going to have 100 mistakes.

We try very hard to create perfect stories for you, but the occasional typo may slip by. If you spot one, you can help by writing us and telling us where and what it is. We'd love to make it right.

So if you find one of those pesky typos, please write us at harbingers777@gmail.com. We will quickly put it out of its misery.

Second, I have always thought that the best fiction is based on fact. My delight lies in taking what is real and exploring possibilities. The fish and bird deaths I featured in *Sentinels* are actually happening. The black-eyed children I featured in *Hybrids* have been reported around the world. And now: fairies.

In the summer of 2016, I was finishing up a historical novel when I learned about something my friend L.A. Marzulli had discovered. His exploration of "the fairy" caught my attention, and the possibilities naturally lent themselves to a Harbingers adventure.

If you would like to see video of the actual creature, visit L.A.'s blog at this link: https://lamarzulli.wordpress.com/tag/watchers-10/

I would also love to share a chapter from L.A.'s latest book, *Nephilim Hybrids*. It contains an interview between L.A. and a veterinarian who examined the actual X-rays of "the fairy."

# FROM L.A. MARZULLI

The "Winged Nightmare" or, as Richard Shaw calls it, "The Fairy," has been controversial to say the least.

As we are getting ready to go to press, Jaime Mausson gave me the X-rays of the winged creature. I had them mounted and presented them, along with other pictures, to a veterinarian who wishes to remain anonymous.

(I have found that many people are reluctant to officially come on the record because of the fear of ridicule.)

The vet looked at the creature and this is what he said:

L.A.: So…we're looking at the wing structure where the wings actually attach themselves to the creature. Can you speak to that, please?

Vet: Yes, I'm looking at the X-rays, the radio-opaque structure that wings attach to. They appear to be some sort of bone and it looks like the thin bones that hold the wing structure together are fused very nicely to whatever that structure is. I assume it's a bone. It looks like they're fused in there naturally, as opposed to someone slopping it together. The only problem is that it's almost too opaque. It doesn't match up with the radiodensity of the other bones.

L.A.: Yes, but wouldn't having a creature like this with the wings protruding from the back, wouldn't there have to be some kind of anchoring to the skeletal structure? Wouldn't the bone be thicker there?

Vet: Yes, it's very possible—could be if this is a flying creature.

L.A.: Which it is.

Vet: For example, chickens [and] birds are going to have a lot less radiodensity in their other bones; in their legs and those bones are more hollow compared to, say, mammal bones. So these bones up here—that hold the wings—could be a little more thick and radiodense and calcified because it needs more stability to keep the wings attached.

L.A.: In your opinion, looking at the pictures and X-rays we've been looking at . . . could this be some sort of a composite, based on four or five different animals? Look at the face and the teeth and the ears. What are your thoughts?

Vet: If it is, it's a very, very good composite. Someone very professional put this thing together. I mean just the way the bones... I can see the joints; I can see where the ribs lead into the sternum. I can see the femur, going into the hip. For someone to put this together would require a lot of work.

L.A.: And for what reason? No one's making any money off this. It's not on the cover of the *National Enquirer* or something, selling millions of papers. That's not the case here. This thing has been in formaldehyde for three or four years.

Vet: I suppose anything's possible. If it's a fake, someone put a lot of work into this to put this together. I can't think of an animal that you could add stuff on too. Very odd.

L.A.: Very unsettling. When we saw it, we were speechless.

Vet: Whatever this is that's trying to hold this fracture together in the tibia [the leg]. For someone to think ahead of time … How would you know where the fracture was, unless you were some sort of medical professional? How did you get that stuff that's holding that fracture together under the skin? It's not an easy job.

L.A.: How would you do that?

Vet: Yeah, that's not an easy job to do, to get that under the skin even though it's not in the right spot.

L.A.: It's a classic gargoyle. It's evil to say the least. Again, when we saw it, it was unsettling. Look at the way the wings are attached. I mean, anatomically it's very proportional isn't it?

Vet: Yes. I don't see the teeth in the back of the jaw…

L.A.: What would be your take away?

Vet: From a medical standpoint, these are real

bones, real joints, and real X-rays. The question is, what kind of animal is it? And if it is a fake, what animals did they use to put this together? It would be a very professional job if it was a fake. You need to get a forensic pathologist, because I'm just looking at some X-rays. They look like real X-rays to me.

L.A.: Closing thoughts?

Vet: I'm perplexed about these round objects in the X-ray.

L.A.: We are, too. Any idea what that might be?

Vet: Perhaps someone shot it with a BB-gun and that's how it died…

L.A.: So you think these round things are metal?

Vet: They look like metal. If I had to guess, metal objects round like this . . . I've seen this before; in animals it's pretty clear. BBs, it could be buckshot. A shotgun. Buck-shot. Someone mistook it for a bird or something.

L.A.: Ah. Ok. That's interesting. Buck-shot. That would really make a lot of sense.

Vet: It's a far away shot.

L.A.: Yes. Wow. Interesting.

Vet: The shot may have broken the bone [in the leg].

L.A.: Thank you for coming on the record with us.

Vet: Nice to meet you.

## Summation by L.A. Marzulli:

So as of June 2016, I will state that I believe the Winged Nightmare is not a hoax and that is the real thing. The fact that the vet was able to state that he believed the BB-like balls showing up in the X-ray were the result of buckshot or bird shot solves a lot of what perplexed us for some time.

In other words, this creature may have been blasted out of the sky by someone with a shotgun.

This explains the broken leg and the BB's randomly placed throughout the body.

More testing needs to be done and I'll be giving updates as they come to us.

We are now in the process of trying to get the creature out of Mexico legally so that extensive DNA testing can be done in the States.

L.A. Marzulli
June 2016

HARBINGERS 16

At Sea

Alton Gansky

Bill Myers, Jeff Gerke,
and Angela Hunt

## ALONE AGAIN, UNNATURALLY

Rocking.

Like an infant in a cradle.

Gentle. Smooth. Even.

Then came a new sensation: Someone had been using my mouth as an ashtray. A vile film covered my tongue and teeth. Still, I wasn't ready to open my eyes. Mostly I just wanted to slip back into the blanket of sleep I had been living in a short time before.

Blanket? I could tell I lay upon a narrow bed but I felt no blanket over me. I was warm. Too warm. Only then did I risk opening an eye. The room was lit but only dimly. Missing was the harshness of an incandescent light. What I saw was natural illumination, enough to see but not read in comfortably.

I forced myself to take several deep breaths. The air was a tad stale and carried a hint of salt. I swung my legs over the side of the bed, buried my face in my hands and tried to focus my thoughts. It wasn't easy. My brain was filled with a thick London fog and my thoughts were as slippery as a sink full of eels.

Lowering my hands, I stared at the thin carpet on the floor. It was a perfectly acceptable beige, which somehow managed to look new and old at the same time. My brain fog lifted a little and I was capable of noticing something that shouldn't be: black, highly polished dress shoes—on my feet. The kind of shoes a man wore with a—

Tux.

Sure enough, I wore a pair of well-tailored tuxedo pants. I stood and touched my waist. Cummerbund. There was also a white shirt with posts instead of buttons, and a bowtie. I had been sleeping in a bowtie. The thing is, I hate tuxes. At least I think I do. Try as I might, I couldn't remember the last time I wore a tux, or why I was wearing one now.

Across the room was a full-length mirror that confirmed everything I had just discovered. I didn't need a mirror to tell me what I was wearing. I puzzled that out pretty quickly. What I *did* need was a mirror or something else to tell me who the guy in the reflection was. He looked familiar. Young and big. Extra big—six-foot-three maybe and tipping the scales at over 250 pounds. That was a guess, of course, but I didn't think I was far wrong. A little wide in the shoulders too. I stepped closer to the mirror and touched its cool, smooth surface. The reflection touched its side of the glass.

A man should recognize his own image, shouldn't he? Why couldn't I recognize mine?

My first question had been: Why am I sleeping in a tuxedo? That seemed like a small question now. What I really wanted to know was who I am. I also wouldn't mind knowing where I was. I didn't recognize anything in the cramped room.

"Well, this ain't right." At least my voice sounded familiar.

I rubbed my eyes until they hurt. Maybe I was still asleep and having one of those hyperreal dreams. I know a couple of people who dream in high-def and technicolor. It sounded cool to me, but they didn't think so. I guess dreams should be dreamy and not too realistic.

I bent forward and rested my hands on my knees. I wasn't feeling any too good. My stomach was in rebellion about something. The rocking of the floor? Somethin' I ate? I had no idea. I took a few minutes to will my stomach into submission then straightened again.

I took in my room: a single bed, made-up but rumpled where I had been dozing. A small dresser was opposite the bed and stood near the full-length mirror. A wood desk was tucked in one corner; the kinda desk you see in a hotel room.

Is that what this is? A hotel? A hotel with a rocking floor? That made no sense, but then nothing I saw or experienced since I crawled out of—maybe I should say *off* the sack—made any kinda sense.

The light in the room was pretty dim. A quick

survey told me that no light bulbs were burning anywhere. The only source of illumination came from a wide but narrow window in the wall. I walked to it. It was set kinda high but I could still see through it without much effort.

Gray. Outside was gray. Gray sky. Gray fog. Gray sea. That last observation explained a lot. I was on a boat, maybe I should say a ship. I tried to think about that some. My thoughts, what few I could lay a mental hand on, were jumbled like a dropped deck of playing cards. Some cards were face up; others face down. Except I had no way of putting them in order. My thinking was as unsettled as my gut.

At least the sea, what I could see of the sea, was pretty calm. My belly was glad for that.

The scum in my mouth still tasted bad. My tongue and cheeks seemed lined with felt. I took a couple of deep breaths and moved to a narrow and short hallway, more of an entry area really, and saw two doors. One was slightly wider than the other. I assumed the wider door led to a hallway; the smaller door had to lead to a bathroom. I guess I should call it a "head." I opened the second door and enjoyed a moment of satisfaction that my assumption had been correct.

The head had the basics of any home bathroom but in a smaller form. There was a glass-enclosed shower to one side. Clearly, it hadn't been designed for a man of my dimensions. If I wanted to get clean inside that thing I would have to soap the walls and spin around in it. That didn't matter now; I was more interested in evicting the taste in my mouth. I paid little attention to the toilet although I was sure I might be more interested in it should my stomach turn traitor.

The sink was smaller than what I would expect and it looked a little out of date. As I thought about it, I could say the same thing for the whole room I had just been in and the rest of the bathroom.

I turned the faucet handle looking for a nice stream of cold water. I got nuthin'. I mean nuthin'.

"Great. Jus' great."

I tried the hot water handle. Again, a great big nuthin'. Maybe the valves below the sink had been cranked shut. No idea why that might be, but I wanted to check. To do so, I needed more light. A man didn't need much light to drink a little water and splash his face a bit, but more than that would require a bit more illumination.

I flipped the light switch and was once again denied. I tried flipping the switch a few times as if I could annoy it into working. No dice.

"All right then, let's try this." I turned on the shower. Well, I tried to turn it on. No water there.

Of course, there was the toilet, but there was no water in the basin, not that I would gargle with it if there were. Now I was getting irritated.

With a mouth that sported a film that tasted like the inside of an old rain gutter, I left the head and exited the room. It was time to find someone to listen to my rants.

The corridor was empty. No passengers strolling to or from rooms. No cleaning crew changing out towels and running vacuum cleaners. No children barreling down the hallway like they were in a human demolition derby. Just a twilight dark and lots and lots of quiet.

That last observation made me wonder. If this was

a ship at sea—and the ocean outside my window pretty much convinced me of that—then shouldn't I be hearing the rumble of mighty engines? Perhaps we were still tied up to the dock. After all, I could only look out one side of the boat.

Still, the boat rocked a little and I didn't think cruise ships did that when tied to a pier. But what did I know? Not much. I had a fuzzy brain, and a scummy mouth, and no memory of the past beyond the moment I woke up on the bed.

I walked through the gloom. What little light there was came from a window at the end of the hall. Sconces were spaced evenly along the walls but not one offered any light. They were pretty and useless.

The light at the end of the corridor drew me closer. Light was better than growing twilight. I walked slowly, feeling a little wobbly as if I had been on an all-night bender. That couldn't be. I had only been drunk once in my life and have avoided alcohol ever since...

That was a memory. Why would I remember that and not my own name? Maybe that was a good sign. Maybe not. My confusion grew. The more I reached for a memory, the more difficult it became to think. Maybe I was having a stroke.

Could that be? A stroke? Probably not. My reflection said I was young. Maybe young guys could have strokes, but I didn't think that was common. Besides, I seemed to be able to think in complete sentences.

I stopped. "Peter Piper picked a peck of pickled peppers." That came out just fine, so the stroke idea seemed unlikely. I shook my head. What did I know? Would a man with a stroke know if he his speech sounded right?

My head was beginning to hurt.

"A concussion. That might be it." My voice rolled down the corridor. Those words brought an odd sensation. I had known people with concussions. I couldn't name one person, but the realization felt right.

"I gotta get some help." I didn't need to say that out loud, but hearing my own voice brought a little comfort.

Twenty-five or thirty steps later I reached the window at the end of the corridor. It was about three feet wide and five feet or so tall. The glass was clear but spotted with watermarks. The view outside showed a thick, wet fog. The ocean was flat and two shades grayer. I looked both left and right and saw no sign of a port. "Definitely at sea."

Below—I guessed I was three stories or so above the deck below—was the front end of the ship. The deck looked smooth and appeared to be something like concrete, not wood slats. What I didn't see were people. Where were the people? Even on a gray day like today, people should be strolling the deck. My attitude was turning as gray as the fog.

The fog bothered me. For some reason, the sight of it gave me the willies, like something might be hiding in the mist. A shiver ran through me as if someone had dumped a barrel of ice water over my head.

I turned my back to the window. To my right was a wide ornamental metal stairway. One side of it went up, the other went down. I chose the steps going down. Why? Can't tell ya. I just did. My hope was that I'd find someone who could direct me to the ship's doctor, and if not a someone, then a sign.

Halfway down the staircase an awful thought occurred to me. Maybe there was no doctor onboard. I hadn't seen anyone else, why should I believe there was a doctor?

There was only one way to find out.

**Chapter 2**

## A BRIDGE TOO NEAR

I WAS FEELING a tad lonely. Was I the kinda guy who was prone to loneliness? I guessed no, but what did I know? At that moment, not much. For all I knew, I might be an emotional cripple. If I was, then this amnesia might be a good thing.

The cause of my loneliness was pretty easy to figure out. I had come to in a room alone. I had searched the ship from the main deck up and saw no one. I called out for help but no one answered. The gray fog was a downer, too. I couldn't see a horizon in the distance, or lights from a city. There was no sun or moon in the sky, just a dull, eerie canopy of mist. When I looked over the rail I couldn't help but notice that the sea was gray, too. For some reason, that didn't surprise me. Not a bit.

I had emerged from the stairway—I think they call it a companionway on a ship (but again, what do I know?)—onto a wide deck. A wide, *empty* deck. I could see almost to the front of the boat and all the way to the back. Nobody. I walked to the back, peeking into every window I came across. I saw nobody. I saw no light. I saw no proof that anyone was onboard. Of course, I hadn't searched the whole ship, but why would this deck be empty of people? The ship was clearly a cruise ship, although it seemed like it was a generation or two older than modern craft. The doorknobs looked old. And the stateroom doors used real, honest-to-goodness keys to lock and unlock them, not those magnetic or chip keycards.

That thought made me realize something. I could remember some things like being in a hotel, several different hotels, but I couldn't remember why. My Swiss cheese brain seemed willing to let some information through, but nothing about me. Seemed a bit unfair.

As I walked to the rear of the boat I read every sign I came across. I was looking for one the said, SHIPS DOCTOR, or MEDICAL, or YOU HAVE ENTERED THE TWILIGHT ZONE. No luck. What signs I did find directed me to decks with odd names like "Promenade," or "Lido," and several that pointed the way to the life boats.

When I reached the stern I found an open area with lounge chairs neatly arranged in rows, a few patio-like tables, and two spas. There was also a bar, but no bartender. The bar was fully stocked. "It's a shame that I'm not a drinker—"

And there it was: another bit of random information about myself. I had nothing to tie the thought to. It just popped into my head. "At this rate, I'll know everything about myself in a couple of years."

My voice sounded slightly off. Kinda muted, like the air was muffling the sound. Didn't matter. I was going to talk to myself until I found someone else to talk to.

I had another reason for moving aft. When I first looked out the window of my room, or whoever's room I had been in, I got the sense that we weren't under power. The lack of lights made that seem like a real possibility. I now had proof. There was no wake. A ship this size should leave a sizeable wake no matter how slow it was moving.

We—I—was adrift.

Alone.

In the middle of nowhere.

Going nowhere.

Now I really wanted a little company.

I looked over the railing and into the gray water thirty or so feet below. From this height, a jumper would get a pretty nasty sting. I waited for the urge to end it all to come over me. It didn't. That would just be stupid. "Can't get into heaven if you die stupid." I doubted there was any solid theology in that thought, but it gave me a tiny reason to smile.

I figured it was time to get back to my search. I was no longer focused on finding a doctor. Aside from the nasty taste in my mouth, I felt fine. Befuddled, sure, and more than a little confused, but physically I felt tiptop.

Before I committed to searching the right side of the deck, I helped myself to a soda from behind the bar. I'd pay for it later if I found someone to pay. I used the soda to rinse out my mouth. It did the trick.

From there I moved up the other side of the main deck doing the same thing I had done on the left side. The word *starboard* rose in my brain. "Starboard means the right side of a boat; port means the left." Why would I know that? Was I a sailor? Maybe I was one of the crew.

I shook my head as if doing so would dislodge a few more nuggets of memory. No such luck. I probably had just learned the terms from a book or a movie or somethin'. Still, it could mean my brain was gainin' some traction.

My starboard side stroll was as useless as the port side. When I reached the bow I began to despair. Despair is fine, I guess, as long as you don't give into it. Nothing to do now except move higher or search the lower decks. I chose to go up. Surely, I told myself, someone will have to be on the bridge. No sailor would let a ship drift at sea.

The bridge overlooked the bow and was several stair climbs higher than the main deck. All the better to see the sea, I figured.

The bridge had been easy to find and to my surprise its door stood wide open. I crossed the threshold. I entered slowly, not sure if I was allowed to enter the brain center of a cruise ship.

It appeared that I had been wrong; apparently sailors would leave the bridge empty. This didn't sit well with me. So far I held out some hope that others were onboard and I would find them sooner or later.

I had doubts before; now I had serious doubts.

I studied the controls long enough to know that I had never been an officer on a cruise ship. I had no clues what the chrome handles and levers did. I did notice that there was no ship's wheel. Instead there was something like a podium with several blank screens and a coupla things that looked like controllers for a video game.

There were other monitors spread around the bridge, all of them tucked in a U-shaped console that filled most of the floor space. It looked like something out of some sci-fi movie. If I didn't feel so confused and alone, I might have appreciated all the high-tech stuff. As it was, I felt only disappointment.

There were two leather seats centered in the room and facing the front of the bridge. I assumed one was for the captain. Between the chairs was a console of gauges and small computer monitors—all dead. There was also a microphone. I doubted that a ship dead in the water without enough power to switch on a light would have an active intercom system or radio.

Still I had to try. After all, I could be wrong.

I wasn't.

A pair of binoculars rested in the captain's chair. I took them. I used them. All I saw was a deep shade of gray in every direction.

Mounted to one wall was a "pigeon hole" case, the kind of cabinet in which a person might keep rolls of plans. Not plans, charts. I was a little confused because the ship's bridge was clearly high-tech even if it was as dead as a stone. Why have paper charts?

"Emergencies?"

I didn't answer myself. The why didn't matter. If those were charts, then I might at least get an idea where I was.

I grabbed several rolls. Beneath the cabinet was a table just the right size for the wide paper. I unrolled one. Yep. Charts. Sea charts. It showed sea lanes and nearby land with ports.

I didn't recognize a single thing. The names of the ports meant nuthin' to me. Place names: nuthin'. I saw a few islands. Nuthin'. Even if I could recognize a place or two, it would do me little good. I had no idea which chart was the right one. There were at least twenty rolls.

"Nuts."

I re-rolled the charts and put them back where I found them. I don't know why. There wasn't anyone around to yell at me.

I took several deep breaths and tried to clear my mind of depression and doubt. I'll admit that I was tempted to sit in the captain's chair and just wait, and wait, and wait. But that passed in a few moments. My gut told me that I wasn't the kinda guy who liked to sit around and wait for things to happen.

"If answers won't come to me, then I'll hunt them down."

# Chapter 3

## OUT OF THE CLOSET

DECISIONS NEEDED TO be made, even if they were wrong. So far, everything I had seen made me think I was the last soul onboard a powerless, drifting cruise ship. I felt alone but I hadn't proved it. Since I was still aboard, there might be other people snoozin' in their bunks dressed in tuxes or some other kinda fancy dress. I had no proof of that. Of course, I had no proof I was wrong. Bottom line: I had spent the better part of an hour searching the topside of the ship and knew less than when I started. Maybe the answers lay below decks. After all, that's where all this began for me.

I left the bridge and made my way back to the main deck. I was gonna take another quick look around when I noticed something that had got by me during my first search. Aside from gazing at the fog that surrounded the SS *Twilight Zone* and the ocean below, all my attention had been turned on the rooms and the deck. That's where the people should be. This time I forced myself to broaden my gaze. In some ways I wish I hadn't.

Spaced along the deck just inside the safety rail were cranes—davits. They were ten feet tall or so and shaped like steel candy canes. A metal cable ran from the base of the davit and up the steel pole, along the crook, hung free over the side of the ship and hovered about five feet above the water. A device on the end the cable was clearly meant to attach to something—something that was no longer there.

"Lifeboats."

My words chilled my blood. I walked the length of the deck examining every davit. The davits were used in pairs, a lifeboat meant to be hangin' between them. Not anymore. There wasn't a life boat to be found. That meant...

"Not good. Not good by a long shot."

The pit of my stomach became a runaway elevator. If it had been possible, it would have crawled out of me and jumped overboard.

The ship had been abandoned.

And I had been left behind.

It shouldn't have been possible, but I now felt twice as lonely as before and I was pretty doggone lonely to begin with.

I circled the main deck again this time searching the sea. Maybe the life boats could still be seen and if they were, then I could... could... I had no idea what I could do in that situation. Still, I strained my vision trying to peer through the fog looking for an emergency beacon or the shape of a boat that could hold a couple dozen people. I had counted the davits and my guess was that the ship carried twenty-five lifeboats. The ship was much smaller than the big monsters I had seen in pictures. Ships with many decks above the main deck and many below. The kinda ship that carried a few thousand passengers. Perhaps that was one of the reasons I thought of the ship as old. It seemed small.

Still, this boat, it seemed to me, could carry several hundred passengers. Maybe even a thousand or more.

I let those thoughts go. They didn't matter at the moment. I had a long way to go before I reached the goal line.

Once I had confirmed that no life boats were near enough to see or hear, I continued on with my plan. I had to. I had no other plan to follow.

Two thoughts rattled around in my head, each wanting attention. One was a sense of sadness. Life boats would have their own source of power, working engines, and radios. The other was a question: What could make the captain and crew abandon ship?

I had no answer and I had a strong feeling that if I found one, I wouldn't like it.

MY PLAN WAS simple. I would search the ship by brute force. Based on the image provided by the mirror in my room—if was really my room—I was a brute force kinda guy. Maybe that was true; maybe it wasn't. For now, I was going to embrace it as the truth. I began one level down. The same level I had

ALTON GANSKY

been on when I came to.

Maybe there was a better way of doing this, but if there was, then I couldn't see it. I began banging on stateroom doors. I also exercised my lungs a lot.

"Hello? Anybody there? Hello?"

Door after door and always the same silence.

There was another problem. I had seen a placard with a drawing of the ship in cross section. Kinda one of those, "You are here," things. I doubted that I was any kinda rocket scientist, but I knew the deeper in the ship I went, the darker it would get. With no power, I would be descending into a crypt.

*Great. My own thoughts are creeping me out. Like I need more creeping out.*

I reached the end of the first corridor and found an in-wall cabinet with a glass front. Inside was a fire hose and, praise God, a flashlight. It was a big one, too. I'm sure it was meant for crew in times of emergency, but I decided to help myself anyway.

I broke the glass which gave me access to a lever that unlocked the cabinet door. I took the light. I flicked it on and it came to life.

"Finally, something good."

I went level by level deeper and deeper into the ship. Some of the levels were below the waterline. I anticipated that and my love for my new flashlight grew.

The beam of light splashed on the walls, ceiling, and floor. If I tripped now it would be because of stupidity or carelessness, not because I was strolling in the dark.

I continued banging on doors and calling attention. I continued to get nothing in return. It reminded me of a flashlight scene from the old *X-*

*Files* television show.

Four decks down from where I started, I heard it. I had stopped to take a breather and to rest the hand I had been using to pound on hard wood doors. It was a soft sound. At first it seemed too distant, but then nearer.

No words. Muffled.

Weeping.

A deep weeping. Not a child. Not a woman.

I closed my eyes and tried to turn up the sensitivity in my ears. A man. Somewhere a man was weeping. It broke my heart.

I moved slowly and with soft steps, like a cat sneaking up on prey. At each doorway I paused and placed an ear near the door. The weeping grew louder. A dozen doors later I located the right room. Well, not a room. It was a closet of some kind. A sign on the door read: CREW ONLY.

I took a few deep breaths and willed myself to move slowly. Whoever was inside the closet was definitely upset and I didn't want to scare the life out of the guy. I was pretty sure that he, like me, was having a really bad day.

I tapped on the door. "Hey buddy, you okay?"

The weeping stopped. I heard a scuffling sound like someone scampering away from the door.

"It's okay, man. I'm a friend."

No response.

"You mind if I open the door?"

"It's locked." The voice sounded fairly young. Adult, but not old.

"Can you unlock it for me?"

"Do you think I'd still be in here if I could unlock it? Don't be dense. It's locked from the outside."

I was beginning to get an idea about why someone might lock the guy up. He wasn't very warm and fuzzy.

"You know something, pal. You and me might be the only two people on this tub. It might be wise to make a friend instead of an enemy."

I heard mumbling. "Yeah. Okay. Right. I'm a little upset."

"Understandable. I'm a bit off my game, too." I studied the door. "Okay, I'm gonna try the doorknob. That okay with you?"

"I already told you it was locked."

"Then it won't hurt anything for me to give it a try. I'm just givin' you a heads up." I gave the knob the once over. It had a place for a key, which made sense to me. I'd expect a room reserved for crew might need to be locked. Still, I gave the brass knob a twist. It didn't cooperate.

"Believe me now?"

Grumpy was getting on my nerves and I didn't have many nerves left.

"And I told you it wouldn't hurt to try—and it didn't." Deep breath. "I don't know how much room you have in there. Can you back away from the door?"

"Yes." I heard shuffling, then, "Well?"

"Well what?"

"I'm out of the way. Do whatever you were going to do."

"Oh, sorry. My X-ray vision isn't working." I was certain I could get the guy out, but every time he opened his mouth I felt an urge to leave him right where he was.

I took a step back, raised a foot and kicked the

door just to the side of the doorknob. It rattled a little but stayed put. This would have been so much easier if I wasn't wearing a monkey suit and dress shoes.

"That's it?" The stranger's voice pressed through the door. "That's your great plan?"

I kicked the door again. I kicked harder than I should and felt pleasure in the exertion. I also felt some pleasure at seeing a chunk of the door with the knob splinter and fall to the deck. The door swung in with an earsplitting crash.

A blur of a man flew out of the closet like an iron ball out of a canon and rammed me in the chest with his shoulder. I back-peddled, surprised by the attack. Then he had his hands around my throat, his fingers squeezing and squeezing. The good news was he wasn't very strong. Still, it was enough to make me drop my flashlight.

The temptation was to grab his wrists and pull his arms down. I didn't. Instead, I raised a hand between his extended arms and took hold of his face. I clamped down—hard. He screamed, so I assumed I had his attention. I didn't wait for retaliation; I brought a quick knee to his gut striking him just about belt high.

Air left his lungs. His arms dropped. He wobbled. It was a good time for me to seize his belt in my right hand, lift, and shove him in the chest with my left. He hit the deck on his back, just as I intended. That was when the war in my brain started. Part of my mind wanted me to kill the little twerp; another part just wanted me to beat on him for a bit; and about half by brain was tugging hard on my reins. Lucky for Grumpy, I felt inclined to follow my more reasonable self. Truth is, I felt like something or someone was holding me back.

I picked up my flashlight. "Are we done?" I watched him roll on the deck for a few moments. "I can do this all day."

He raised a hand. "I know when I'm beat." He sucked in a barrel full of air. "Did you have to kick me so hard?"

"I pulled that kick, buddy. It coulda been worse, much worse. Besides, I seem to recall your hands around my neck." That's when I noticed his right arm. It sported a dragon tattoo that looked very familiar.

"Sorry about that." He stopped rolling around but spent a few more moments moaning. "I thought you were someone else."

"Best I can tell, pal, we're the only two people around."

"It's not people that worry me."

I didn't know what to make out of that. Maybe he hit his head when I put him on the floor.

"What's your name?"

He gazed at the ceiling. "I don't know."

"At least we have that in common." I extended my hand to him. "Need help getting up?"

He shook his head. "I can manage."

He rolled over and pushed himself up until he was on all fours and made several attempts to stand, but couldn't quite manage it.

"Okay, maybe I could use an assist."

I grabbed an arm and lifted him to his feet. He swayed a little, then looked at me.

"You're a big one, aren't you?"

He was young, looked in pretty good shape, and had the kind of looks girls seemed to go for. He wore a formal white shirt, the kind with ruffles over the buttons. Like me, he wore tuxedo pants and dress shoes. No jacket, though. I imagined that it was in the corner of the closet. His shirt sleeves were rolled up. "That's some tattoo. Where'd you get that?"

He looked at his arm. "I don't know. I don't remember much."

That I understood. I moved to the closet and shone my light in. It didn't take long for me to recognize a simple janitor's closet.

"How did you get stuck in here?"

"Don't be an idiot. I didn't get stuck. I was imprisoned."

I let the insult pass. "Okay then, who imprisoned you?"

"My dad."

"Your dad locked you in the closet? I take it he's never parent of the year."

He looked at me with an odd mix of anger and sorrow. It was kinda heartbreaking.

"Where's your dad now?"

"He's dead."

I didn't like the sound of this. "He died on the boat?"

"No, he's been dead for a while."

"How could he... Never mind. Let me ask you something. Do I look familiar to you?"

"You hitting on me, big guy?"

That did it. "If you don't shut that smart mouth of yours, I'll be hitting on you, but not in the way you think."

A wave of guilt washed over me. He just stared at me, looking a little like a scolded puppy. The guy could switch from mean-spirited to the verge of tears in a heartbeat. I felt sorry for him. It also made me think he might be a little unhinged.

"Sorry." I gave a little shrug. "It looks like we've both had a rough day. I'm a little edgy. What say we start over?" I extended my hand. "I'd introduce myself to you but—you know—I have that whole amnesia thing going on."

Grumpy nodded and took my hand. "Same here."

Then        the        ship        shuddered.

## Chapter 4

SHUFFLING THE DECKS

I HAD BEEN just about to ask him how his dead father could lock him in a closet when he disappeared. In fact, the whole hallway vanished. Gray light surrounded me, which meant I had somehow made it back to one of the upper decks. The problem was, I hadn't planned to go back to the upper decks.

Something else was different. I was no longer on my feet. I was on my hands and knees, swaying like a drunk dog. I didn't feel any too good, either. I proved that point by emptying my stomach on the deck. I hadn't puked in years. I don't know. Maybe I had and just couldn't remember it.

Once I was done decorating the deck with my last meal, I tipped over onto my side, then my back and waited to see if more retching was to come.

*Slow breaths. Even breaths. Relax. It will pass.*

The nausea did pass, but my stomach continued to cramp a little longer. When I opened my eyes I saw the fog-shrouded sky again, except it was different somehow. A different shade of gray. And brighter.

"There you are."

A familiar voice. Grumpy's voice.

He had more to say. "Now, that was weird. I mean off the charts weird—eww." He pointed at the deck. "Did you do that?"

"Of course not, I just like to find a puddle of puke and lay down next to it." I sat up and wrapped my arms around my knees. I took a few more deep breaths praying that I wouldn't puke again—especially in front of Grumpy.

"To each his own, I guess."

"I was kidding. Yes, I'm responsible for the mess. Apparently being snapped from one place on a ship to another upsets my tummy."

"Tummy? Really? What are you, six years old?"

I struggled to my feet and tried to look even taller.

Grumpy raised his hands. "Okay, okay. Just trying to be friendly."

"You don't have many friends do you, smart mouth?"

"How would I know? I'm as blank as you. Well, maybe I'm not that blank, but I have the same memory affliction you do. Remember?"

"Let me guess. That's supposed to be a joke."

"Nope, but I've got to admit, it was clever." He walked to the rail. "I have a point to make."

"Yeah? And what's that?" I joined him at the rail and noticed another difference. The ocean was green and a little choppy. Still, I could tell the ship was dead in the water.

"First, see if you have a handkerchief in that tux of yours. It's difficult enough looking at you as it is. The addition of vomit dribbles makes it worse."

*As if I wasn't already embarrassed enough.* Turns out, I did have a handkerchief in the inside breast pocket of my coat. I used it as requested.

"Why are we in tuxes?"

He shrugged. "One mystery at a time, Big Guy. First, I have a question or two, assuming you're done spewing."

"Let it go, pal. What's your question?"

"What's the first thing you remember?"

I gave that some thought. "You mean today?"

He looked at me like green ooze was coming outta my ears. "Can you remember anything before today?"

"No, I told you... Okay, I get the point." I looked at the soiled cloth in my hand, then tossed it overboard. It wasn't the kind of thing that becomes a keepsake. "I remember waking up on the bed in my stateroom, or someone's stateroom."

"You were in bed?"

"No. I was *on* the bed. Fully dressed. Shoes and everything."

"Tell me everything from that point on."

"First, I have a question. Whatever happened back there put me on the deck and made me sick, yet you look unfazed. What's the deal?"

He smiled. I was surprised he knew how. "Didn't bother me a bit. In fact, it seemed kind of familiar." His smiled widened. "Don't hate me because I'm rugged."

Since arguing seemed the least productive thing to do, I caved and told him how I had come to in the stateroom, my search of the upper decks, and how I found him. He nodded.

"Is anything different now?"

"Yeah, I was transported from one of the lower decks back up here. That's pretty different."

He looked disappointed in me. "I mean different from what you saw before."

"The sea is green. Before it was gray."

"Anything else?"

"I haven't looked around since…" I motioned to the mess on the deck.

"So the sea is a different color?"

"Yep. And it is a little more active. Choppy."

"Uh-huh." He raised a hand to his face and tapped his lips with his index finger.

"Uh-huh what?"

"Try to stay with me on this—"

"Do you have to be so condescending?"

"Ooooh, that's a big word."

"One you don't seem to understand." My temper was swelling. "I could throw you over this rail, you know."

Grumpy shook his head. "No, you can't. It's not in you. You're not that kind of guy. You're one of those gentle giants."

"I wasn't gentle when I put you on the deck a short time ago."

"Yes you were, Big Guy. You could've beat me into a pile of goo, but you didn't. You took care of business. That's a fact and I have the bruises to prove it. You even apologized to me. Thugs don't do that."

My head was starting to ache. I don't think I could beat this guy in a battle of wits. He was mouthy, annoying, self-centered. I learned that in less than ten minutes with him. In addition to all of that, he seemed to be hiding a brilliant brain behind his barbs.

When he did speak, he carried on as if he were lecturing a class. "First, my memory goes back about as far as yours, but while you were trying to figure out how to open the door to the hallway, I was being locked in a closet by my dead father."

"I know how to work a door… I been meaning to ask you about that whole dead father thing."

"Not now. First things first. Our memories go back about the same amount of time. Have your forgotten anything since you awoke on the bed?"

I gave that some thought. "I don't think so, but then again, how would I know what I forgot?"

He looked disappointed in me. "Gaps, Big Guy. Gaps. You just described a moment by moment sequence of all that happened since you woke up, right? Any gaps in that story? Did you come up on deck, then find yourself in the galley or some other place?"

"No."

"Okay, that's good. It means that our brains are still working the way they're supposed to. Well, mine is anyway."

"That water looks awful cold, dude."

He raised a hand. "Sorry, apparently I'm not a very nice guy."

"I get that feeling. Where ya goin' with this?"

"The fact that we can remember anything tells us something about our problem. Our memory loss isn't from brain damage. We can remember, just not past a

297

certain point. We can talk intelligently…well, I at least—"

"You really want to test your theory about me being a nice guy?"

"Nah. I don't see that ending well for me. Besides, we need to work together. My point is this: I feel a little groggy, but not so much that I can't reason. You too?"

"Yeah, but my brain is clearing as time passes. No important memories, but at least my thoughts aren't crashing into each other anymore."

He nodded. "That's a good thing. We're not brain damaged, but something is interfering with our ability to recall events prior to just a few hours ago. And what are the odds that two people would have the same affliction at the same time on the same boat and both be dressed in tuxes? You see what that means."

"I think so."

"There's a good chance we've been drugged. Probably something in our food."

"How do you figure that?"

"The tuxes, Big Guy. We're both wearing tuxes. And where do guys wear tuxes?"

"You mean like a banquet or something."

Again a nod. "On the nose. Right on the nose." He stepped away from the rail and walked to the spot where I tossed my cookies. "Look here."

"You want to study my vomit?"

"Why not? Vomitus can reveal a lot. You're not queasy are you?"

"Since I just vomited all over the deck, I guess you could say yes."

"Ah, point taken." He looked at the vile goop. "Anyway, I can tell you that you ate not many hours ago, so you could have ingested some drug."

"Why would anyone do that to me? To us?"

"I have no idea." He stepped back to the rail.

"Did they poison all the passengers?"

"I can't know that. Not yet anyway."

Thoughts began to bubble in my brain. "Did you notice that all the life boats are gone?"

He looked up and down the deck. "I haven't had a chance to look around, but you seem to be right. That means that we were rendered unconscious, had our memories stripped away, then were left behind while the crew and passengers took off in the life boats. Rude, if you ask me."

*Rude* wasn't the word for it. "Okay, smart guy. How did we get transported from the lower decks to the main deck?"

"How? No clue. But you said the fog is a different shade of gray, and that the sea is a different color. Right?"

"Yes, and it feels warmer now."

"I don't think we were transported up here. I think that was a consequence of something else. I think the whole ship was moved from one place to another."

"Like where?" I wasn't sure I wanted to know, but knowing was better than blind ignorance.

"I have no way of knowing."

I looked over the green sea. "You know what strikes me as odd?"

"I would think that all of this strikes you as odd."

"It does, but somehow I don't feel surprised. It's almost familiar. In a way, I'm surprised by my lack of surprise."

A moment of silence passed between us. "I suppose you think that's clever."

"It's the best I can do at the moment," I said. "Come on."

"Where are we going?"

"To look for others."

He frowned. "What makes you think you can find anyone else?"

"I found you, Grumpy. If I hadn't, you'd still be in a closet weeping. Now let's go before everything shifts again."

"Okay, but I want a different nickname. Grumpy isn't doing it for me."

"Whatever you say, Grumpy."

## JUST BECAUSE YOU DON'T BELIEVE IN GHOSTS

THE CLOSET WAS the logical place to start. After all, it's where we left off when the ship shuffled or whatever it did.

"Let me get this right," Grumpy said. "You want us to start another search from this spot because it was as far as you got last time."

"You got it. It's only logical." Based on his tone, I

figured he had a different opinion.

"Think about it, Big Guy."

"What?" I retrieved my flashlight.

"Just give it some thought. It's about time you gave thinking a go."

We were standing outside the now-broken door that had held Grumpy prisoner a short time ago. I looked at the closet. I looked at him and narrowed my eyes. Then I looked at the closet once more.

He held up his hands like a crook surrendering to the cops. "Okay, okay. Maybe that was a little harsh."

I couldn't have locked him in the closet if I wanted to, and I didn't really want to. Even if I did, I had busted up the part of the door with a knob. That door wouldn't be locked again anytime soon.

I leaned against one of the walls. "Okay, genius, what am I missing?"

"Last time we were here, what happened?"

"We ended up on the upper deck."

"Yep, with you puking all over—"

"I know what I was doing. I was the one doing it." This guy had a way of pushing my buttons. I was starting to regret finding him.

A half-sec later I realized what he was getting at. "You're saying if there are other people on board they could have been transported, shuffled, whatever into a room I've already checked."

"Bingo! Give the man a cigar."

That was disheartening. So what should I do? Start over? "You might be right, but let's assume you're not. We start from here and keep working our way down."

"I don't see the logic."

"It's simple. This is where we are right now, so this

is where we pick up the search." I started down the corridor banging on doors, calling out, and jiggling doorknobs. All the doors were locked and no one replied to my calls.

We made it through the hall with me doing all the work and Grumpy following behind with a dog-eatin'-red-heart grin. I was beginning to question the guy's sanity. He might not be crazy, but he was pushing me in that direction.

We made our way down a level and started the whole process all over again. After banging on what I guessed was the twentieth stateroom on this deck, something caught my eye. Someone—no—something was standing at the end of the corridor. I raised my flashlight and aimed it down the corridor. The thing looked human-ish, stood at least seven feet tall, was pale, and if I was reading its expression correctly, a little put out about something.

Grumpy squeaked something, but my attention was on the thing at the end of the hall. It seemed I had three choices: turn and flee (I kinda liked that one); stay put and see what it did; or march up to it and see what it would do. I chose the last option. Don't ask why. It just seemed the kind of thing I would do.

I took a step forward. "Um, excuse me."

Grumpy almost choked. "What? You say *excuse me* to that thing? Are you planning on asking directions or something?"

I kept walking at a slow pace. No need to spook the ...spook. The odd thing was that all this seemed almost normal. I shoulda jumped outta my skin, but I didn't. Don't get me wrong, I was apprehensive enough for ten people, but I was shocked. Shouldn't I be shocked? I mean how often does a guy share an empty ship with a ghostly thingamajig?

"What are you doing?" Right behind me, Grumpy seemed terrified enough for both of us.

"I have no idea." I kept moving forward. My heart had turned into a jackhammer. If it beat any harder, it would break a rib or two.

As I drew closer I could see more detail; detail I didn't want to see. Its eyes were about the size of tennis balls. Fortunately, it had only the two eyes. *Be thankful for small things.* Its mouth was too wide for what passed for its face. It had lips: chapped, puffy, bloody looking lips. I prayed I was wrong about the bloody part. The thing's skin was pale, almost see-through and looked like someone had too little skin to offer so he stretched what little he had.

It wore clothes: torn, tattered, covered in something. I had no interest in knowing what. It stood on bare feet. I have big feet, but this thing made me look tiny.

Grumpy cleared his throat. "Um, listen Big Guy—"

"Hush. I'm trying to concentrate."

"Yeah, but—"

"Feel free to hang back. Or run. Whatever."

To Grumpy's credit, he stayed with me. Maybe he wasn't so smart after all.

When we were about fifteen feet from the visitor, it turned and fled down the side corridor. Of course I chased it. It seemed the thing to do. Chasing running people seemed normal for me, but I doubted I had ever chased a ghost or a zombie or an alien or whatever. At least that I could remember.

It took only three good strides for me to reach the

end of the corridor and turn in the direction of the thing. It was gone. There was a stairway a short distance down the abutting corridor, but I had doubts about the thing's ability to reach them and disappear that fast.

"Okay," Grumpy said, "I'm going on record as being totally creeped out."

I turned. "Let me ask you something, buddy. Have you ever seen anything like that before?"

"Not exactly. My father looked pretty terrible, though."

"Your dead father that locked you in the closet?"

"Yep. That's the guy." He looked at me. "Don't stare at me that way. Just because you don't believe in ghosts doesn't mean there aren't any."

"That thing looked more like a demon than a ghost."

He cocked an eyebrow. "Seen many demons, have you?"

"Says the guy who sees his dead father."

He opened his mouth to say something, probably something snide and deserving of a fist to the nose, but he didn't. He closed his mouth.

I looked down the corridor again. "Back to my question. When you first saw that thing, did it seem a weird thing to see, or did it seem like you've seen things like that in the past?"

"What difference…" His eyes shifted from side to side a few times. The guy was thinking. "I see where you're going with this. No, it didn't seem abnormal. It scared me all right. I'm still scared."

"I had the same feeling: more of a *not again* than *this can't be possible*. Know what I mean?"

"Yeah, I know. What I don't know is why we

would react that way."

I scratched my head. "I ain't got a clue. Not about that thing, not about this ship, not about why we can't remember."

"Hello?"

A voice.

"Anybody there?"

A woman's voice.

# Chapter 6

## THE BLACK LADY AND THE REDHEAD

SHE STOOD AT the top of the stairs. The same staircase the bogyman had used to escape us. I couldn't tell if he left outta fear (doubtful) or just because he couldn't be bothered with such puny beings like us.

The woman held a flashlight, which told me that she had been hanging around on the lower decks. I aimed my flashlight at her. She returned the favor. I let my beam linger on her face for a moment, then lowered it. Her beam in my face made it hard to see, so I assumed my light was doing the same to her. Once I moved the beam off her face and lowered it to her shoulders, she did the same for me.

Before me, at the top of the stairs, was a youngish

black woman with dreadlocks. Her face made me think that she had seen some hard things in her life. She wore an evening dress, but no shoes. My guess was that women's heels weren't all that good for wandering around a ghost ship.

"Who are you?" Her tone was hard like steel and had an edge to it. To be honest, she scared me some.

"Really, lady? That's your question?" At least Grumpy was consistently rude to men and women.

"Don't mess with me, pretty boy. I ain't in a good mood."

"Clearly," Grumpy said.

I shone my light in his face. "Maybe you should let me do the talking."

"Why?"

"Because you have a tendency to make people hate you."

He pushed the flashlight away. "You're blinding me, moron."

I moved the light back up the stairwell and addressed the stranger. "That's the problem, ma'am. We don't know who we are, or where we are. We don't have any answers."

"You don't know who you are? You expect me to believe that?"

"Do you know who *you* are?" Grumpy said.

She didn't answer.

"I didn't think so."

I thought it better if I continued to do the speaking. "I know this is a little strange, ma'am, but do you know your name?"

She shook her head.

I nodded mine. "I guess we're all in the same boat." I cringed at my own words. *Of course we're all in the same boat—literally.* "What I mean is, we're all facing the same problem. May I come up the stairs?"

"I don't own the ship. You can climb any stairs you want."

"Thanks." Grumpy and I climbed the treads. I held out my hand for a friendly shake. The woman looked at it like I had leprosy. I lowered my hand.

She studied me a little more. "Wow, you're built like a tank, aren't you? I assume the most expensive bill in your house is the one from the grocery store."

"I've never been to a grocery store that sent bills. At least I don't think I have."

"What's going on here?" she asked. "I want to know what you know."

I guessed her to be a little older than me, but not by many years. She was pretty in her own way and came loaded with attitude. I told her what little I knew, what we had been doing, and finished with the ghoul in the corridor.

"Didn't see no ghoul. I've been up here for a while, but I was in a room before…I don't know how to describe it."

"Before you were miraculously transported someplace else." Grumpy smiled. I could see the smile because the woman blasted him in the face with the beam from her flashlight.

"Yeah, somethin' like that."

Grumpy turned to me. "Hey look, Big Guy, there is someone on a deck you already checked. It appears that I was right—again."

The woman looked at me. "You're a big guy, why haven't you squashed this jerk yet?"

"I've been wondering the same thing. It just doesn't seem to fit who I am—whoever that might be."

"Well, if you ever change your mind," she said, "let me know. I'll lend you a hand."

Grumpy snickered. "You don't scare me, lady."

She turned and closed the yard that separated them in one stride. I could tell she had no respect for personal space because her nose was an inch from his. "Really? And here I was thinkin' you at least had some brains." The words were cold enough to give me a chill.

Grumpy backpedaled. "Ease up, woman. I'm not your enemy."

"Yeah? We'll see about that."

Grumpy looked at me and all I could do was shrug. I managed not to laugh and that was no easy task. Truth be told, I started to feel sorry for the guy.

Several unusually long seconds passed before the black lady stepped away. She seemed to soften as she moved a few steps down the corridor and stopped to study one of the walls. I moved in her direction and shone my light on the wall. We had some light from a window at the junction of hallway and stair landing, but I wouldn't want to try and read a comic book in it.

My light revealed a series of drawings on the walls. They reminded me a little of those wall drawings in Egypt—hieroglyphs. Yeah, that was it: like hieroglyphs in a pyramid. "You do this?"

"Yep, but I don't know why." She extended a hand to touch one of the sketches. It was the image of a boy. The kid looked like he was maybe ten years old. I don't know how much a man can glean from watching someone touch something, but I got the distinct impression that she was feeling a strong emotion. If I had to guess, I would say she gave it a loving touch.

At the base of the wall were several pencils and pens. A quick look at the number of drawings made me think that she had been at this for some time, but that didn't make sense. I had been in this hallway not all that long ago and she wasn't here. That meant she was fast, and to be that fast meant she had been drawing stuff most of her life.

Grumpy joined us but stood on my left with the woman on my right. I guess I make a pretty good obstacle.

I tried to take in all of what I was seeing on the wall: a boy, a woman, a house, what looked like the exterior of a school or an institution, a few people and animals without eyes—that creeped me out—and some sharped toothed monsters. There was a tall, scary looking man similar to what we had seen a short time before.

I also saw the figure of a very normal looking man. There was enough detail to make me think he was older than us. He looked confident, proud, and a little superior.

Nearby that sketch was another of a woman and superimposed over that was the image of a girl. They looked an awful lot alike, as if the woman was the little girl all grown up. There was a spooky mansion and even a pirate ship.

"It looks like you had a few things on your mind," I said.

"Maybe. I don't know." All the bluster had gone from her voice. She touched the old man image then moved back to the boy.

"What's that?" Grumpy pointed at what I first

assumed was a basketball but under my flashlight beam I could see it was some kinda mechanical sphere. She had drawn it so that it looked like it was flying.

"I don't know. I don't know what any of this means." Her voice trembled a little. "I just had to draw the images. They're important."

"Important how?" Grumpy spoke softly, a skill I didn't know he had.

She put a hand to her mouth. "I don't know. I keep askin' myself that question but I come up empty every time. Why can't I remember? Why? Why? Why?"

I put a hand on her shoulder, slightly afraid I'd pull back a stump. She allowed it. "We'll figure it out."

She drew a hand under one eye. "You really believe that?"

"Yes. I choose to believe that. Believin' otherwise won't help."

"They look like tattoos." Grumpy leaned closer to one of the drawings. "These are pretty good. You show some real talent—"

He snapped up straight.

I had to ask. "What?"

"You did all of these?" Grumpy sounded a lot less cocky.

"Yes."

"Every one of them? There were no drawings here before you began defacing the walls?"

"Watch it, pretty boy." Anger had replaced the woman's softer moment.

"Not everything is a confrontation, lady. Answer the question. Were there drawings on this wall before you started drawing?"

"The wall was blank, I tell you."

Time for me to speak up. "What are you getting at, Grumpy?"

He pointed at one of the images I hadn't seen before, and I coulda swore his hand shook a bit. I looked to the spot on the wall where he was pointing. I saw it: a dragon. I moved my eyes from the wall to Grumpy's arm where the same tattoo glared back at me. The woman saw it.

I don't know what I expected. A gasp? A cry of surprise? A question? An accusation? Instead she swore. I don't mean she let slip a bad word. No sir, she spit out curses like a machine gun spits out bullets.

Grumpy appeared stunned, but managed to move down the wall. I walked with him, shining my light on scores of sketches. At one, he stopped, stifled a scream, backpedaled to the other side of the hall, then dropped to the floor. He pointed a finger that looked like it had palsy. He could barely speak. I had a feeling I had seen terror before, and this was it.

I redirected my light to the drawn image of an old man; a man with the devil's own smile, and hatred in his eyes. I don't know how the woman did it, but I could have sworn the evil image moved.

"Run! RUN!"

A woman's voice rolled down the corridor. I glanced to the far end and saw a young woman with wild red hair speed around the corner of the T-intersection of corridors.

We stared at her as she sprinted toward us. "This isn't a drill, people. Run!"

All this would be strange in anyone's book, but what I saw next kicked strangeness up a notch. Not far behind the woman was one of those flying basketballs I had seen on the wall. It carried too much speed and slammed into the corridor wall. It slowed for a second or two, then picked up the chase again.

I grabbed Grumpy's collar and lifted him to his feet. "Go. Get."

He didn't argue. The redhead shot past us and he was right on her heels. The wall artist was on the move, too.

I decided on a different approach. I might be able to outrun the thing, but sooner or later it would run us down. So I ran—straight at it. When I was in tackling distance I leapt forward, arms out wide and tried to take the thing down.

There was a flash and I landed face down on a hard floor.

The carpet was gone.

The hallway was gone.

The people were gone.

I was alone in a wide room. A glance around told me what I suspected to be true: the ship had shuffled again.

## PUTTING HEADS TOGETHER

I PUSHED TO my feet and took a quick look around for that globe thing, that—sphere. I didn't see it. "Thank God." I took another look around. No ghouls either. All I saw was the wide, raised wood floor I stood on, a bunch of rows of padded seats, and some musical instruments on stands. There was also a drum kit.

The light was dim—nothing new there—so seeing detail was tough. Still, enough light pushed through partially open curtains along one wall. The curtains looked heavy and thick. It all made sense: I was in a theater of some sort. Didn't cruise ships have a place where bands played or entertainment personnel put on shows? I was pretty sure they did and this last shuffle had dropped me center stage.

The nausea I had felt the first time I was teleported or whatever you call it came back with a vengeance. I had been a little too frightened when I first hit the floor to notice anything but my heart pounding like an airplane piston. With no sight of the flying metal basketball thing, my belly decided it was safe to complain in the only way it knew how.

I sat on the stage for a moment, then lay on my back. A few minutes of slow, easy breathing calmed the storm in my stomach. I tried closing my eyes, but I was afraid I'd open them and see the hallway critter drooling on my face. That did nothing to soothe me.

Fortunately, I was very much alone and I'll admit—for a few moments if felt very, very good.

Once I knew my stomach was settled enough not to embarrass me again, I sat up. "What to do now?" I had no answers for myself, but sitting around waiting for something to happen didn't seem all that wise. I rose and walked to the windows, most of which were shrouded with heavy curtains. I figured that curtains were needed to darken the place for whatever kinda shows they put on in here.

I glanced back over the seating and guessed that the place could hold maybe five hundred folks or so. It kinda reminded me of a church, but with more comfortable chairs. Dim as the room was, I was able to make out two pair of double doors on the far wall.

I turned back to the window and stared out. A face was staring back in. I let out a whoop and jumped back. A hand that I assumed belonged to the face waved. The face smiled.

"Grumpy!"

He held up a finger then disappeared. Two other bodies passed by the window: a black woman and a redhead. It appears they had found each other after the shuffle.

"Big Guy!" Grumpy was all smiles as he entered the theater through a pair of double doors. "Did you miss me?" He came to a sudden stop and held out his arms to hold back the women. "You didn't... I mean..." He studied the floor.

"No. Not this time."

"What are you goin' on about?" The artist pushed past him.

"Turns out, Big Guy here has a sensitive tummy. Last shift, he puked his guts up. You should've seen it. It was amazing. A guy his size—"

"We get the picture." The red head glanced around the room like she was scanning it for clues. She looked at me. "You okay?"

"Yep. Thanks. You?"

"Peachy. Ended up in the men's bathroom. Never been in a men's bathroom. Don't want to go back, either."

I looked at the graffiti artist. She shrugged. "Kitchen."

It was Grumpy's turn. "Atrium, I guess you'd call it. Skylights. Wide room where people can gather and move around."

Red had a question: "Exactly where did you end up?"

I thought I had answered that. "Like I said. I ended up here. Well, specifically, I ended up in about the middle of the stage."

"Interesting."

"What's interesting, Red?"

She glared at him. "My name's not Red."

"Okay, what is it?"

She inhaled deeply and exhaled loudly. "You got me there."

"We gotta have some kind of name." Grumpy looked from person to person as if seeking agreement. "I mean, we can't keep saying, 'Hey, you.'"

Grumpy stepped next to me and faced the women. "Look, I call him Big Guy. Why? Because he's a big guy. Get it?"

"Don't patronize us," Red said.

"Fine. He's Big Guy. I'm Spartacus—"

"I've been calling him Grumpy." I tried not to smile when I said it.

"I don't deserve that name. I want a new one."

"Okay," the hall artist said. "We got Big Guy, Grumpy, Red, and me. Maybe you should call me Queen of Sheba."

Grumpy laughed, his voice echoing in the theater. The laugh stopped abruptly when the woman slugged him in the arm. Grumpy screamed, "Ow," then followed that with some very sour language. "What's with you, woman? You some kind of female ninja? Man, that hurt." He raised his hand and wiggled his fingers. "I can't feel my hand."

"Just for the record, gentlemen," Red said. "If push comes to shove, I'm with her."

"Me too," I said.

Grumpy made the kinda face a man makes when he's just guzzled sour milk. "Once again, it's the good looking guy against everyone else."

"Sketch," the artist said. "I was sketching when I first heard you guys. I can live with Sketch, but the first one that calls me Sketchy gets a pencil up the nose."

I believed her.

Red tugged at her hair. "You guys have a little more history together. That makes me the odd person out."

"We haven't spent much time together. We just met Sketch." I glanced at Grumpy. "We met not more than an hour or so ago, I'm guessing. Time seems different in this place."

Red chewed her lower lip for a minute. "I have a question for you, Big Guy."

"Shoot."

"Were you right behind us when we were running?"

"No. I ran the other way."

Red raised an eyebrow. "It was in a hallway. Are you saying you ran toward the sphere?"

"I guess so."

"You're not guessing, Big Guy," Red said. "That's exactly what you did. Why would you do that?"

I shrugged. "At the time it seemed the right thing to do. Doesn't matter. We shuffled before I could reach it—or it could reach me. Whatever."

"Interesting." Red looked at the floor as if someone had spilled a bag full of answers there. She looked at Sketch. "And they found you drawing?"

"On the wall." Grumpy was still rubbing his shoulder. "Really, who draws on a wall?"

Sketch took a step toward him and Grumpy took three steps back.

"I need to see those drawings." Red started for the door, then stopped. "Well, you guys coming or not?"

"Hang on," I said. I jogged to one of the walls

next to the door and found a metal case set in the wall. The case held a fire extinguisher and a fire ax. I helped myself to the ax. I lifted it for others to see. "Just in case one of those flying balls comes looking for us again. I want to give it something to remember us by."

## A PICTURE IS WORTH A THOUSAND WORDS

I LED THE WAY, the others behind me. I had convinced Grumpy to take up the rear. He was antsy enough to be an alert rear guard, always glancing over his shoulder. That's what we needed at the moment. I searched the corridor looking down connecting corridors to be certain seven-foot tall ghouls weren't having a card came with flying spheres. All was clear. For the moment.

We made our way out of the theater and down stairways until we were on the deck where Sketch had been defacing the wall. *Defacing* might be the wrong word. There might be something to those wall tattoos.

Red wasted no time studying Sketch's graffiti. We found and made use of more flashlights. The corridor wasn't pitch black, but it was pretty dim.

While Red gazed at the drawings, I gazed at Red. There was something about her and I couldn't deny feeling some emotion for the red-headed woman. I didn't know why. If she felt any kind or warmth for me, she kept it under wraps.

"How long did it take you to do this?" Red kept her eyes on the wall. It looked to me like she was sucking in each image like a Hoover sucks up dirt.

Sketch shrugged. "I don't know. I seem to have lost my sense of time. Maybe an hour. Maybe two. For all I know, I was up all night making this mess."

"That couldn't be," I said. "I've been up and down the corridor a couple of times and I didn't see you."

"Maybe." Grumpy didn't seem convinced. "Remember, this ship shuffles. Maybe it does more than move us, it moves the decks and rooms too. This deck might have been higher or lower than it is now."

I wanted that to be a stupid idea, but I couldn't come up with any argument that would prove him wrong.

"Can't be much lower," I said. "The deeper we go into the ship, the less light there is. She had to have some kinda light to see what she was doing."

"Maybe," Grumpy repeated.

Red looked my direction. "Do any of these images mean anything to you?"

"Sorry, no."

She posed the same question to Grumpy. "Nah."

I cleared my throat.

Grumpy gave one of those theatrical sighs that people use to show annoyance. "Okay, a couple of them make me feel something. You know, a little emotional twinge."

"Why do I feel you're holding back something?"

He shrugged for effect. "Beats me. Maybe it's your time of the—"

Sketch pivoted and raised a finger as if it were a knife. "So help me, if you finish that line I will drag your skinny butt up the stairs and throw you overboard, and I'll be smiling the whole time."

She was loud. Her words were hot. And she scared me a good bit. It was a little hard to tell in the dim light, but Grumpy seemed to shrink by a few inches and his face turned pale.

Grumpy, to his credit, used his brain and took a step back, hands held at half-mast. "Okay, okay, I'm sorry. This whole thing has me off my game."

Red cocked her head. "You can remember your *game?*"

Girl doesn't miss a trick.

"No, I just meant... I'm gonna shut up now."

"Before you do," Red pressed, "tell me what you meant by a *twinge.*"

"Most of these seem somewhat familiar. Some more so than others. And there's one—" He pointed down the hall to the spot where he had crumpled to the deck. "There's one down there that frightens me."

"Show me," Red said.

"I'd rather not."

"Show her," Sketch said.

He moved the few steps that would take him to the image that undid him. I noticed he walked near the opposite wall, as if a coupla feet of distance would

es

ALTON GANSKY

protect him. He pointed.

The image of the old man with the horrible grin and evil eyes stared back at us. The hair on my arm stood up.

"This?" Red pointed.

"Yeah …that's it."

Red put her face close to the drawing and shone her light on it. "Ugly cuss."

"You should have known him when he was alive." Grumpy's tone was softer than usual.

"You know who this is?" Red straightened and turned her gaze on Grumpy.

"He's my old man."

"And you're afraid of him?"

"If you knew him, you'd be afraid too. He was a monster."

"Interesting," Red said.

"I don't think so." Grumpy kept his back to the opposite wall.

"You don't get it." Red stepped to the center of the corridor. "Does anyone else remember their father? Or mother? Or pet dog?"

I said, "No." So did Sketch. Red admitted she couldn't remember any family members. She felt sure she had them, but she couldn't summon a name or conjure up a face.

"Why is it, Grumpy," Red said, "that you can remember your father?"

"You don't forget an animal like that," he said.

"Could it be because his dad is dead?" I wasn't sure that had any bearing but it was all I could muster.

Red thought for a few moments. "I want to say no, but I don't have a clue. I'm just trying to find a pattern. You know, make connections."

A couple moments of silence filled the space between us.

"I have an idea." Red moved back to the bulk of the sketches. "Gather round. I want to try something. Hold your questions until I'm done. Agreed?"

We agreed.

"Okay, I'm going to point at images at random. You tell me what you feel. Does the image make you feel good or bad; positive or negative. Clear?"

I had no idea where she was going with this, but she seemed like a pretty smart lady so I and the others went along with it.

"First, an easy one." She pointed at the drawing of the sphere thing.

"Bad." We said it in unison.

Next she pointed at a sketch of an eyeless man. Again, "Bad."

She thrust a finger at odd drawing of a little girl superimposed over an adult woman. I hadn't noticed first time I saw it, but the little girl was barefoot.

"Good." Again, we were in agreement. I had more than a good feeling. I felt sadness, longing, maybe even a family kinda love.

The test continued. Red pointed at what looked like large, flying things that were human-like but had a stinging tail, at a man in some kinda cloak (that one kinda freaked me out), and critters that looked to be swimming in the air and had a head full of sharp teeth. That one made my stomach turn.

There were two special images. The first was the one of the old distinguished-looking guy. Red paused on that one, then touched it. "I feel like this guy is important. Very important." We all agreed with that. Then...

"Anybody feel like we should know the kid?"

I said yes. Sketch could only nod. She looked heartbroken. To my surprise, Grumpy seemed moved, too. Truth be told, I felt very strong emotions, positive emotions, when I looked at the image. There was love there.

"We have to find the kid," Red said. "I can't be sure, but I have a feeling he may be the key to everything. Him and this gentleman." She pointed at the old guy again.

I had a question for Sketch. "What made you draw all this?"

"I don't know. I kept seeing images and it seemed the right thing to do, like it's natural to me."

"That fits," Red said.

"Fits what?" I asked.

"I'm not sure yet. I'm starting to sense a pattern, but I need more time to percolate. My brain is still in first gear."

"Wow," I said, "if that's first gear, I can't wait to see fifth."

Grumpy cleared his throat to get our attention. "I have a suggestion. We should have a place to meet. I don't know how or why the decks shuffle, but we have to assume it's going to happen again. If we get scattered again, then we could all meet in the bridge. It's an easy place to find." He turned to Red. "If you want, I could hold your hand."

"I don't want." Red picked up the discarded pencils and pens. "Let's go where we have more light. I have another idea."

## RED HAS IDEAS

RED IMPRESSED ME big time. She was smart and wasn't afraid to show it. I was going to have to defer to her in the brains department. Still, I couldn't figure out why she picked up the pencils and pens and carted them out of the corridor.

We went topside where the light was bright. Still gray, mind you, but brighter than what we had available in the corridors, even the ones with windows at their ends. I was glad for it. I needed a breath of fresh air, but the air never seemed fresh on this tub. For the first time I noticed that it smelled like day-old bread.

Red didn't lead us far once we got on the main deck. "I'm going to run off at the mouth for a minute.

Just let me do it without interruption. We can discuss later. Okay?"

I saw no reason to disagree. "I'm good with that." Grumpy and Sketch just nodded.

"Good. That's good." Her eyes danced around as if reading something only she could see. "Here's what we've got so far. The best we can tell, we may be the only ones on this ship."

"We haven't searched the whole ship yet—"

Her head snapped up and she shot me a harsh glance. "I thought we agreed I wouldn't be interrupted."

"Yes," I said. "Right. Correct. Sorry. I didn't mean— This is me shutting up right now."

The corners of her mouth ticked up a notch. What a relief.

Again, she tilted her head down a few degrees and I could tell she was wandering the corridors of her mind.

"Big Guy is right, there might be more people to find. My gut tells me that at least one other person is onboard. The boy."

Sketch started to say something, but reigned it in. I had already come to the conclusion that very few things frightened her, so I had to conclude she was being polite.

"I can't be sure, but our response to the image makes me think we know the kid. I also think we know each other. Maybe we're friends, coworkers. I don't know, but we're all connected by something.

"We saw some strange images down there," Red continued, "but there's something stranger still—the fact that we didn't find the images strange. Okay, that's a lousy sentence, but you get my point. We should have been repulsed or, at very least, questioned Sketch's sanity, but we didn't. We accepted it all as if it was nothing new. Why is that?"

Red began to move her head back and forth like a metronome. The movement was subtle, but noticeable. She was weighing heavy thoughts.

"We each have amnesia. A specific kind of amnesia. There are a dozen or more types of amnesia. Most are caused by physical trauma or a disease like Alzheimer's. Our heads look to be in pretty good shape and it's doubtful we would all manifest the same form of amnesia at the same time or the same place. So, what does that leave?"

Grumpy took the question to mean the silence law had been lifted. "Drugs. Like what they use for some surgeries."

"Exactly. If we all had suffered some kind of injury, then we would be having problems remembering anything at all. As it is, we can't remember ourselves or our past, but we can still think, reason, communicate, and—this is a big *and*— we still have impressions. All of us responded to Sketch's drawings in the same way. We agreed on those images that represent something bad and those that represent something good."

"I think I'm falling in love with you," Grumpy said.

"If I'm lucky, I'll forget that comment too." Red got back on track. "Someone did this to us. I don't know why. Maybe we all know something that someone wants us to forget. That idea has problems. It would've been easier to kill us than to get us on a ship like this. Missing. Too much missing stuff."

"Yeah," I said, "but you're making sense. Some

knowledge is better than no knowledge at all."

"Why am I the only one who can remember his father?" Grumpy's tone sounded a little more civil than I had come to expect.

Red stared at him for a long moment, as if trying to decide if she should tell him what was on her mind. "Trauma. You're afraid of your father. That kind of lasting fear has to be rooted in something." She paused then spat it out. "He abused you when you were a child. Does that seem right?"

"I-I guess."

"I'm sorry to be so blunt, but I have a sense that things are going to get worse before they get better. If they get better at all."

"No sweat," Grumpy said. I didn't believe him.

Red stepped to Sketch. "I need you—no *we* need you to do something." She handed her a pencil.

"Where? I don't have any paper."

"You don't need it. You've proven that." Red pointed at a wall behind Sketch. It was metal, but had a thick coat of grayish-white paint. "Think of the boy. Keep him in mind when you draw."

"Oh, come on." Grumpy's quiet moment had passed. "What do you think she is, some kind of psychic?"

"Yes, I do. *Psychic* might not be the right word, but she has some kind of gift. I'm guessing we all do. And don't ask. I don't know what they are. I'm working on impressions and patterns."

"Pattern-girl," Sketch said.

That sounded familiar.

Red cupped Sketch's face in her hands like they were old friends. "You can do this. The boy's life might be in danger. Go on. Give it a go."

She did.

Chapter 10

## IN THE BELLY OF THE BEAST

FIRST, A BOY appeared, then came details of a room. Sketch was amazing to watch. Once the pencil started moving along the paint, she seemed to be a different person, fully absorbed by what was happening in front of her. It took only ten minutes for her to complete the task, and only one minute for the rest of us to say, "Engine room."

"I'll lead." I still had the fire ax and a flashlight. We had already seen a flying orb-sphere-basketball-thingy, a seven-foot-tall ghoul with big feet and a bad attitude, and Grumpy had seen his dead father. I had to assume that other creepy things waited for us. No one questioned my decision to take point. I guess it seemed as natural to them as it did to me.

We entered the innards of the ship and started down the stairs. Sketch's drawing showed enough detail for us to know that the kid was in the engine room, and the engines in the engine room drove propellers, and propellers were at the bottom of boats so...what little logic I possessed said to go into the belly of the beast.

We had descended as far as we could and, as luck would have it—or providence maybe—there was a handy-dandy sign with an arrow pointing the way: ENGINE ROOM.

We found the door to the room. It was big, made of steel, and reminded me of a bank vault door. It also had a large padlock and hasp.

"That's not good." Grumpy took a close look at the lock system. "The padlock and hasp are new. I doubt it's been open more than once or twice. No scratches, no aging. Yep, brand new. And worse, the hasps cover the screws that hold the backplate in place. It was designed that way, of course—"

"Everyone step back," I said. "Grumpy, keep your light on the lock."

"Sure, Big Guy, but you can't cut through hardened steel with a fire ax—Whoa!"

I raised the ax and brought it down like someone's life depended on it. For all I knew, it did. The sound of ax head impacting hasp assaulted my ears.

"Good try," Grumpy said. "But the lock is still—"

I let the ax fly again, this time putting all my weight into it. On the floor lay the lock, still attached to the hasp. I didn't break the lock or hasp, but I did break the screws that held it in place. Not my original goal, but I would take it.

Sketch started for the door, but I held out an arm and stopped her.

"He'll be scared," she said. "That was enough noise to wake up an entire town. So move it or lose it, Big Guy."

"Not yet. Let me go first." Part of my reasoning was to keep her safe; the bigger part was to shield her from the sight of a dead boy.

"Well, snap it up, or I'll find a new use for that ax."

I didn't doubt her for a minute.

I retrieved the flashlight I had set on the floor before I began destroying private property, took one deep breath, and opened the door. The engine room was black as a tomb. Not very welcoming. I plunged into the dark, casting my light around as I did. Inside sat engines, silent and still, safety rails, pipes and things that a non-mechanical guy like me can't name.

"Hey, little buddy. It's me. I think we might know each other."

Nothing.

"I've come to help. Sorry about all the noise."

"Tank?" The voice was tiny but strong.

"Is that you, buddy? We've been looking for you."

A kid I made out to be nine or ten appeared from a narrow space between two metal cabinets. I had the light in his face and he raised a hand to protect his eyes.

"Oh, sorry." I shone the light at my face. "Recognize me?" I expected him to say no.

"Of course."

He ran to me and threw his arms around my thick middle. Man, that felt good. It also felt familiar. I couldn't tell you how, but I knew this kid. I knew him well and loved him.

"Let's get outta here, kid. There's more people for you to meet."

When the boy saw Sketch, he broke into tears and ran to her. She dropped to a knee and pulled him into her embrace. The kid cried. Sketch cried. I might have cried a little, too.

"Mom. I was so worried."

I looked at Grumpy. "Mom?"

He shrugged. "It's the twenty-first century, man. After all we've seen and experienced so far, I'd say this is the least shocking."

"Let's get out of here," I said. "It's hard to fight in such an enclosed place."

Ten minutes later we were outside on the upper deck again. Everything looked pretty much as it did before except for the fog. It was closer and denser.

After the kid hugged everyone two or three times, he settled down enough to field a few questions. I took the lead with that, too.

"Okay, little buddy, strange question. What's your name?"

"You still can't remember?" He seemed bothered, but not hurt.

I shrugged. "Sorry, but no."

"I had memory problems too, but it didn't stick. I'm Daniel. You're Bjorn Christensen but everyone calls you Tank. You used to play football."

Grumpy snickered. "Bjorn." He snickered some more.

The sound drew Daniel's attention. "Your name is Chad Thorton. You're real smart. Mom calls you obnoxious because you are."

"You know how to make a guy feel good, don't ya, kid?"

Daniel ignored him and addressed Red. "You're cool and really smart, too."

"What's my name, sweetie?"

The kid didn't hesitate. "Andi Goldstein. We like to stay at your house in Florida."

"What about me, kiddo?" Sketch asked.

The question seemed to make him sad. "I call you Mom now, but your name is Brenda Barnick." He turned back to the rest of us. "She's a tattoo artist. And a really good one, too." Sadness covered his face. "She won't let me get a tattoo."

"You're just a kid." Even as I said that I knew I was wrong. He might be a kid, but he seemed a whole lot more.

Well, there it was. I was Tank, Grumpy was Chad, Sketch was Brenda, and Red was Andi. It was good to have real names.

The situation allowed me a moment to feel good; to feel like we were making progress.

Then Daniel screamed.

## OUTSIDE AND EXPOSED

I SAW HIS EYES widen and his face go pale. It was the scream, however, that hurt me the most. I couldn't tell you how or when, but I had heard him scream like that before. Something about his back. Something was stinging him. The sound of it dredged up a whole lot of impressions. Not real memories, but the feeling that something bad had happened to the boy—to all of us.

I looked at his eyes, saw the direction he was looking, and turned to face whatever bogeyman was coming our way. I crouched, fist clinched into tight balls of flesh and bone.

No bogeyman. Just fog. Just gray, rolling, thick, smoke-like fog. And it terrified me.

Then I saw what the kid must have seen: something in the fog. Not just *in* the fog, but swimming in it like a person might swim in the ocean—only better, and faster. It was like watching dolphins swimming in the sea; dolphins with big heads, big mouths, sharp teeth and claws on the end of spindly arms. They looked hungry, fast and mean.

I stood welded to the deck. My brain refused to believe what I was seeing while my heart said I had dealt with these things in the past and it wasn't good.

"Inside!" Daniel was the one that said that. I tried to say it when I first caught a glimpse of those things, but my mouth wouldn't work.

"Everyone this way." I used the fire ax to point down the deck to where a door way led to the theater I had been in earlier.

No one argued with Daniel's advice or my direction. They ran next to the superstructure; I stayed between them and a fog that seemed to somehow gain speed. It was as if those things could move the fog bank at will.

It was only twenty or thirty feet to the doorway, but it seemed like a two-mile sprint. My heart was like a wild, captive animal trying to break free of a cage. I felt the chill of a cold sweat and I had to remind myself to breathe. This was industrial-strength fear.

A glance to the side revealed what I didn't want to see. The fog was closer and closing in on us at an unbelievable rate.

It was twenty feet out.

Fifteen feet.

It was at the railing. A hideous corpse-like face

poked out of the wall of fog. I swear it was smiling or leering. It had the expression of a starving man looking at a plate of steak and potatoes.

The fog poured over the rail.

"Faster!" My voice rebounded off the fog on the one side and the metal wall on the other. Don't ask me to explain that. I'm no physicist, and frankly I don't care.

Another face. Then three. Five. Twenty. The wall of fog turned into a sneering mass of faces, each chomping at the air.

One face disappeared, then reappeared followed by its stringy body. It was headed for Andi.

She screamed. I yelled and put on the breaks. The thing was graceful in the fog, but outside the fog it was more like a trout flopping around in a rowboat.

That was a mistake on my part. It couldn't swim in simple air. I guess it needed the fog for that, but the thing could scramble pretty good.

It grunted, snapped, and headed for Andi.

I had the ax.

I used it.

I doubted killing things is my style. Guilt filled me as I put the ax in motion, but there was no time for self-reflection—even if I could remember more of my past. I made an appointment to talk all this over with myself when we reached safety. If we were ever safe.

The ax did its job. It was like hitting a cantaloupe. The creature's bold choice to leave the safety of the fog hadn't worked out like it planned, but that didn't stop others from trying. They might be fearsome, but they weren't any too smart. Each one that sprang from the fog hit the deck pretty hard. That would all change in about thirty seconds because the fog had just passed the rail. Only five feet or so separated us from it and the horrors it held.

One of the overly eager critters leapt from the deck and reached for Daniel. It caught the kid by the collar, but his claws missed any flesh. Daniel screamed that scream again and the coals of anger and fear in me burst into flame.

I bolted that way, then heard another scream. Not one of fear, but fury. A woman's voice. An angry mother's kind of scream. Brenda had the creature by the back of the neck and yanked it off Daniel before it could bring claw or tooth to bear. Then Brenda slammed the thing face-first into the deck. I knew she was furious because she slammed its head several times to drive home the point.

It stopped moving. I glanced back to the other creatures and saw those on the deck back up a few feet. I don't think they've ever seen anyone like Brenda do in one of their own.

Their caution evaporated a moment later. Short memories, I guess. The momentary pause was all we needed. I sprinted to the one closest to our party and gave it a sample of my shoe. It felt like I had kicked a ragdoll. It flew down the deck like one.

"Get in. Get in." Grumpy—Chad—had reached the door and opened it. The guy was full of surprises. I had him pegged to be one of those guys who scream like a little girl and do everything they can to save themselves.

I couldn't have been more wrong. He held the door open, held it in its place with his shoulder, turned to the mass of hungry murderers and tensed like a man about to take on a barroom full of bikers.

Daniel crossed the threshold first, followed by

Brenda, then Andi.

"Move it, Tank."

I didn't need the encouragement. The moment I was through the door I spun back to the opening, grabbed Chad by the back of his shirt and yanked. He stumbled in and I grabbed the knob and pulled the door shut, but not before one of the little monsters got his grubby mitt between the door and the jamb. I closed it anyway. I closed it hard, putting all my weight and strength behind it.

A scream came from the other side of the door. I don't know if it was a scream of anger, frustration, or immense pain. I didn't spend much time thinking about it.

"Into the theater." Chad was again holding open a door. "Bring the ax."

I did and plunged past him. The door he held open was one of two. The entrance to the theater was through the set of double doors I had seen my first time in the room.

"Thanks," I said.

"Save it. Those things might figure out how to open a door." He was leaning back, a hand on each U-shaped handle. "Use the ax."

"You want me to chop—"

"No. Put the ax handle through the door handles. We need to barricade these."

I did as he said. After all, it was a good idea.

We checked for other doors, found the other pair of double entrance/exit doors, and used one of the metal cymbal stands from the drum kit to keep those doors from opening out.

A brief thought occurred to me. "You'd think they would have a way to lock these doors until they were ready to let people in."

"There are a lot of things about this ship that are off. That's the least egregious."

"Something else I can't argue with." I moved to the windows. I did so because I thought it was wise. I really had no desire to look outside.

The windows were covered with thick curtains to keep out the sun during performances and maybe to keep passengers from peering in. Chad joined me. The women and Daniel had moved as far from the doors as possible.

Deep breath, then I pulled the curtain back. A mass of milky-white faces was pressed against the glass. So many ugly faces.

They were *licking* the window. I closed the curtains and bent over, resting my hands on my knees.

"You going to hurl again?" Since it was Chad speaking I expected a little more mockery, but he sounded almost concerned.

"Nah. I'm just trying to—I don't know. I just need a moment."

When I straightened I got a good look in Chad's eyes. There was fear, but there was something else.

"You did good out there, Tank. You saved a life or two. Maybe all our lives."

"You done good too, buddy, holding that door and all. You're quick on your feet." I slapped him on the shoulder.

The girls and Daniel were seated on the floor of the stage. Brenda held Daniel like she was afraid he'd run away.

We walked to where they were seated.

Brenda looked up. "Now what?"

I had no idea what to tell her.

Then she—all of them—were gone.

## Chapter 12

### BACK IN THE CLOSET

LAST TIME I got shuffled I ended up on the stage of the ship's small theater. Before that, I landed on the main deck where I left a pool of biology, something Chad hadn't let me forget. This time I was in a pitch- dark compartment.

"Swell. Jus' swell." I had landed on my fanny, which isn't all that comfortable for big guys like me. I put my arms out to my sides. The space was narrow. I couldn't extend my arms to their full span. I felt a wall on one side and something I took to be a shelf. I pushed myself up until I was standing.

Then I heard something. Something moving. Something shuffling. In the dark closet with me. I thought of the bogeyman we had seen in the corridor.

Worse, I thought of the fog creatures. Being stuck in a confined space with one or more of those couldn't be good. Not good at all.

"Who are you?" The voice was a tad timid but wore a veneer of bravery.

"Chad?"

"Is that a question or an answer?"

Yep, Chad. "It's me, Tank."

"Good to hear, Big Guy."

"Do you know where we are?" I wished for my flashlight. No telling where that was now.

"Oh, yeah, I know. I remember the smell." He sniffed. His voice was a little wonky.

That's when it hit me. "The closet?"

A sob. "Yes. Same closet." He wasn't hysterical, but he was zeroing in on it.

"Okay, okay. No problem." I took a breath. I was getting a little claustrophobic myself.

"I hate closets. I've spent way too much time in them."

"What does that mean?"

The sobs came in rapid succession. I was beginning to feel his panic. "My old man, moron. He used to lock me in closets. Sometimes for days at a time."

Before I could respond I felt his hands on my arms pushing me back. "I've got to get out of here. I'm losing my mind. You—you're breathing all my air." His voice softened. "Please, Daddy, I'll be good. I promise. I'll be good."

"Easy, Chad. I'll have us out in a couple o' moments. Just take a deep breath and—"

The punch hit me in the gut and it was hard enough to knock the air out of me. When I first met him we had tussled, so I knew he had decent strength, but the punch was harder than I thought him capable of. My stomach hurt, my head pounded, I was on edge, and I had had all I wanted of this ship. No way was I gonna let this guy wail on me.

I reached forward, felt cloth in my hand and guessed I had him by the front of the shirt, I pulled him forward then slammed him back. It sounded like I had just rammed the guy into some shelves. That had to hurt.

I clinched a fist, pulled it back. I had a good idea where his face was and I was gonna tenderize it. After setting my feet I started to let the punch fly.

But I didn't.

I stopped before my fist moved an inch. This wasn't right. I may not remember who I am, but this seemed way outta character for me. This was the second time I felt this. New emotions flooded my brain and my heart. Anger gave way to pity and a truckload of conviction landed on me.

I lowered my fist. "Ease up, Chad. Give me one minute and I'll have us outta here."

"Really?" Man, he could be snide. "How are you going to do that?"

"How did I get you out last time?"

"You're going to kick the door down from in here."

"You know something, Chad? For a smart guy, you can be really dumb." I reached forward and found the door, then ran my hand slowly down the side of it until I felt shredded bits of wood. "I don't need to kick anything down. The door is still broken."

The door swung open easily enough. "Viola!" I moved into the dim hall. A half-sec later, Chad was out of the closet and looked like a man who had just crawled free from a coffin.

He looked at me. "Um, listen. About what happened in there…"

"Forget about it."

"Maybe it could be our little secret—"

His eyes went wide and his mouth went slack. That could only mean one thing: something butt-ugly was standing behind me. I turned.

There are times when I hate being right.

A man stood behind me. Sorta a man. He was taller than me by a foot and a whole lot uglier. His face was misshaped, as if it had been made of wax and held under a hair dryer. He had a black mustache covering about half of his upper lip and one eye was twice the size of the other.

For a moment, I thought my heart had just given up and stopped. But since I didn't drop over dead, I figured it was still working some.

"No, Daddy. Please no. Leave me alone. Leave—"

Chad was on the run. I glanced his way, then looked back at the meanest dad I had ever seen. Except he had disappeared.

My brain lit on fire while my blood ran cold. If I weren't so terrified and worried, I mighta stopped to figure how that worked. I didn't take the time. An image splashed on my mind: Chad racing up the stairs and onto the main deck—the place where we saw a thick fog full of round-headed, sharp toothed monstrosities. That image was replaced with one of a dead, gutted Chad dead on the deck. He was outta of his mind with fear and I was the only one who knew what or who stood a chance of catching him.

I stopped thinking and started running. Running

down the corridor to the spot where the big bogey man had been; running up the stairs where we found Brenda; running onto the deck where we had seen and barely escaped the creepies in the fog.

The door to the deck had just closed when I reached it. Then I did the dumbest thing in my life, I charged outside without a thought. It might have been brave, but it was also tempting fate. Maybe even tempting God.

I balled my fists so tight I could feel tendons strain against bone. I had no plan, no scheme, just a goal: find Chad and drag his fanny back inside before he became monster chow.

Three steps outside the door, I paused long enough to notice that the fog was gone and with it the infestation it carried. That was good. Everything was still a dull gray and I could see fog in the distance, but for now the fog-sharks wouldn't be jumping on deck anytime soon. Now I needed to find Chad before his terror drove him to do something stupid.

I asked God for help. I pleaded with God. I begged him. The prayer came naturally to me and felt familiar. Apparently, I was used to walking on hallowed ground.

Which way to go? I chose forward. We had walked that way earlier, so there was a chance Chad would choose the familiar.

My feet pounded the deck. My breathing came in great gulps. My mind ran to Andi and Brenda. Mostly it ran to Daniel. My fear felt like an animal with long tentacles was taking hold of my guts, my stomach, my heart and lungs. I could feel it moving, wriggling, churning.

*Chad. Find Chad. Focus. Focus.*

Most people paid little attention to me, once they got used to my size. I have never been the smartest guy in the room, but I have my insights and knew I could only chase down one lost sheep at a time. Still, I worried about the others.

The thing in my gut tugged at my innards some more. It was as if my fear had come alive.

No matter. I had my mission. I had my goal. Find that smart-mouthed, egotistical, chucklehead and save his bacon if I could. I might fail, but it wouldn't be for the lack of trying.

I pressed on, glancing into windows, looking up to the higher decks where I could, but no Chad. Then I reached the bow.

And there was Chad—straddling the safety rail that ran around the ship. Except here it wasn't a rail made of tubular steel. It was more of a parapet with a wood cap over a short steel wall.

A moment's relief. He was still alive. Then more tension and fear when I realized he wasn't taking a break but giving some serious thought to going over the edge.

I slowed to a walk, but continued forward. To my right was the wall that enclosed a room we hadn't been in.

"Chad. Dude. Whatcha doing? That doesn't look all that safe."

He ignored me. He didn't even bother to look at me. Something else held his attention. I reached the open deck of the bow and to my right stood the focus of Chad's attention: his father. Uglier than before and twice the size any man should be. One eye was now the size of a saucer and the other, although closer to the correct size for a guy standing twelve feet tall or so, oozed something milky-white. His face was even more twisted and his skin was almost see through. I could see things crawling just beneath the surface.

No wonder Chad was considering taking a dive. For a moment I considered doing a swan dive over the edge myself. If I could have put the guy down right then and there, he would still win. I'd be seeing him in every dream from now till heaven.

"Leave me alone, Dad. I haven't done anything to you. Why do you hate me? Why?" Chad broke into tears.

Dad raised a hand and pointed over the bow, encouraging Chad to jump.

"Look at me, Chad." I tried to sound calm although a hurricane of emotion raged within me.

Nothing.

"Chad!" My voice echoed off the hard surfaces and rolled over the water. "I said *look at me*."

He turned his face my direction. His expression nearly broke me. His face showed a lifetime of hurt, of pain, of rejection.

"Help me, Tank."

I could barely hear him. That's when I noticed the blood. It ran from his nose and a nasty cut on his right cheek and right half of his forehead. I noticed some blood on the one hand I could see. My guess: he had tripped while running and did a header into a bulkhead or into the deck.

Chad turned his attention to the ghoul he called *Dad*. Then he leaned a little more over the edge.

"Don't do it, Chad."

"It's the only way out. Death. Blackness. Nothingness. That's better than this."

"What if death isn't the end, Chad?"

He didn't respond other than tipping a few more inches toward certain death.

"Chad, I'm here. I'll stand by you. I'll stand with you. Just trust me."

"You'll stand against that?" He pointed at Dad. "No one can stand up to that."

I was lost for words. That thing could flatten me in a second if it had a mind to.

"Chad, if you go over, then so do I. No man should die alone. I'm gonna be with you on the deck or in the ocean. You are not alone. We are never alone."

His eyes drifted back to me. "I'm no good, Tank. I never have been. I'm a loser. I was born a loser. I'll die a loser. You don't like me. I've done nothing but antagonize you."

I nodded. "Yep. You're good at that. It's your super power."

"See?"

"What I see, buddy, is a man in the need of a friend. I'm that friend."

Tears trickled down his cheek. "What about him?" He nodded at Dad. "We can't stand up to that."

"Resist the devil and he will flee from you." I don't know where that came from, but it felt right.

"What?"

"Don't ask me. I can't even tell you how old I am." I looked at Ugly who was no longer content to point at the sea but was now gesturing for Chad to finish the job of killing himself.

Chad straightened on the rail. He was no longer leaning over the ocean.

I had had enough of standing around. I started toward Chad without giving a glance to Dad. If he wanted to kill me mid-step, I couldn't stop him. I resigned myself to death. Even that seemed familiar. I couldn't recall my past, but I guessed my life wasn't boring.

Chad eyes widened again. "What are you doing?"

"Resisting the devil, buddy. Just resisting the devil."

## SHIFT, SHIFT, SHUFFLE

SEVERAL IDEAS RAN through my weary brain. I could rush Chad, grab him, and pull him onto the deck. Chancy. That struck me as a stupid idea. I'd do it if I had no choice, but instead I went with something less Hollywood. I held out my hand. "Come on down, Chad. You're giving me gray hair."

"What about him?" He nodded in the direction of Ugly.

I gave the ghoul a glance. "He will do what he will do. Even if he kills us, we will die on our own terms."

Chad thought about that for a moment and I thought about yanking him off the railing. I chose not to and prayed that I wouldn't regret it. Crawling off on his own would let him feel like he made the decision to live and hadn't been forced into it.

He took my hand and planted his feet on the deck. I took him in my arms to give him a manly bear hug, but then held him a little longer than was natural for me.

I felt a warmth in my body. The fear that had been tugging at my guts disappeared. My eyes stayed closed but I could tell we were covered in light.

"Um, Tank, this is a little awkward."

"Right. I don't know…" I stared at him. His wounds and the blood were gone. I couldn't tell where the cut on his cheek and forehead had been. I told him about it. He had been healed.

Dad let out a furious wail that could be heard a mile away.

"Oh, shut up," Chad said.

That made me laugh. I had no reason to laugh. I still didn't remember my past, was still on a dead ship adrift in the ocean, and the rest of our group was still missing. Sometimes, if people get frightened enough they laugh. Maybe that was me. I didn't have enough energy to care.

The giant bent at the waist and put his ugly mug close to our faces. He was real enough and his breath smelled like he had been lunching on raw skunk.

"Maybe we should run," I suggested. Not that I thought we'd make it.

Chad swallowed hard. "No way, Big Guy. I'm done running. If I'm going to die, it's going to be against my will, not because this thing forced me into suicide.

I began to question my sanity. After all I had seen, I probably should have done that sooner, but this brought the point home. I had to be nuts because Dad seemed to shrink some. Chad noticed that too.

"All my life, you have abused me in every way possible." Chad was getting hot under the collar. "I put up with it because I was too young to do anything about it. Well, I'm not a kid anymore. I don't have to put up with you for another minute."

Scary-Dad shrunk a little more. I remembered nothing of childhood, or for that matter, my adulthood, but Chad seemed to be dredging up horrible memories from his past. Maybe having amnesia was better.

"Go ahead, Dad. You're big and bad. Do something to me now. You might get away with it, but I won't give you the satisfaction of seeing me afraid again."

The incredible shrinking dad shrunk even more. It was as if it had been empowered by Chad's terror, but starved in the face of Chad's courage.

Chad must have put those two ideas together because he got louder and bolder. He let loose with a string of insults and curses that would have sent the sailors on this ship running, if there were any sailors on this ship.

Before my eyes what had been a deformed giant of a man reduced to normal size. He stepped back from Chad. I'm pretty sure I saw his swollen lip quiver.

Chad kept venting, and as the specter of his father diminished Chad's courage and intensity grew. Somehow, Chad's external injuries had been healed; no doubt his emotional injuries were being cured now.

The Dad ghoul grew smaller and smaller. When he reached the size of a child, he up and disappeared.

We stared at the spot where he had been standing.

"Okay," I said. "Now I've seen everything."

"You haven't seen anything." It was a new voice. An angry voice. A threatening voice.

A man in a red robe rounded the same corner I had and moved onto the bow deck. Dread filled me from toes to skull.

"Who—" I began.

Red Robe raised his hand.

He was holding something.

A gun?

No, it looked like a television remote control. He pressed a button.

*Shift.*

I stumbled down a half flight of stairs. I managed to stay upright, but my body lodged a serious protest in my knees, left ankle, and lower back. Still, I had to be thankful I didn't go head first down the metal treads. That would have been a good way to pick up a few dozen bruises, a broken bone or two, or even a busted neck.

It took me a moment to stop swaying. It was dark. Like I was locked inside a lightless vault. I wished for my flashlight. I had no idea where that was. It went missing. *Okay, I stumble down so if go back the same way I fell, I'll be moving up toward the light—*

*Shift.*

My nose hurt and for good reason. I was face down in the dark again. Judging by the pain in my head, I had landed face first on the steel floor.

I could smell oil. Oil and diesel. The engine room. Daniel had been locked in the engine—

*Shift.*

The theater again. At least this time I had a little light to judge my situation—

*Shift.*

A bed. Except I was crossways in it with my feet hanging off the side leaving me in a kneeling position. Some light through portholes. Gray. Large room. Nice. A white officer's style cap rested on a desk near the head of the bed. Captain's quarters?

*Shift.*

Kitchen.

*Shift.*

Flat on my back on top of the superstructure. Gray sky overhead. Gray horizon—

*Shift.*

Dark again. Standing. Stumbled back into what felt like shelves. A few touches later I judged that I was in a storage room for linens and towels.

*Shift.*

Cold. Metal all around. Smell of meat. Inside a large industrial refrigerator. I heard no compressors. Cold, but not freezing. No power.

*Shuffle.*

On my hands and knees. Puking again. Praying that this would stop. Dizzy. Unsteady. In pain. Ready to collapse. I raised my eyes enough to see I was out in the open again. I wretched a few times more.

Someone else did the same. Then someone else. I wasn't alone.

I pushed back from the mess I made and sat on the deck, my arms around my knees, my head resting on those arms.

Breathe. Deep breath.

"Tank?"

I lifted my head and looked to my left. There was Red, Andi, with an impressive mess in front of her. "You okay?"

She cut her eyes at me. "Sure. Don't I look just swell?"

"No, but you're still beautiful." I eased myself down so I rested on my back. Man, I needed to rest.

"I bet you say that to all the vomiting girls." That was Brenda. She was behind me somewhere. I didn't bother looking. That would have meant moving and moving meant more yakking.

"Where's Daniel?" I asked Brenda.

"I'm here, Tank. I'm okay."

It was great to hear his voice. "I guess you tossed your cookies, too."

"Nah," the kid said. "I never throw up. That's for babies."

"Okay, buddy boy. I'm gonna tickle you until you turn purple."

He chuckled but I was pretty sure it was a courtesy laugh. "Bring it."

That gave me a reason to smile. "Okay. You free next week, 'cuz I'm gonna need a little time."

A shadow fell over me. As much of a shadow as a body could cast in the gray light. It was Chad.

"Hey Chad. I know, I know. I did it again."

"We all did, Tank."

"Not me," Daniel said.

I sat up and looked around. We were higher than the main deck and a few deck chairs were scattered around and few patio style tables. I worked myself to my feet. The deck was maybe twenty-five percent as long as the main deck. Rising from the middle of the deck was one of the ship's smoke stacks. No smoke. That was to be expected since we had been without power since I woke this morning, or afternoon, or whenever it was.

"Sun deck," Chad said.

The others joined us. Not to put too fine a point on it, we carried a bit of a stink with us.

I was tense. I kept waiting to blink and end up somewhere else in the ship. That didn't happen, but I hadn't wasted my worries. The guy in the red robe appeared at the top of the stairs, the stairs that led down to the next deck. Man, he looked familiar, and not in a good way. The robe was open in the front revealing an expensive looking three-piece suit. Like everything else, it was gray.

Daniel stepped behind me. Brenda was at his side, her hand on his shoulder. "Slick doesn't get close to Daniel. Got it, Tank? No matter what, Red Robe doesn't get within twenty feet of the boy."

"Yes, ma'am." That was all I could think of to say.

"I have had enough of you." Red Robe took two steps closer. I moved to the side to stay between Nutcase and Daniel.

"Yeah?" Chad said. "I don't even know you and I've had all I can take of your face."

Red Robe turned to stare at Chad. "True, we haven't met face to face yet, young Chad, but I know about you. I know all about you. You are a problem."

He turned to us and his eyes turned a glacial blue. *His eye color changed.* That seemed familiar, too. I was getting sick of hints about my past. I wanted real information.

"You all are a problem to us," Red Robe said. "And we will stand for it no longer."

"Us?" Andi said.

"The Gate." It was Daniel that answered. "Long story."

I hoped to hear it someday.

"And the kid. We hate you most of all, Daniel."

Brenda snarled. "One step closer, Slick, I'll separate your head from your body."

"Sure, you will." He didn't sound convinced. "I'm not afraid of a tattoo artist." He did take a step back. "I have something to show you. You, Brenda, and you, Chad, should enjoy this."

He raised the remote control in his right hand, gave us a sick grin and then, like some old time actor, shouted, "Behold."

## Chapter 14

## GRAY SKIES ARE GONNA CLEAR UP

THE MOMENT RED ROBE said, "Behold," the gray skies went black, a black filled with funny lookin' stars and other things I couldn't quite figure out. One thing I *could* figure out: they were gettin' closer and I didn't have a good feeling about that.

"What the..." Chad said.

Then things got weird.

A hole appeared in the sky. Like someone took an ice pick and gave the heavens a good poke. The hole drew closer and grew bigger.

"Should we run?" Andi sounded a little on edge. If she hadn't, I would have been worried. I was on edge.

More than that. I was paralyzed with fear.

"Run where?" Brenda said. "There are creeps wherever we go."

The hole turned into a tunnel. I could see down its middle. It reminded me of a long train tunnel, except it was rotating, expanding, and moving.

"Wait," Brenda said. "I know this. I've seen this." She pulled her eyes away from the thing in the sky and stared at Chad. "You. This has something to do with you, doesn't it?"

Chad stood statue-still for a moment, not hearing, not moving, not responding. His mouth opened and I half-expected words to come out. No words came from him, but a gut wrenching, eardrum bustin' scream did. He clamped his hands on the side of his head as if shutting his ears would make him blind to what was before his eyes. Of course, that makes no sense, but nothing on this ship made sense.

The ship rose. I mean that in the most literal way I can. The ship lifted out of the water. The deck heaved beneath our feet. Andi fell, Brenda stumbled, and I had to shuffle my feet several times to keep my balance. Oddly, Daniel seemed to ride the deck just fine. Youth.

The tunnel, the tube, whatever you want to call it, swallowed us whole. It swallowed the entire ship.

"Ain't no way this is good." It wasn't profound, but my statement was accurate.

Brenda steadied herself and looked to be on the edge of panic. Daniel had said we all knew each other and I believed him, but I remembered so little. Still, I had the feeling that Brenda didn't scare easily, and seeing her terror made me even more afraid.

The ship moved through the tube bow first.

Around us the tunnel spun. The wall seemed to move as if it were alive. Then I saw the first face. A frog-like face. A demonic face. It reminded me of one of those statues people used to attach to old gothic churches and buildings. Gargoyles. That was it. I was looking at the face of a butt-ugly gargoyle. It opened its mouth.

Then there was another, then another. The place was alive with them.

The ship began to flip over like it was capsizing in slow motion. That got our attention. Any moment we would slip from the deck and fall into the sides of the tunnel and become gargoyle food.

But we didn't. We turned over all right, but we didn't fall. It was as if there was no gravity. We just stayed in place.

I struggled to come up with a plan of action. I could probably reach Red Robe, but then what? I guessed we might need him to get back home, and if not home, a better place than this.

We emerged from the rotating tunnel into a black space filled with giant slowly spinning snowflakes. Each snowflake was large enough to hold a man. In fact, I saw people in them. Something else that made no sense.

"Look familiar, boy?" Red Robe moved close to Chad. "How about it? This is the place you visit when you do your remote viewing thing. Look around you, boy. You move yourself here when you do your astral projection thing, but you are a mere amateur. Nothing more. You wade in the shallows, Mr. Chad Trenton, while the Gate swims in the deep waters. Look, I moved a whole ship from one multi-verse to another many times and I can do it again."

He raised the remote control. "I can do all that

and more. And if I want—and *I want*—I can move just myself and leave all of you right here. Alone. Helpless."

"Why?" Andi asked.

"Ah, the lovely Andi Goldstein. Always searching for answers and patterns and connections." His lips parted. "Because I want to, Ms. Goldstein. Because I can. Most of all, because I have grown weary of you and your friends destroying our work."

Over the bow I could see snow covered cliffs and a huge, black surface, like a wall.

"We don't even know who you are." Brenda added a colorful but not endearin' reference.

"Well, that's to be expected with the memory loss." The wicked smile came out again.

The ship shuddered and the space around us lightened a tick or two.

Red Robe continued, apparently enjoying his own voice. I missed his first few words because one of the giant snowflakes drifted close to the safety rail. It spun slowly on its axis. Inside were several children. Children with coal black eyes.

"…around you," Red Robe was saying. "This is your new home…"

Another snowflake drew close. Inside it was a swarm of "things." They were about the size of a child's doll and looked like small people but with large lumpy heads, spindly arms and legs, and leather skin. They also had skin-covered wings. Worse, they had tails equipped with nasty looking stingers.

A movement near the steps to the sun deck where we were caught my attention. I braced myself for more terror. Instead, a man in a suit slowly ascended the steps and moved onto our deck. He glanced at us and smiled. He was tall, had gray hair, and oozed intelligence. Of all the things I had seen since waking up on this ship, he seemed the most familiar.

The man moved slowly and silently. For some reason the snowflake with the black-eyed kids in it backed away. The one with the swarm of uglies in it stayed in place.

I don't know what the new arrival had in mind but I sensed he was on our side. To keep Red Robe's attention on us and not on the man he had yet to notice, I asked, "You're going to abandon us? What about Daniel? He's just a kid."

"Your good and kind heart, Tank, is what makes you stupid. I don't care if Daniel is a kid. Leaving him here will be the greatest joy of all. We have grown weary of all of you, but none more than Daniel. We hate him the most. You can't win. Not even with Daniel on your side."

"Excuse me, Dr. Trenton," the stranger said.

At least he was polite.

Red Robe—Trenton—turned sharply and got a face full of fist for his effort. The stranger put some weight into it. So much so, that Trenton's head snapped around and he dropped like a sack of rocks. Judging by the way his head bounced on the hard surface, I was pretty sure he was unconscious before he hit the deck. The remote he had been holding bounced a few times and skittered five or six feet away.

The stranger stood over the body like a heavy-weight boxer over an opponent. Impressive. Then his mood changed. "Ow, ow, ow." He jumped around shaking his hand. "I didn't know punching someone could hurt so much."

"Professor!" Daniel raced from his protected spot behind me and threw his arms around the stranger. "Professor. I miss you so much."

The stranger embraced him like Daniel was his grandson. Brought a tear to my eye. Then he pulled away and retrieved the remote. "I hope this isn't broken. I hadn't thought about it being dropped. Stupid of me, really."

I looked at Andi, then Brenda, then Chad. Each shrugged. "Familiar?"

"Very," Andi said.

"Friendly good."

"Daniel thinks so," Brenda said.

The professor walked our way. He held his boxing hand a few inches from his side. It was swelling. No doubt there was a broken bone or two in that hand. Still, his mitt worked well enough to hold the remote.

"Who are you?" I asked. "I mean Daniel knows, but I don't have a clue."

"I'm a friend."

"He's the professor," Daniel said.

"Not now, son," the professor said to Daniel. "Our time is limited. You will all remember soon enough."

The snowflake with the swarm of toothy fairy things began to shake. Whatever they were, they wanted out.

He turned to Brenda. "Barnick, you are a royal pain." He leaned forward and kissed her forehead. "Don't ever change." He set his good hand on Daniel's head. "Protect him. He's the key."

"Of course. I will."

The professor looked like a proud father.

The buzzing of wings and a hundred tiny screams

came from the human-like bugs in the snowflake.

The professor turned to me. "Tank, you were right about everything. I was wrong. Thank you. Whatever you do, stay the course."

"I don't understand."

"I know." He gave me a sad lookin' smile. His eyes were extra moist. "I need you to remember something."

"I ain't been so good at remembering lately."

"You can remember this." He spoke loudly, no doubt hoping one of the others could recall what he said if I failed to remember. "Revelation 9:14–15." He paused, then, "Say it, Tank."

"Revelation 9:14–15."

"Good. Very good." The professor took a deep breath.

Chad stood in silence. I think it was the longest span of silence he had ever endured.

The professor held out the undamaged hand. Chad shook it. "I wish we could have worked together." He motioned to us. "These are your friends. Believe that. They will annoy you and try what little patience you have, but don't turn on them. They need you as much as you need them. You are not alone, son. You never have been."

Chad just nodded.

"Something else, young man. This will make no sense now, but it will soon. Losing something we have doesn't mean we're lost."

"I have no idea what you mean."

The professor didn't respond to that. He looked at the vibrating snowflake thing. It was bulging.

"We're almost out of time." The professor took a few steps back before speaking. "All you've been through, all the missions you've been on, all the dangers you've faced, have been for a reason. In a way, it's been training. Every battle, every skirmish, every threat has been a prelude to the war that must come. The war you must win."

Puddles formed in his eyes. I had puddles in my own.

"Have a good life; stay true to the mission. Your journey is not done. Heaven and Earth need you." He looked at Red Robe. "Trenton is not the one you're looking for. He's a flunky and nothing more. There is someone else you must find." Then he said a name: "Ambrosi Giacomo."

The name meant nothing to me.

"Come with us, Professor." Daniel was in tears. "Don't leave again. Please don't."

"I can't, son. Too much to do. Too much to learn. Too much to discover. I'll do my part wherever I am." He moved between us and the flying stingers. He lifted the remote. "I love you all. I always have."

The snowflake contraption gave way and the swarm emerged.

"Professor, look out!" I started for him.

Everything was gone.

ROCKING.

Like an infant in a cradle.

Gentle. Smooth. Even. Familiar.

I opened my eyes and saw the ceiling of my room. I sat up and hung my legs over the side of the bed. My feet were clad in dress shoes (scuffed up pretty good) and I still wore my tux. I hate tuxes.

I rubbed my face for a few moments and let the memories settle in. I'm not a drinker (made a few mistakes in the past) but I felt a little hung over or maybe drugged. I searched for my latest memory and it came to me easily. I was on a 1950s cruise ship sailing around the Gulf of Mexico on its last voyage. We had received invitations in the mail and it sounded like fun. And boy, did we need some fun together. We were getting on each other's nerves just hanging around our Dallas Hotel.

Someone knocked on my door. I could hear people talking in the hallway and outside. A bright sun poured light into the room.

"Just a sec."

I stepped in front of the mirror and took a good look at myself. My tux was worse for wear. It musta been a hard night.

I opened the door. Andi and Brenda stood before me, both in evening gowns which seemed entirely wrong for the time of day. But then again, I was in a tux. Daniel stood between them. Behind them moved a stream of passengers. For some reason, it struck me as a good thing to see. One of those passengers was Chad. Yep. He was in a tuxedo too, but no coat. He always was smarter than me.

"Hi, guys."

"We need to talk." Andi said.

"Did you have a dream, Big Guy?" Chad asked.

"Yeah. It was a doozy. The best part is I dreamed about the professor." It all came back to me in a tsunami of memory. "It wasn't a dream, was it?"

I stepped aside to let my friends enter. It was too many people in the small room but we could, at least, talk in private.

Andi sat on the edge of the bed, Brenda stood next to Daniel like they were tethered to each other.

Chad leaned against the small desk.

"So it was all real," I said.

"Yeah," Chad said. "Every stinking minute of it." He hung his head like a scolded dog. "I'm a little embarrassed."

"Don't be." I stood in the middle of the room. "I wasn't at my best, either."

"You did great, Big Guy. Your big heart stayed true even when your memories abandoned you. I guess a psychologist would conclude that we are not the sum of our memories."

"As a man thinks in his heart so is he," I said. "It's a Bible verse."

Chad smirked. "Yeah, I kinda figured that."

Andi crossed her arms. She didn't have to say she was heartbroken. We had all seen the professor and now felt like we had lost him all over again.

"Speaking of Bible verses," Andi said, "what was that the professor gave you?"

"Revelation 9:14–15. You're right, it is a coupla verses from the last book in the New Testament." I stepped to a backpack I used for luggage and removed a Bible. I never travel without one. The others have teased me about it. There was no teasing now. I read the verses:

> "'Release the four angels who are bound at the great river Euphrates.' And the four angels, who had been prepared for the hour and day and month and year, were released, so that they would kill a third of mankind."

Brenda sighed. "I don't get it. What's that

supposed to mean, Cowboy?"

"I think it means things are about to get serious. Real serious."

**Read all of the Harbingers books:**

Harbingers #1—*The Call*—Bill Myers
Harbingers #2—*The Haunt*ed—Frank Peretti
Harbingers #3—*The Sentinels*—Angela Hunt
Harbingers #4—*The Girl*—Alton Gansky

Volumes #1-4 omnibus: *Cycle One: Invitation*

Harbingers #5—*The Revealing*—Bill Myers
Harbingers #6—*Infestation*—Frank Peretti
Harbingers #7—*Infiltration*—Angela Hunt
Harbingers #8—*The Fog*—Alton Gansky

Volumes #5-8 omnibus: *Cycle Two: The Assault* (or *Mosaic*)

Harbingers #9—*Leviathan*—Bill Myers
Harbingers #10—*The Mind Pirates*—Frank Peretti
Harbingers #11—*Hybrids*—Angela Hunt
Harbingers #12—*The Village*—Alton Gansky

Volumes 9-12 omnibus: *Cycle Three: The Probing*

Harbingers #13—*Piercing the Veil*—Bill Myers
Harbingers #14—*Home Base*—Jeff Gerke
Harbingers #15—*Fairy*—Angela Hunt
Harbingers #16—*At Sea*—Alton Gansky

Volumes 12-16 omnibus: *Cycle Four: The Pursuit*

Harbingers #17: *Through a Glass Darkly*
Harbingers #18: *Interesting Times*
Harbingers #19: coming

Harbingers #20: coming